Co

PART ONE

ONE

The Monster of Geneva Towers

Barney Blatz, a white man, stares at his bony fingers on the keys of the manual Olympia typewriter. "Babe. Do you think the title should be 'Fight Racism' or 'Smash Racism'?" he asks. He's slouched at his self-made, wood-stained door of a desk which takes up much of the living room of their apartment in Geneva Towers.

Linda Jean Blatz, a black woman, Barney's wife of four years, gazes thoughtfully out their 15th floor window at the twinkling lights of the neighborhood below, her hands clasped behind her back like an umpire. "Fight," she says. The Towers, a twin high-rise, low-income complex sticks up incongruously from the floor of Visitacion Valley in the southeast corner of San Francisco, two blocks from the Cow Palace.

"Smash," he returns, squinching his wire-rimmed glasses up on his nose.

"Fight," she says without raising her voice.

"Smash," he says. He runs his fingers through his greying sandy hair. He pecks out the letters, S-M-S-A-H, on the smelly blue wax of the mimeograph stencil. "Shit." He brushes over the error with the rubbery correction fluid. He doesn't wait long enough for the stuff to dry, so when he types in the correction, it will onomatopoetically read "smush" when the ink seeps through the stencil on the mimeograph machine.

The buzz of the fire alarm snaps the air like a whip to the ears.

"Another goddamn garbage chute fire," Barney growls. Lighting fires in the garbage chute is one of the favorite amusements of the preadolescents who roam the halls of the Towers at all hours.

The alarm reflected in her chestnut face, Linda Jean turns toward Barney and says in her voice with a touch of rasp, "What if it isn't, Barney? What if it's a real fire?"

The alarm goes on too long and the smell is different from the orange-peel stink of the usual garbage fire. Barney slides open the glass door and steps out on the rarely used balcony. He stumbles over the Big Wheel, the barbecue, the dead potted plants. The winds from the valley blow smoke, black and plasticky, in his face. He sees that the smoke is coming from an apartment a few floors directly above theirs. Oh-oh, he thinks. It's well known that these apartments are fire traps.

"Maybe we should check it out," Barney concedes.

He opens the apartment door. The wind blasts from the hallway, as if they were in an airliner at thirty thousand feet. The noise from the alarm now stabs like an icepick to the eardrum. The other tenants are converging on the center of the hallway in front of the elevators, where a sign clearly reads "In case of fire use stairs."

As Barney and Linda Jean make for the stairs, Linda Jean shouts at the crowd, "Hey! You're supposed to use the stairs!"

They then find themselves at the front of a mass of people thundering down the pissy concrete stairwell, with panic accelerating the crescendo, overpowering the wail of approaching sirens. Linda Jean is the first to slam into the bar handle of the emergency exit door. The door opens six inches until it catches on the length of chain holding it locked shut.

"Hey! We're locked in here!" Linda Jean shouts without thinking, her words spreading more panic through the crowd as quickly as fires have been known to sweep through these apartment buildings.

A crush of people piles up against them, squeezing them against the door. They are in danger of suffocating.

Usually shy, Linda Jean hollers commandingly at the crowd, "Hey! Let's not panic here. Everybody! Take a deep breath!" The crowd gets control of itself. "If a bunch of us would push against the door, I think we can bust the chain without any one getting hurt."

About ten of the people in the front of the crowd huddle against the door. Linda Jean shouts, "One, two, three, push."

The bar handle breaks, the chain slides off, and the door flies open. Linda Jean and Barney tumble onto the hard concrete as the others pile on top of them. Barney is sure he is dead.

You were in second grade on the playground when your classmates, all of them white, screamed "nigger pile on Barney!" and jumped on top of you, smothering you, grinding your head into the asphalt, creating what may be a perfect metaphor for US society, as you peed in your pants at your first taste of claustrophobia.

The crowd pulsates with the red flash of the fire engine lights. Like others in the crowd of spectators, Barney watches the black smoke pour from the balcony and the orange flames lick the underside of the balcony above. He knows only that there are children in danger and that confusion and chaos are in charge. He does his best to avoid feeling it, but he can't help experiencing real fear for the children's lives, a fear that recalls the primeval terror of running away from his own house when it burned to the ground when he was four. An image of melting faces dancing in the flames brings him to the edge of panic again.

Built in 1967 by Joseph Eichler, who populated the suburbs with his innovative designs, the Towers began idealistically as a racially mixed middle income complex of some 576 units, but the too-small apartments and the notorious fires – as well as the general nationwide failure of integration – scared most of the whites away. The developer went bankrupt, and HUD took over.

As if suddenly remembering her, Barney sidles up to Linda Jean and holds her hand against the fear. She smiles at the unexpected attention. They watch together as the fireman scurries up the ladder from the hook and ladder truck telescoped as far as it will go. He enters the apartment and reappears with a child under each arm. He holds the smaller one, lets the bigger one climb down the ladder himself, followed by a woman, presumably the mother.

Once the family is safely on the ground, the fireman climbs back up and floods the fire with his hose until the black smoke stops billowing.

Meanwhile the TV cameras arrive. Barney lets go Linda Jean's hand and pushes his way to the front of the crowd, which numbered over a hundred people. He asks one of the cameramen what was going on.

"The fireman that rescued the family? That's Dan White. You know, the guy running for Supervisor."

"Hmm," Barney says, not that impressed.

When Dan White, the hero, returns to the ground, he takes the older one of the children he rescued, a boy of about four, and climbs back up the ladder about a third of the way in order to pose for the cameras.

They interview the mother. She says her name into the microphone, "Cali Robinson." A small woman, she's wearing nothing more than a grungy blue quilted bathrobe with neither buttons nor sash, which she has to hold closed against the wind in her tight little fists. "We were so scared. The windl! The wind puffed up the flames like crazy! We thought we were goners!

They, the Towers Management, they gotta do something about these winds!"

After her speech, she comes right up to Barney, perhaps singling him out for being one of very few whites there (who isn't a fireman or a newsperson), perhaps for his reputation as an organizer. "It's time we pinned these motherfuckers to the wall," she says in his ear.

He nods his head, right on. Her anger transforms his fear into excitement.

It's the first time she's actually spoken to him, though he has of course noticed her before – Cali Robinson gets noticed, wherever she goes. Her small body and large eyes radiate sexual energy.

He is acutely aware of Linda Jean, standing a ways behind him watching the drama. His politics preclude any fooling around, and, as one of the few whites who lives in this complex, his activities are not inconspicuous – particularly since he also works as a teacher in the on-site childcare center.

"We'll talk," he tells Cali.

"Yes we will," she answers. "They put me in 1911, right above the old place."

You are a man driven by an anxious compulsion to know what is real. You took Mao's dictum that reality can only be known by acting upon it to the extreme of a constant, restless, and sometimes reckless activity. The minute you stop acting, the anxiety catches up with you and threatens to overwhelm your ability to act forever. Therefore, when, three years earlier, your first wife, Cynthia, tried to slow you down and get you to at least consider your family responsibilities in your revolutionary deliberations, you acted against the anxiety that gives your life it's unreal cast; you acted against the feeling that you were not doing enough to keep the world from collapsing around you; you acted against the sense that you would suffocate in your own fear if you didn't keep moving; you acted in line with your understanding that reality must be constantly tested. You left. You left your wife, you left your children, you left your home to pursue the struggle on the front lines. You moved into this all-black housing complex thinking you will organize "these people" for the revolution. "Divorce, revolution, suicide – it's all the same thing," your father wrote you regarding the break-up of your marriage. You thought of yourself as an expatriate living in the Black nation. You couldn't imagine what they thought of you, a lone white man invading their turf.

It was one o'clock in the morning, and the security guard at the desk by the door was asleep. You were returning from a marathon meeting that put together a newsletter for teachers. You waited for the elevator. When it came, you noticed that all the buttons had been pushed again, another favorite trick of the Towers' preadolescents who roam the hallways even at this hour. The walls of the elevator were covered with burgundy carpeting that must have once looked elegant in a kitschy sort of way, but now the carpet was ragged with knife slashes. You pressed the button for the 15th floor, even though it was already lit. You wondered as you had before at the fact that there's no 13th floor in such a modern building, at the tenacity of superstition. The elevator went down. At the first subbasement, there was a garage filled with old cars whose owners no longer much cared what happened to them. At the second subbasement, there was another garage, but this one was abandoned and littered with Twinkie wrappers and such deposited there by the swirling winds. Three dark young men with hardened faces and rags on their heads strutted onto the elevator, glaring at you with glazed-over eyes. Your whole body stiffened with terror, all the worse for you wanting with all your soul not to let it show, yet knowing they could see it in the tremor of your hands. With your fingers, you combed back your sandy hair, parted Jimmy Carter style, as if to reveal the two inch scar on your forehead above your left eye that you got from a policeman's billy club when you were arrested last year with a group of your comrades, a scar which made you look tougher than you really were. You pushed your wire-rimmed glasses up on your nose to enhance your attentiveness. The elevator started, stopped, started, stopped, agonizingly slow, lurching like a stick-shift car driven by a student driver. But you were cool. You retreated to a corner of the elevator, pocketed your hands, and, with a gentle smirk, tried to ignore the young men. They ignored you back and exchanged high-fives with each other as they discussed the basketball game from which they were returning, in a lingo you were just beginning to understand. You hoped they couldn't hear the thumping of your heart.

2.

It is in his capacity as the vice-president of the Tenant's Association that Barney meets Cali again the day following her fire, in her new apartment on the 19th floor, just above her old one, from which you can still smell that lingering, stockyards-stench of the incinerating blaze. It's his task to hear her grievances against the management resulting from the fire, particularly the ones which might translate into general demands, such as for the exit doors to be unlocked at all times or for a serious wind-break.

Cali had moved to the Towers from Brooklyn two months ago, bringing with her the inimitable accent and those invaluable New York street smarts. It's her Brooklyn-Black English that establishes her primary ethnicity as black, though in skin color she could pass for white. Her hair is not at all coarse, but soft, puffy, and gently curly, though short, and bleached orange, pale enough not to look punk, tipped, the hairdressers call it, so that just the ends of the hair are colored. She's a small woman, five-foot-two, slender, slightly bony. Her skin, when seen in the fluorescent lighting of the Towers' hallway as she opens the door, possesses only a hint of tan, the color of the outer shell of a walnut, without the wrinkles, in fact as smooth as yogurt. She has a sprinkling of freckles across her pug nose and a mole on her cheek (perhaps created by her own pencil) reminiscent of Marilyn Monroe's. Her eyes, emphasized by dark eye-brows, are large and colored a startling gray.

For an instant, he's struck with the image of flames darting through her hollow eye-sockets.

On this warm afternoon, she's wearing red hot-pants and a yellow halter top with black polka dots. She wears lipstick of shimmering violet. Her small feet are bare, her toenails done in Day-Glo pink.

He introduces himself. "Barney Blatz."

"I know who you are." Whoyare.

The living room is barren, glaring white. She has only a few folding chairs, loaned by the management, and they sit on two of these, facing each other. When she looks at him with her penetrating eyes, it feels as if she's undressing him, or even looking through his skin, and he shifts his feet nervously. He looks away from her and gazes through the sliding glass doors to the balcony at the valley stretching out below, from the shipyards on the bay to the east, along the beige ridge of the hills of McLaren Park, to the colorless barracks of the Sunnydale Housing Project to the west, the view muddied by the brown smog from the suburban oil refineries.

She offers him a drink. "Bull?" Schlitz Malt Liquor.

"No thanks, it's a little early for me."

She flashes her eyelashes. "Suit yourself." Yasef.

He can hear children arguing in the back bedroom, over the drone of the replacement TV someone has given her. "Quiet back there, you'll wake the baby," she shouts, plenty loud enough to wake the baby herself.

Then she says, "What gets me, Barney Blatz, is how fast" – fa-ast – "the damn fire" – fi-ah – "spread, you know?"

"How did it start, Mrs. Robinson?"

"Cali, please. Robinson's my no-account white trash father's name, you know? His name was Calvin. He wanted a boy. When he got me instead, he named me Calvina and then split. I ain't seen him since."

Playing to my liberal pity, Barney thinks. Meanwhile, she hasn't answered his question. "Do you know how it started?" he persists, trying to carry out his duties responsibly.

She averts her eyes. "Cigarette. A damn Kool 100 down the couch."

"Polyurethane?"

"Polly-who?" She cocks her head at him skeptically.

"A lot of couches are stuffed with this highly flammable plastic stuff called polyurethane. Was there a lot of really black smoke at first?"

"She-it, Barney Blatz, I don't remember. I was asleep. What are you trying to say here? That it was my fault the fire nearly killed my kids and burnt up everything I own in a matter of seconds? Whose side are you on here?" Yon, heah.

"I'm on your side, Mrs. Rob...Cali. I just have to know what happened so I can get some idea of what management's response will be. I know these apartments are firetraps."

"Well, between you and me, that cigarette is a secret, okay? I ain't told no one but you about it. Far as management and the fire department is concerned, this fire ignited spon-tan-eously, know what I mean? The place was so totally destroyed they'll never know the difference. Can you keep a secret, Barney Blatz?"

"I can keep a secret," he says, smiling involuntarily.

3.

The next time Barney sees Cali is about a week later when she comes to enroll her two boys, Barney and Darnell, in the childcare center. She is wearing stretch-tight jeans and a red western shirt with the tails tied together, showing her midriff and a long gash of a navel.

"Barney?" he exclaims when she introduces him to her older son, whose name is also Barney.

She stands about three inches away from him in the office doorway, seriously invading his space, making him so nervous that he drops the pen he's using to fill out her children's emergency cards. "That's my husband's name too. My *estranged* husband. You take care of my children, Barney Blatz. They're all I got."

One look and Barney knows they are going to be a handful. Darnell, just over two and constantly drooling, doesn't waste a second in pulling down all the puzzles from the puzzle shelf, while Barney, with his mother's eerie gray eyes, knocks down the blocks. Barney tries to redirect their attention, a tactic teachers use, especially in front of the parents.

Seduced by her self-evident power, Barney decides on the spot that he will groom her to lead the parents' group.

He hates that the boy's name is Barney. Whenever he does something wrong, which is frequently, one of the other teachers calls his name in a way that makes the hairs on the back of Barney's neck stand up. If your name is John or Mary you get used to this, but when your name is unusual, you don't expect to hear it referring to someone else.

The childcare center is only two years old now, opened by the local school district in the days when it had a surfeit of funds for such purposes. It's constructed to conform to the exigencies of the "open classroom" approach to teaching, three large rooms in a row, like a New York City railroad flat, with large open doorways between them, and sliding glass doors opening onto the yard. The small office and kitchen are tucked in the corners as you enter the center, either from the 2nd floor hallway or from the yard outside. The walls are freshly painted a cheery yellow, the wooden blocks and Fisher-Price garages are shiny new, and the teachers are full of the enthusiasm engendered from creating a school from scratch. They spend hours in staff meetings debating the merits of freedom versus structure in the curriculum, ways to give the children choices without the situation descending into chaos.

Barney himself is involved in a Super 8 mm. film project with the children.

"Tell me about our movie," he asks the children during his small group time. "You remember how it goes?"

"There's a monster!" squeals one of the twins, Tenisha or Ronisha, identical dark-skinned dolls with short naturals, gold studs in their ears. The staff lets them alternate between the small groups on a random basis because it's too hard to figure out which is which, especially since they both frequently say that they're the other one.

"The Monster of Geneva Towers!" Little Barney, Cali's son, spits as he speaks.

The eight children in Barney's group work on developing the plot and the props. Barney tells them the story, for the umpteenth time. "Once upon a time there were eight children who went to Geneva Towers Children's Center. Their names were: ..." He lists their names.

"There also lived in Geneva Towers, deep in the basement by the abandoned parking garage, a horrible monster. That monster looked like a bear and a wolf all mixed up together, but bigger, as big as you can imagine. Every day that monster would growl down the hallways of the big apartment building, drooling with hunger.

"First he'd go to Ronnie Rodgers' house – what's that number, Ronnie?" Barney asks him.

"Thousanone Vis'tacion, 'partment twothousan' one-B."

"Good, Ronnie. And what do you feed him?"

"Pork chops," says Ronnie. The story goes on like this, with each child feeding the monster his or her favorite food.

They make a monster out of two sheets of butcher

paper stapled together, stuff him with newspaper, paint him brown with white teeth and a red tongue. To film the movie, they go to the door of each of the children's apartments to show the number, and then they film the action at Barney's apartment, 1001 Visitacion, Apartment 1505- A.

In the story, the children hold a meeting and decide to "get rid of that monster, once and for all." Each child gets to pick a weapon. Ronnie chooses a plastic samurai sword, Little Barney picks a broom to knock him over the head with, and whichever one of the twins tries to tie him up with a rope.

Each of the children fails to capture or kill the monster on his or her own of course. They have another meeting, and decide to join forces and work together. They all gather in Barney's apartment, which they pretend is Ronnie's apartment, and after Ronnie lures the monster inside with his promises of pork chops, the children jump him all at once and exuberantly tear him to shreds.

TWO

Split

1.

On another one of those early elevator rides, you met a black woman comrade from the Party, Linda Jean Hudson, who, it turned out, also lived in the complex. She was a husky woman, not fat, but big boned and big hipped; about five foot four, with chestnut skin, smooth except for her hands which were rough from overwork. She wore her hair in a natural of medium length. She had full lips, a smile bursting with warmth, dancing eyes, dimples in her cheeks which revealed themselves in her shyer moments, and a round face that evoked the dark side of the moon.

You made a coffee date and agreed to sell your newspapers together, "the Communist paper," you told people, the organ of your small but militant Party, an uncompromising group which split from the Communist Party to side with China in the Sino-Soviet debate, and then split with Mao when he invited Nixon to visit. You sold a lot of papers door to door in the Towers the next Saturday afternoon, and you asked her to the movies. You saw "The Spy Who Came In From The Cold," Richard Burton, straddling the wall. You criticized the "revisionism" of the movie's politics (you considered the USSR already capitalist), and on the way home your red Volkswagen bus overheated, as was its wont. "I didn't plan this," you said, putting your arm around her. You felt at once a certain strangeness at the contrast of your skin color, yet also a rush of electricity, as if the current between you increased in charge with the distance between the poles. You kissed her passionately as the car's engine cooled. Later that night, your mutual animal magnetism pulled you into bed.

It didn't take long before you realized that you had differences which went beyond race. She was six years older than you, those years spanning World War II, a generational watershed. Her father was a railroad worker, yours a prominent ophthalmologist. She finished high school. You had a master's degree. She worked as a domestic. You were a teacher. She liked Victoria Holt; you liked Franz Kafka. She liked Frank Capra movies (without knowing his name); you liked Goddard. She liked Johnny Mathis; you liked Motown. She liked the Beatles; you liked the Rolling Stones.

But, you had your differences in common, and a limitless commitment to the struggle. Overcoming barriers and achieving unity was what the struggle is all about, in love as well as revolution. With the revolution only 10 years away, there was nothing you couldn't do.

As time went on you discovered that she had a way with children, and you loved how she was with yours, firm and loving all at once in a way that eluded you. She was so good in fact that you persuaded her to get a job as an assistant teacher in the schools, which she did, without, however, giving up her job as a domestic. She had a son of her own, Darryl, a man now in his late teens, who nevertheless moved in with you and Linda Jean one day on his own. He worked nights at a gas station, kept the family's cars going, and stayed out of trouble. The product of a teenage fling on the part of his mother that got her ostracized from her own family, he was now what his grandmother would call a "fine young man," a tribute to Linda Jean's child-rearing skills.

Only five months had passed since you left your first wife, Cynthia, and you had hardly begun to grieve. You didn't even know it was necessary. Knowing your feelings was not one of your strengths.

You and Linda Jean clung to each other as leaves cling to a tree in a windstorm. You couldn't deny that her color was an asset. You liked to think that you were attracted to black women the way some men were attracted to blondes, but there was more to it than that. She was a good woman and your being with her proved you were a good man, relatively free from prejudice. Being with her lent you legitimacy as an organizer in the Towers. And, she had an innocence about her that was at once disarming and profoundly endearing.

You were married six months later on November 22, 1974, in your 15th floor apartment at 7 in the morning, in the company of your three children, Darryl 18, Jason 4, and Ramona 2. The ceremony was performed by Leonora Jackson, a proudly fat woman from your school who was associated with Rev. Jim Jones' People's Temple, but who had also been credentialed (for $1.00) as a minister for the Universal Life Church (and was therefore legally qualified to perform a marriage). The date, the anniversary of the Kennedy assassination, was your idea, a cynical joke mocking the sanctity of marriage and death. "At least we won't have trouble remembering our anniversary," you joked.

You composed your own vows. Linda Jean said: "Barney, as a Communist I promise to love you forever, to pick you up when you are down if you will support me in my weakness."

You said: "Linda Jean, I commit myself to revolutionary love for you. Marriage is a great contradiction, and it is in contradiction that all things come into being and flourish. I promise to struggle with you in the name of the revolution. Together we'll fight to change the world."

You prepared a tape to go with your vows which included musical selections from Minnie Riperton ("Loving you is easy cuz you're beautiful" – Linda Jean's choice), Gladys Knight ("For once in my life" and "It's got to be that way" – your choices), and Al Green ("Let's get married" – a consensual choice) – but you forgot to start the cassette player.

You honeymooned at the Timber Cove Inn on the Sonoma Coast north of San Francisco, a delightfully decadent hostelry overlooking the ocean, with a hot tub and fireplace in the room, a gourmet restaurant with a cathedral ceiling suspended from massive redwood beams, and a phallic Benjamin Bufano sculpture gracing its most prominent cliff. For 24 hours at least, you wallowed in the contradictions of being revolutionary Communists in this post-scarcity advanced capitalist society. You decided against reporting on your trip in much detail to your Party comrades. You were happy.

Your favorite record was a long piece by Charles Mingus called "Meditations on Integration." The piece was a triumph for Mingus when he performed and recorded it in 1970 at the Monterrey Jazz Festival, an outfit which for years had shunned him. The music veered back and forth from

cacophonous disharmonies to a manically powerful me-
lodic line, representing "integration" in every sense of the
word. Your life – living, loving, teaching, and organizing all
within the multiracial organic unity of Geneva Towers – had
achieved just the kind of "integration" that that music so
transcendently proclaimed.

2.

Cali and Barney develop a relationship in the ensuing
months of 1977 characterized by her trying to get him
involved in the Dan White for Supervisor campaign
and him trying to get her involved with the Party, in
various campaigns around the schools and for rent
control in the city. They wrangle good-naturedly, because they both know that her gut-level politics are
way to the left of White, and she's supporting him
primarily out of gratitude for his having saved her
children. "No one's ever done anything like that for
me," she says. For his own sake (or for the sake of his
marriage), he's glad to see her get hooked up with a
big, muscular, dark-skinned man named Mike Davis.
He's a former cocaine addict who used to finance his
habit by fencing stolen cassette decks, but who has
been "saved" by Jim Jones, and has risen through the
treacherous hierarchy of the People's Temple to become the head of its youth program.

The Tenants' Association holds numerous demonstrations, but can't get management to agree to build
a wind-break or improve the fireproofing of the
apartments.

"Let's just let this one go," Barney tells Linda Jean one night after a frustrating tenants' meeting. "It's not, like, the most exciting issue in the world."

"Barney, there are lives at stake here, what's more important than that? Everything can't be exciting and that there. We need to go all the way on this one."

"Okay, it's important, but we're not getting anywhere. It's not a winnable demand. What do you suggest?"

"How about a rent strike?" Linda Jean answers a devilish gleam in her eye.

The idea scares and thrills him at the same time. "I don't know. I suppose we could try."

Linda Jean has a stubbornness about her which is infuriating at times but which makes her a dependable ally to Barney in the political realm. He can be easily demoralized and at such times tends to give up. She has a larger picture of the struggle, which he attributes to her working-class background.

They discuss the rent strike proposal with their Party comrades and, not surprisingly, they think it's a great idea. Barney and Linda Jean plan to raise it at the next Tenant's Association meeting.

With the election less than a month away, Cali has invited Dan White to the meeting, and Linda Jean and Barney meet him for the first time. Barney is wary of him because he's an ex-cop, and the police are supporting him as one of their own, but he does respect his heroism as a fireman, and he is struck by his sincerity.

"Cali tells me you're quite an organizer here," White says to Barney, flashing his smiling blue eyes. He looks exactly like his picture on the billboard near the freeway, a ruggedly handsome fellow a couple years younger than Barney, say 32, with short dark hair, neatly kempt, and a muscular body. "She recommended you to me. Are you interested in working on the campaign?"

Is he naive or what, Barney wonders. Doesn't he know I'm a fucking Communist? he thinks. He's hardly kept it a secret. It's the policy of the Party to be as up front about their politics as possible to undercut red baiting. Rather than plead the Fifth Amendment like people from other organizations, their members told HUAC during its hearings some years ago things like, "Are you asking if I'm a Communist? You're damn right I'm a Communist!" They would follow this declaration with an argument for why a revolution was needed in the U. S.

Barney tells White, "I don't think so. We're not into electoral politics."

Barney insists that Linda Jean make the proposal for a rent strike, since it was her idea and will fare better coming from a black person. She is a shy woman and nervous about raising her voice. She waits until the last minute, while the meeting drones on, with White talking about "community block grant funds" and the Tenant's Association president, Cora Jimenez, a woman whose straightened hair is so gooey with hairspray that even the Towers' wind won't mess it up, complaining about all the welfare mothers here who don't care how the building looks. Finally, Linda Jean raises her hand and says, "I'd like to propose a rent strike," her dimples giving away her embarrassment.

The meeting falls silent. "I'm going to rule that out of order," Cora Jimenez says, the first time she's invoked any kind of procedure all meeting.

"I think you're out of order," Linda Jean snaps back.

"Very well." Cora smiles insincerely. "The meeting's adjourned."

Though they've encountered such reactions to their proposals in various contexts in the past, Linda Jean focuses her eyes on the floor, clearly hurt. Embarrassed for her, everyone avoids her as the meeting breaks up, except Dan White, who speaks to her as if it were her that was simply naive. "I can appreciate your frustration," he says. "But those kind of confrontational tactics don't work anymore. The sixties are over."

When they report on this meeting to the Party's local leadership committee, they are surprised that it ignites a big debate, with far-reaching consequences. There are two factions, those who think they should work with Cora Jimenez and Cali, if not White, and those who think that if the Party put forward the correct line of a rent strike to the "masses," they will follow. Most of the local leaders, including Linda Jean and Barney feel the party should unite with the Tenant's Association, but there's a significant minority that wants the Party to go it alone, and they appeal to the national leadership.

There is an ominous rancor to the debate, and Linda Jean and Barney cling together anxiously, overcome with the sense of their neat little world unraveling.

The Party operates by the principle of "democratic centralism," which means, in this case, that whatever the national leadership says goes.

While waiting for the National Committee to rule, Barney gets Cali's friend Mike to set up a meeting with Jim Jones, the head of the city's Housing Authority, a post he was given as a reward for helping to elect Mayor Moscone – a somewhat desperate move on Barney's part to resolve the matter short of what could be a disastrous rent strike. Linda Jean and Barney meet him in his office in the People's Temple, a domed, former synagogue, built of mustard- colored brick, in the ruins of the Western Addition Urban Renewal area, surrounded by vacant lots.

The walls of his office are covered with proclamations and awards for community service, as well as pictures of Jones with politicians, from Mayor George Moscone to Roslyn Carter. Jones wears dark glasses, but they don't hide the intensity of his eyes. His brown hair falls repeatedly over his forehead despite him constantly combing it back with his fingers. He's dressed casually, in a white cotton, short-sleeved, slip-over shirt without buttons, and pale gray slacks. Linda Jean and Barney are both nervous, unused to being in the presence of such self-assurance.

"You're from Geneva Towers," he states in a voice that seems to come from deep in his viscera, a voice that reverberates through your brain as if he were in touch with some subliminal energy that commands you trust him absolutely.

"That's right," Barney says. "I'm the vice-president of the Tenant's Association." Barney thinks he can see his eyes narrowing, as if recognizing in him some commonality with him in their relationship to black people. "We were wondering if the Housing Authority might be able to do something about management's reluctance to build a wind-break out there. The wind is a terrible fire hazard."

"I've heard about it," he says. "But it is out of the jurisdiction of the Housing Authority. We only deal with city-run public housing, and believe me, we have our hands full there. Tell you what though. I've got people out there from the church. We can look into making a church project out of your struggle there. Might take some time."

They're interrupted by an old black man, thin, bent over, who removes his Giants' baseball cap as he enters the office, and bows his head humbly.

"Yes, what is it, Brother?" Jones asks.

"I'm sorry to bother you, Sir..."

Jones interrupts him. "Don't ever be sorry, Brother. Be proud!"

The man stands straighter. "I got laid off the job and got no money for the rent."

"Your name's Reeves, isn't it?" Jones asks.

"That's right," the man says, visibly pleased that Jones would remember his name.

"Six great kids, a loving wife: ask, Brother and it shall be given unto you." He scribbles a note and hands it to the man. "Give this to Sister Henderson outside and she'll take care of you."

The man smiles broadly and suddenly looks ten years younger. "Thank you, Reverend! Thank you!"

"That's what we're here for, Brother. I know you'll pay us back tenfold in service to the struggle." Jones turns back to us. "Now, where were we?"

Barney stammers, unable to believe what he's just seen. This man is some kind of saint, he thinks. "We... we were thinking about calling a rent strike," Barney tells him, incautiously.

"Whoa, you better wait on that until we've had time to look into it. Work with Mike Davis. We'll be in touch." He stands up from his cluttered desk, shakes their hands. His touch vibrates through Barney in a way that makes him think this guy really could heal the sick. They leave his office, dazed with wonder.

Somehow the National Committee of the Party gets word of this meeting with Jones and accuses Barney and Linda Jean of "uniting with the class enemy" for attempting to build an alliance with a "bourgeois sell-out preacher." They are told that the Committee's decision is that they should go ahead and call the rent strike in the name of the Party, to "rely on the working class, not its enemies."

This accusation makes Barney feel like a naughty

little boy again, as if everything he does is wrong, wrong, wrong. It makes him hunger for what Jones seems to have, that sense of being able to do *no* wrong.

With extreme reluctance, in the name of "party unity," Barney and Linda Jean swallow their "bourgeois individualism," and issue a leaflet in the middle of the holiday season calling on all residents of Geneva Towers to withhold their rent until the management agrees to build a wind-break.

The results come swiftly. Within days, Cora Jimenez calls an emergency meeting of the Tenant's Association without inviting Linda Jean and Barney, which votes to remove Barney as vice-president, to kick him off the board entirely, and to demand that Linda Jean and Barney be evicted unless they rescind their leaflet. Cali pays them a visit, flush with her victory in electing Dan White – he's gotten her a job in the Board of Supervisor's secretarial pool – and while she is not unfriendly, she does inform them that many tenants are highly upset with them because their rent is just about fully subsidized by the federal government through Section 8, making such a rent strike not only ineffective, but downright foolhardy, jeopardizing their subsidies. She tells them that Mike is angry too. He had thought they had an agreement to consult with him.

Meanwhile, the local Party leadership attacks the national leadership for their "sectarian" decision regarding this situation in a way that the leadership decrees violates "democratic centralism" and gets the locals expelled. Most of the Bay Area membership, Linda Jean and Barney included, quits the Party in protest. On the one hand, Barney feels exonerated and liberated. On the other hand, suddenly, from now on, they are on their own.

Sometimes it was hard for you to tell what's real. Sometimes you couldn't even tell what you were feeling. There were mornings you lay in bed and you couldn't tell whether you had just fallen asleep or just awakened. Such moments were fraught with terror, and your pillow case was stained with sweat from the struggle of sorting things out. On your own now, you were once again adrift without mooring or anchor. Only four years previously you walked out on your first wife and family to follow this flawed vanguard. Ironically, it was Cynthia who got you involved with the Party in the first place, "love me, love my dogma," she quipped at the time, but then she became disillusioned herself when she noticed that the role that she wold be allowed to play in the movement, as a woman, was limited to typing the leaflets written by the men, and making the coffee. You didn't like this either, but you felt the Party would best be changed from the inside.

You had other questions too, but you believed that the Party was committed to ending racism, which coincided with the mission that you'd been on ever since the civil rights movement crystallized your vision of what the world could be like. You weren't sure how your own destiny and that of the movement became intertwined, even confused. Certainly you remembered hearing Martin Luther King back in the late sixties, when the civil rights movement was becoming the Black Power movement, answering a reporter who had asked him what role white people should play in the struggle. King got kind of mad and said, "Well it's like this: if you see a man stuck in a deep pit, what do you do? You help him out of the pit."

But you knew there was more to it than that. At age 12 you read Billie Holiday's autobiography, and you spent your adolescence in an all boys' boarding school listening to her mournful songs and pining for her kind of passion. Your favorite song was "Strange Fruit;" your favorite line from that song:

Scent of magnolia, sweet and fresh,
Then the sudden smell of burning flesh.

On an illegal weekend, you snuck into New York and lost your virginity to a black prostitute.

In your first year at Berkeley, there was an argument between the students and the administration over whether it was legal to collect money for the civil rights movement on campus, and you found yourself drawn into the fray, arrested along with 800 others after following Joan Baez singing "We Shall Overcome" into Sproul Hall for a sit-in, an event which precipitated the Free Speech Movement, an experience which exposed the bankruptcy of liberalism before your eyes. Then the Vietnam War followed shortly thereafter from the same liberal premises and shattered whatever remaining vestiges of faith you might have had in the system. Ho Chi Minh, Fidel, Mao Tse Tung, and the ever elusive People they represent will shape the history of the future. You questioned the dictatorial policies that your heroes pursued, but you developed a rationale: it was a trade-off, political freedom for economic freedom. Which was more important, after all, in the broad scheme of things? If, like the vast majority of the worlds' peoples, you had nothing to eat, what good did it do to have the right to complain? And it was amply clear from the events in the South, that even where political rights were "guaranteed," only the rich and powerful really had access to them.

There was still another dimension which sometimes revealed glimpses of itself in these early morning moments of heightened awareness, an idiosyncratic vision which you couldn't really discuss with anyone, a notion you had that the Communists were putting into practice what for centuries the Christians only preached: unity in universal love – a boundless energy released by uniting the largest group of humans on earth, the international working class. It was up to you and your comrades to finally realize the Kingdom of Heaven on Earth. And, there were moments lying close to Linda Jean in bed that you had an image of this new world streaming jointly out of your eyes and her eyes, a vast, luminous city reminiscent of El Greco's "Toledo," Diego Rivera's depiction of the Aztec city of "Temochtila'n," or even the picture of New Jerusalem that blues singers' Sonny Terry and Brownie McGee invoked with rasping harmonies in the song "Beautiful City."

That you and your former comrades were now sworn enemies was disturbing, but the vision was still real, and you would continue to pursue it even if you had to do it by yourself.

"Barney, the sixties are over," Cynthia said to you in one of your final arguments, and it was true, the second half of the seventies witnessed droves of activists giving up the dream and settling for modest lives of raising families. But not you. You couldn't let it go. You had to know what's real, and the only way you could tell was to keep acting upon reality, trying with all your might to change it. The movement was you and you were the movement. You had merged yourself with the People. You would never give up. Never.

3.

Linda Jean and Barney involve themselves that bleak winter of 1978 in various efforts to organize a new group and unite with other groups on the left, but most of the people who left the Party with them are sick of the struggle and drop out.

Not Barney and Linda Jean though. There's a trace of desperation to their efforts as they shop around for issues and allies. What would they be forced to feel if there were no struggle in which to bury their feelings? Whatever it is, they are in no hurry to feel it.

Fortunately, by spring, they are rescued by two re-actionaries from Southern California named Howard Jarvis and Paul Gann. These two gentlemen spear-head a grass-roots movement for reduced property taxes, based jointly on the legitimate grievances of mid-dle-class homeowners and on the thinly veiled notions that most of their tax money is being "wasted" on mi-nority people in welfare programs and in the schools.

As the June election approaches, Linda Jean, Cali, and Barney go door to door in the Towers with literature against Proposition 13, as the Jarvis-Gann tax relief initiative has come to be called.

School boards are asked by the State to list the cuts they would need to make if proposition 13 passes. One of the cuts that the San Francisco board proposes involves the closing of sixteen small schools, including the Geneva Towers Children's Center.

On June 6, 1978, Proposition 13 passes overwhelmingly in the state of California, marking the beginning of the end.

4.

On the night of the "victory" party for the "No on 13" campaign, Linda Jean and Barney find themselves in the kind of mindnumbing funk you can sink into when you have given the struggle your all, and still the forces of reaction are closing in on you from all sides. They can't dance, though ordinarily they love to; they can't get drunk, though they are good at that too; and they can't talk – which isn't all that unusual.

They have a mild argument. "Let's go home," Barney says. "I'm exhausted."

"Now? They haven't even counted all the votes yet. It looks bad, but we can't cave in so easily, Barney."

Her stubborn streak again. "Fuck it, Linda Jean, I've had it. Face it, will you? We've lost. Badly."

"Barney, it's just one ballot proposition. You've got to be stronger than that. If we give up this easily, then they really will have won, more than just one battle. I thought you wanted to be a leader and that there. You have to set some kind of example."

Barney knows she's right, but her being right just now is making him sick. He wants to collapse. Times when she drips with self- righteousness like this he can't stand to be around her, so he turns his back on her and walks away.

He runs into Cali Robinson, in a leather miniskirt, smiling, boring her startling gray eyes right into him, that gray an eye color which black culture sometimes associates with devilment. "What are you so happy about?" Barney says.

"I'm just happy to see you is all. What's the big deal? So it's all going to hell on a sled, so what? It's always been that way for poor folks."

"Happy to see me, huh? Where's that big hunk of yours?" They've come to flirt more and more over the past few months, but it doesn't mean anything.

"He's around here someplace with his Temple buddies. He's in love with Jim Jones."

"I always wondered how you two were able to reconcile your different politics," he says.

"It's easy, Barney. We're two different people, you know?"

"Do you know they're planning to close our child-care center?" he tells her.

"No shit?"

"No shit."

"We can't let them do that, Barney Blatz."

"No, we can't, Cali."

By the time he gets back to Linda Jean, she is fuming. "Let's go," she says.

"I thought you wanted to stay."

"I saw you talking to her. I saw how you looked at her. You think I was born yesterday?" This is the first time she has acted this way about Cali. He had no idea she was the least bit jealous.

"Jeannie, please. Don't do this. There's nothing between us. I'm not that kind of guy. Really. Trust me," he says.

They leave the party and sulk to themselves all the way home.

In bed, he reassures her some more. "Linda Jean, I promise you I'm not even attracted to women like Cali. All that 'sexiness' is usually a cover for frigidity, you know. To me, you're the hottest thing on two wheels." This isn't just flattery. He's thinking that he's increasing his commitment to her in the face of his doubts.

Whatever his motives, his words light a fire in her furnace, and they make love, hard and sweet.

"It's just that I love you so much," she says, cuddling next to him in the afterglow. "I'm scared of losing you."

"I know," he says.

After a few minutes of warm silence, she speaks in a confessional tone, with tears in her voice. "I had this cousin Felicia who lived with us back in Pennsylvania. She was, well, you know, slow, retarded, and that there. She was older than me, but she was my best friend. One day, I...I couldn't find her. I looked all over the house. Then I heard some noises in the bathroom. I peeked in

through the keyhole. It was her. And him. My own father. They were.... I ran outside and threw up in the
street.

"I've never told that story to anyone," she con-
cludes, her voice cracking.

Barney doesn't know what to say, so he just holds
her. I'll never leave you, Linda Jean, he thinks, but he
doesn't say anything.

THREE

Juneteenth

1.

"Who knows what special day it is today?" Barney asks the children during circle time.

"Christmas," answers Clarisse, with all the braids.

"Halloween," screams Dathan, who has a long, narrow face.

"No," he tells them, "it's a day called 'Juneteenth,' which stands for the day the slaves were freed in a place called Texas, June 19, 1863, a long time ago, before you were born, before I was born, before my mother was born, even before Leonora was born." I wink at my colleague, who scowls back good-naturedly as she bustles about, making preparations for our Juneteenth party. "Who knows what slaves are?"

"I've got slaves on my shirt," says Dathan.

"Not quite, Dathan. That's close though. Those are 'sleeves.' A long time ago, most black people were slaves, which means they were forced to work without getting any pay by the mean, rich white people."

One of the twins, Tenisha or Ronisha, who are very dark- skinned, says, "I'm not black. I'm brown."

"Let's see. I better start at the beginning. A really,

really long time ago, the first people lived in a beautiful place called Africa. The first people in the world were black people, because Africa is hot, and people needed dark skin to protect them from the sun. More and more people were born and Africa got crowded, so people began to move all over the world. The people who settled in a place called Europe developed light skin because Europe is cold, and they needed the warmth from the sun." The children are fidgeting, untying each other's' shoes. "Then there was a war. The light-skinned people from Europe fought the dark-skinned people from Africa, and the light-skinned people won and captured the black people, made slaves out of them, sold them like cattle to white people in America, who made the slaves work for nothing. Then there was another war, and the slaves were freed. In Texas, that happened on Juneteenth. They had a big party, with barbecue and everything, just like we're going to have this afternoon. Ribs, potato salad, sweet potato pie."

"Can we go outside now?" little Barney asks.

"Do you see Leonora out there? She's cooking the ribs. We'll go out in a little while. But there's one more thing I want to tell you."

"Oh, man," sighs Dathan.

"The slaves were freed, but they weren't given any land or money, so black people stayed poor and weren't really free."

"I'm not poor," says Ronnie, light-skinned and pudgy-faced.

"The point is," I continue, "people still have to fight for freedom. Like remember I told you they want to close our school? We have to fight to keep our school open."

"I know kung fu," says Ronnie, and he starts to demonstrate on Dathan who slaps him in the face. Ronnie cries. Barney decides circle time is over. They go outside and have their barbecue.

2.

On the cold, foggy morning of the summer solstice, Linda Jean, Cali, and Barney drive downtown to meet with Dan White in his office in City Hall, a domed, Italianate structure reminiscent of the Vatican – how appropriate in this Catholic city – with marble floors that echo with their footsteps as they pass through the metal detector (installed after Sara Jane Moore took a shot at President Ford some years back elsewhere in the city). They ascend the sweeping central stairway.

White sits at his desk, empty except for a phone and a picture of his wife and baby. There's a tacky photo-mural on the wall next to him, depicting the woods in autumn colors, the way they never get in California. He's reading the *Chronicle*. He greets them nervously and seats them awkwardly around him so he can't see them all at once but has to keep turning his head.

With a gleam in his eye, he shows them, without comment, the picture in the paper of Harvey Milk, the gay Supervisor (and the first openly gay elected official in the US), gleefully pointing to a massive glob of dog doo-doo on his shoe to publicize his "pooper scooper" law.

"What can I do for you?" he asks finally, blinking his bright blue Irish eyes. He's wearing charcoal slacks and a pale blue dress shirt, no tie or jacket.

Cali begins, "They want to close the childcare center in Geneva Towers, Dan. We need your help to stop them."

"Who is 'they'?" he asks. "And what are their reasons?"

Barney answers, feeling immediately guilty for stealing the floor from Cali. "The Board of Education. They only opened the place three years ago. They want to move the children to another place a mile up the hill. And you know the reason. Prop. 13."

"So the children won't actually lose their service?"

"No," Cali says, "except that that mile up the hill happens to be through the Sunnydale housing projects, which you ought to know are the roughest in the city. And you know how fragile people's lives can be when they're living at the poverty level. Many won't make it up there." Barney notices how perfect her English has suddenly become.

"Are the teachers losing their jobs?" he asks me.

"We don't think so; presumably they will be transferred up the hill too."

"I don't see why this cut is so terrible if no one is losing service or jobs," White says.

"You miss the point, Dan," Cali sharpens her tone. "Geneva Towers is *our* community, and this center is *our* center. It's a good school, and with all the bad schools out there I don't think we can afford to lose a good school. Besides, Dan, you owe me."

Their eyes meet and sparks seem to fly off of them from the history of their relationship. Barney wonders if they ever slept together. White, as if reading his mind, turns red. "Cali, you know I don't play that way. This 'you scratch my back, I'll scratch yours' business is what's wrong with politics in this city. I've got more integrity than George and Harvey put together."

Barney assumes George is Mayor George Moscone and Harvey is Supervisor Harvey Milk, but he can't figure out what they are doing in this conversation.

White continues, "I'll look into the merits of the case. It does seem reasonable that the Towers have a childcare center since it has the facility. If no reduction in staff or service is involved, there can't be that much of a saving. What would they be saving by closing the center, anyway?"

"Rent," Barney answers, "about $600 a month plus maintenance. Chickenfeed."

"Why don't you talk to the management of the Towers and see if they'll reduce or even write off the rent? I'm sure keeping the center is in their interest, too."

"That's a good idea," Barney gushes, taken aback by getting more than he expected from this Boy Scout. He nods at Cali and Linda Jean and they all nod together.

They express their thanks and good-byes. "Keep me posted," he says. "I'll do what I can. I'll talk to the school board members, let them know my concern."

3.

The Head Teacher at the childcare center, Marcia Mason, is a mousy black woman, a former radical who isn't about to rock the boat. This leaves it up to Cali and Barney to organize the fight against the center's closing. They issue an urgent flier calling for a meeting of all the parents.

Marcia surprises them by inviting the Director of the program from the school district, Sylvia Conners, an elegant black woman, a formidable opponent, who drives a yellow Mercedes 450SL convertible.

Cali opens the meeting without recognizing Sylvia or Marcia. She goes right to the point. "I called this meeting for the parents, so we can organize our response to the threat by the school board to close our center. I'm here to tell anyone who might be listening that this center will not close."

I'm scared of you, Cali, Barney thinks, an expression he picked up from her ("skahd a you" she says). He curbs his urge to dominate the meeting and looks around to see who the fighters will be. There are a good 30 people at the meeting, not bad for a school with only 48 children. The twins' mother Alice with a gruff voice like a man's is clearly the most militant, ready to storm the administration building. Ronnie's mother Latricia is educated, articulate, trained in the civil rights movement. She will be their spokesperson before the board. Sue Ann from the South, mother of Dathan and Clarisse, is illiterate, shy, but solid as a rock. Charlene, also quiet, mother of the withdrawn Rhonda, but a close running buddy with Cali, who will go along with whatever Cali says. This, along with Cali, Linda Jean, and Barney, looks like the hard core. He thinks, we are in good shape.

There's also Cecilia, Angela's mom, an ardent Jehovah's Witness, a saintly figure who wears ankle length skirts, and her brother Eddie, an odd fish, lanky and awkward, who volunteers at the center and seems to enjoy playing at the children's level: these two are not likely to oppose the parents.

They have invited a few nonparents as allies, including Reggie Johnson, the Rec Director, who works with the teenagers in the complex (they call him "Rec" – or "Wreck"), Cora Jimenez, the president of the Tenant's Association, and Cali's Friend, Mike Davis from the People's Temple. Cali also invited Dan White, who promised to come but never does show.

They make plans to circulate a petition in the Towers, to lobby the School Board members, to meet with the Tower's management, to coalesce with other groups fighting for survival. Mike Davis makes a statement. "I think I can get the People's Temple to help us out here. They have a lot of influence." The gathering applauds enthusiastically.

Latricia, a tall woman with an elegant Jheri curl, perks up. "You're involved with them?" she says to

Mike. "I am too. I'll help you with that."

Finally, Cali can no longer avoid letting Sylvia speak her piece. The director stands, confident and stately, taking her time. "It's wonderful to see such energy coming from parents, and I want you to know that I share your concerns. Ever since this Proposition 13 passed, I've been meeting with the board and with Sacramento to find ways to avoid cutting back our service. I'm happy to say that we've been largely successful. I can promise you this much: *there will be no cutback in our service to parents,* not here in Visitacion Valley or anywhere else in this city. Believe me, it has not been easy to hold to this position. The one concession we've had to make is to agree to operate more efficiently. This is one reason why we're proposing to close this site – along with fifteen other similarly small sites in the district – and combine it with other sites in the area into one large site. I realize this is an inconvenience for those of you used to riding the elevator to your center, but like many of you, I'm from the south, and when I was coming up, I had to walk 3 miles to the black school when the white school was only 2 blocks away. Compared to that, your having to ride the bus up the hill isn't so great a hardship..."

Unable to hold his tongue any longer, Barney interrupts. "That's not the point, Sylvia. The point is that this is a step backward, and the people here are not in a mood to go back to the days before the civil rights movement. This school is *our* school, and you don't have the right to make this decision for us. The vote on Prop. 13 was a racist vote, and we don't intend to go along with it no matter how popular racism has come to be again..."

Sylvia interrupts him back. "I can't speak for the others here, Mr. Blatz, but I personally resent you speaking for *us*, as a white man. I don't think you understand at all the kinds of compromises people have had to make in order to just survive. *We* can't afford the luxury of your privileged radicalism. Most of us don't appreciate you coming into our community and telling us how to think. Furthermore, there's another reason I've recommended that this site be closed. It isn't safe." She reaches into a shopping bag and pulls out a circular barbell weight, marked "25 LBS." She continues. "Two weeks ago, someone dropped this weight off one of the balconies above the center's play yard in the middle of the afternoon, while our children were playing out there. Can you imagine what would have happened if one of our children – your child – had been hit? Think about it."

Barney is dumbstruck by her attack on him. His stomach ties itself in knots. He's seething with rage but too terrified to vent it out at her. He can tell by the buzz through the meeting that she has succeeded in sowing confusion. He glances at Linda Jean, who, surprisingly, considering her shyness, has risen to speak.

"'*Our* community?'" she says. "You come here in your $30,000 Mercedes and talk about '*our* community?' I think we have a little better idea than you do about who our friends and enemies are."

She doesn't say much, but it feels to Barney as if she has saved the meeting. Actually, it feels as if she's saved his life.

Tensions are high and no one is raising their hands anymore. Cora Jimenez speaks next. "The sister from the school district has a point, though, about the danger. We've been trying for years to get management to get rid of the irresponsible tenants here, and until we do, none of us is safe." This is a favorite theme of Cora's, exploiting the class divisions in the Towers between those who work and those on welfare.

Latricia ignores her and speaks to Sylvia, with a conciliatory tone, cleverly positioning herself between the warring factions, yet clearly remaining on the parents' side. "Mrs. Conners, I am personally gratified that you are so concerned with the safety of our children. And I share your dismay over the behavior of some of our tenants. But I need to point out to you that we live here, along with about 1000 children. Even if there's no childcare center here, there will always be plenty of children playing on that yard near enough to the balconies to get hit if someone drops something. At least with a center here, these children get a certain amount of supervision. And, I wonder how difficult or expensive it would be to build a roof over that part of the yard that's dangerous. I'll bet we could even get a grant from someone for something like that."

Cali, who has been uncharacteristically silent through this debate, now moves deftly to give it closure. "We've heard from the administration. I think we know what's what. I'd like to bring the matter up for a vote so we all know where we stand. All those in favor of keeping the center open no matter what, please raise your hand." About two-thirds of the gathering does so. "There's your answer, Mrs. Conners. Take that back to your bosses. This center will not close." There's loud applause.

On impulse, as the meeting breaks up, Barney starts to sing: "We shall not, we shall not be moved..." and the others join in. He gives both Cali and Linda Jean a hug.

4.

They are having one of those discussions, Linda Jean and Barney, one that Barney initiated because the silences between them have become painfully loud and the sex consequently routine. "One thing I hate," Barney says, "is always being the one to do this, to bring up the tough stuff."

They're lying naked in bed, having just watched the 10 o'clock news, new revelations about People's Temple, Jim Jones using chicken guts to fake a cancer cure. Linda Jean and Barney figure Jones is being persecuted for his socialist views and political activism. COINTELPRO.

"What's wrong now, Barney? You bring stuff up because you're always dissatisfied. Things seem fine to me."

"Well, sex, for one thing."

"Sex? What's wrong with our sex? I love our sex."

"Oh, it's okay, I just want more variety."

"Just tell me what you want, Barney."

"I don't mean that way. I don't mean like new positions or something. I mean I want to try other partners. This monogamy thing is a drag."

"Oh," she says, looking hurt. "Anyone in particular you had in mind?"

"No, not really."

She's silent for a time. Then she says, "You want to meet my friend Al and his wife? You know, I told you about that New Year's party I went to at their house."

He remembers. An orgy, she called it. She came with a friend without expecting anything but an ordinary party. When everyone in the party started taking off their clothes, she was terrified, but she went along and kind of enjoyed it. The prospect does excite him. "Are you serious?"

"Sure. Why not?"

Her suggestion seems so out of character that he is suspicious. "Are you sure you want to do this? You're not just doing this to please me?"

"It was my idea, wasn't it, Barney? I'll call them."

He listens while she calls. The usual pleasantries. Then she says, unbelievably. "We were wondering if you wanted to get together. My husband and I...we share sex." She makes a date for a few days hence. She hangs up and smiles at Barney proudly. He loves her profoundly at that moment, and they make love amid visions of all kinds of other bodies.

⏝

Al and Ruby live in one of the newer co-ops in the Western Addition Urban Renewal Area. Their apartment is decorated in what Barney calls, to Linda Jean's dismay, Afro-American kitsch. Plastic African masks, a bust of Nefertiti, a sappy picture of Martin Luther King surrounded by teary-eyed children. Dark paneled walls, ornate lamps, a gold living room set covered with clear plastic.

Al is short, pudgy, dark-skinned, balding, and Barney's first thought is, to his heterosexual surprise, he's cute. Ruby is tall, dignified, smooth-skinned, lovely.

"Drink?" Al asks in his gravelly voice.

"Brandy," Barney and Linda Jean both answer.

They talk about People's Temple – Ruby's mother is in Guyana; and Prop. 13 – Al works for the city. Barney doesn't exactly know how this is supposed to happen, but he's anxious to get started. "Well?" he says, proud of his boldness.

"Yeah, let's go upstairs," says Al.

They follow him up. They undress. They get into the king size bed. Al gives his attention to Linda Jean. Barney works on Ruby. The whole thing seems on the perfunctory side, too matter of fact. Ruby and Barney make love, and somewhere in the middle, Barney feels Al's hand on his balls. He's surprised, but not shocked.

When Ruby and Barney are done, they lie back and watch Al do it to Linda Jean. This is a strange feeling, watching another man make love to your wife. What's even stranger is it affects Barney hardly at all.

On their way home, though, Linda Jean is furious. "You seemed to enjoy her more than you ever do me."

"Jeannie," he whines. "It was your idea, remember?"

"You just weren't supposed to enjoy it that much."

"I didn't," he says, not really lying.

FOUR

The Fourth of July

1.

He wears his black velour three-piece suit with flared trousers and a wide, red paisley tie. He knows he looks sharp. Linda Jean wears a dark lavender silk wrap-around dress that she made herself.

"Linda Jean, you look gorgeous," Cali gushes as she answers her door four floors above their apartment. She wears her stretch jeans and a white jersey top that shows off her skinniness. Mike, with muscles like a body builder, also wears jeans, a Navy blue ribbed turtleneck, and a tweed sport jacket.

Linda Jean and Barney glance at each other. We're overdressed, that glance says.

Mike gives us the once-over. "It's not like a regular church," he says. "But that's okay. Your outfits might help you get through security. We've had to beef things up since all those attacks have appeared in the paper. My vouching for you will help, but you'll still have to be interviewed, you understand. They have to be especially cautious with Angela speaking." Angela Davis, under indictment for supposedly helping Black Panther leader George Jackson lead an aborted escape attempt from Soledad Prison in which Jackson was killed, is the morning's featured speaker.

"It's been awhile since we've been in any church," Barney apologizes.

As they drive in Barney's van through the Western Addition, a formerly all-black neighborhood near downtown, now filled with the long fallow vacant lots of urban renewal. Barney comments, "It looks like a war zone. It makes me furious to see all this desolation. These used to be beautiful Victorians. It's so obvious that all they're doing is moving the black people out so the speculators can make a killing on the real estate."

"You got that right," Mike says. Barney has sensed that Mike has viewed him with suspicion ever since that rent strike fiasco, but his role in the fight to keep the childcare center open has won him Mike's grudging respect.

The entryway to the Temple is blocked by a phalanx of men and women in burgundy berets, many with leather jackets. They produce an opening for Mike, but challenge Cali, Linda Jean, and Barney. "They're with me," Mike explains. "They're new."

"They'll still have to go through orientation," one of the men says. He speaks into a walkie-talkie. "Follow me." The man takes the three of us to a room off to the left.

"You haven't been here before?" Barney whispers to Cali, reluctant to be intimidated by all this security business.

"No. Dan insisted I stay away. You know how he hates these people and their liberal influence."

Scattered about the carpeted orientation room are quartets of folding chairs, in which interviews are being conducted. On the walls are giant posters of Jim Jones, Martin Luther King, Malcolm X, Angela Davis, Sitting Bull.

The man leads them to one of the interviewers, a sweet-faced, dark-skinned, fat woman in a black satiny dress. "Welcome to People's Temple," she says through clenched teeth. When she catches Barney staring rudely at her mouth, she chortles. "My jaw is wired shut so that I can lose weight. I can eat only liquids. It's a marvelous program, among the many the Temple has for our members' welfare. For the first time in my life, I've lost over ten pounds." She makes the whole speech moving only her lips. "Why did you want to attend the celebration this morning?"

The three of them look at each other. "We came with Mike Davis," Barney says. "We wanted to hear Angela. And, we're from Geneva Towers. Marceline invited us, through Mike, to make an announcement about our upcoming demonstration at the school board." Marceline Jones is Jim Jones' wife, in charge of the San Francisco operations now that Jones himself has moved to Guyana.

"Oh yes, I've heard about it. How do you feel about the attacks against the Temple?"

"Lies, of course," Barney says, startled that she would be so direct and obvious. In fact, he has some questions about some of the charges, but he knows that this is not the place to raise them.

"Good," she says. Let me see if we can't cut this short and let you in. She goes off to consult with a slender white man in dark glasses, his hair slicked back to cover his bald spot, watching over the proceedings. He has a pencil-thin mustache and no eyebrows at all.

He comes over and sits in her chair, while she stands next to him, smiling serenely. "My name is Larry Cordell, chief of Temple Security. How do you feel about the attacks against the Temple?" he asks, peering at us warily. Cali and Linda Jean both shuffle their feet in impatience, but Barney glances at them to cool it. "We think the Temple is being persecuted," Barney says.

He looks at the others to measure their response. Cali says, "I go with Mike Davis, you know, so I know what's up." Her impatience creeps into her tone.

He looks at Linda Jean. She stammers, "We...we support what Jim Jones is doing," she says. Barney gives her a slight smile, pleased that she recognizes when to be less than completely candid.

"Well, we can't be too careful," he says. "Clear them for entry," he directs the wired-jaw woman.

Once they are seated in what would be the nave if this were a normal church, Barney whispers to Linda Jean and Cali, "They seem a little paranoid."

"Shhh," both of them answer.

Looking around, Barney spots Latricia and Ronnie from the school three rows behind them. He waves at them.

The service begins with a medley of songs from the civil rights movement, "Oh Freedom," "This Little Light of Mine," "We Shall Not Be Moved."

Marceline introduces Jones himself who speaks via a static-filled short-wave radio connection from Guyana. "We're building a beautiful, beautiful world here for all of you to come to whenever you're ready, whenever you decide you can't take one more minute of the war-mongering, racist U.S. society. We're building a world that's ruled by love, where all men and women, all women and men are truly equal. It's true the stories you hear about us working hard, but we work hard with a great joy just bursting out of our breasts. We bathe in the light of our own salvation. Tell the people back home, people, are you happy here?"

A resounding "Yeah!" crackles over the loudspeaker from Jones' apparent audience in the jungle.

A shiver runs through Barney. There's something about his voice that makes Barney wish he was with him, creating this new world. He remembers meeting him, how completely sure of himself he was. He thinks of that song again, Sonny Terry and Brownie McGee, "Beautiful City." Jones is onto something. The church is crowded, with mostly blacks, a smattering of Asians and Hispanics, the rest white. The whites are mostly long-haired and scruffy. Barney is tempted to join this movement. The Marxists' biggest mistake has been to ignore religion. Tapping into the spiritual dimension like Jones does, like the liberation theologists of Central America do – this is what will make a difference in the coming period. He often thinks in terms of "the coming period," an old habit.

Jones is no fool. His ability to turn out voters may be responsible for the relatively progressive look in City Hall. Mayor Moscone might not have been elected without Jones turning out his minions to vote for him, which is how Jones got to be chairman of the powerful Housing Authority, a post which he kept until he fled to Guyana. The proposal to elect Supervisors by district, which was responsible for putting Harvey Milk and other progressives (as well as Dan White) in office, probably wouldn't have passed without Jim Jones' ardent support – some say ardent to the point of voter fraud. At least until the press tarnished his image with revelations from ex-Temple members of faked healings, beatings of disobedient followers, intimidation of critics, tax and voter law violations, Jones could claim with some authority to be heir to the tradition of Martin Luther King, leading a progressive political movement with deeply religious roots. It was the press harassment that led to the threat of a grand jury investigation, and that threat in turn to Jones fleeing to his utopian socialist colony in Guyana.

Angela Davis, her afro piled precariously on the top of her head (the same afro she'd been accused of using to smuggle a gun in to George Jackson) speaks in an east coast whine that is hard on the ears. She makes a disappointing appeal for freedom for the Wilmington 10, a worthy cause and all that, ten black

Delaware men no doubt falsely convicted of inciting a riot, but the issue is so remote to peoples' lives, Barney feels like running up to the podium and shaking her: "Get *real*, Angela!" he wants to say.

Suddenly it's their turn. Cali has agreed in advance to make the pitch. She panics. "Barney! I can't do this! You do it. Please?" She's doubling over as if she has a pain in her gut.

"You can do it, Cali," Barney says to her calmly.

"No, I can't!" She starts to tremble and cry all at once.

"Cali!" Barney gives her a severe but confident look.

Marceline Jones is introducing them. "We have some folks here today from Geneva Towers Children's Center to share what their struggle is about. You know what Jim teaches us. 'One struggle, many fronts.'"

Cali stands to leave, but everyone looks at her as if she has stood to speak. She sighs. She speaks. Her voice is soft and shaky at first. She gives the details of the threat. Then, her brilliant gray eyes light up. "It's our school. It's our community. We will not let them take it away from us!" Her words are plain, but the power behind them echoes off the dome of the church. "We'll be having a demonstration at the school board meeting three weeks from Tuesday and we want all of y'all to be there." She's loudly applauded.

She collapses into her seat, holding her chest. Linda Jean sits between them, but Cali's and Barney's eyes meet behind Linda Jean's neck. He's proud of Cali's power. He's glad for her success. He's excited about her energy. But, there's something more in that look. They both blink it away. They will deny that anything happened. But something has happened. For all their flirting back and forth, and Linda Jean's accusations, this is the first time Barney realizes that he could fall for her. Oh-oh, he thinks.

2.

He picks the wrong day to be late for school. He would have been almost on time, but some kid has punched all the buttons on the elevator again, and it takes him twenty minutes to get from the 15th floor in the A building, to the 2nd floor in the B building where the center is located. Waiting in the office for him is Sylvia Conners, the director of the Children's Centers program.

"Mr. Blatz," she starts right in, fluttering her eyelashes at him in that annoying way that she has, "I see you don't sign in when you come to work."

"Oh, I must have forgotten."

"It looks like you've forgotten for the past two months. That's part of your job description. You have to follow the rules like everyone else, you know."

"Of course."

"I've come to see you to reiterate what I said at the meeting. Some people don't like how you go around here speaking for the black community. As a school district employee, you are under obligation to conduct yourself in a professional manner at all times, even outside of your work place. It isn't a good idea for teachers to get too personally or politically involved with parents. It creates a conflict of interest."

"Why are you telling me this, Sylvia?" he asks without concealing his impatience.

"I'm telling you this for your own good, Barney. Don't get too involved. As a school district employee, you also have an obligation to support administrative decisions, and certainly not to organize against them. It's not worth jeopardizing your career."

His body stiffens. "Is that all, Sylvia? Because I have to go to work now. The children come first, you know?" He's shaking with anger, but he doesn't really know quite what to do about it.

"That's it, Barney, just stay out of what doesn't concern you."

He stands. "Thanks for coming all the way out here and taking the time out of your busy schedule." He gives her a big grin, dripping with sarcasm.

As soon as she leaves, he calls the union. The woman from the union advises him to write a letter to Sylvia, thanking her for her visit, but suggesting that attempts at intimidation are out of line, with copies to the union and the superintendent, her boss.

While the children go wild waiting for him in the next room, he takes time out of his busy schedule to peck out the letter on the manual typewriter which the school still has to use. He put it this way: "I welcome your visit any time, as well as your comments and criticism. I'm sure the intentions of your visit were benign, but I do have to say that I will ignore any attempts to intimidate me as a violation of my constitutional rights and my rights as an employee under the National Labor Relations Act."

He sends off the letter and returns to work, satisfied that he has turned her hamhanded tactic back on her and actually increased his power in the situation.

3.

Barney has trouble with the 4th of July as an orgy of jingoism in celebration of what amounts to a slaveholder's revolt, but in his teaching, he emphasizes the need to fight for freedom and self-determination. "Independence Day," he tells the children. "It's about controlling our own community. It's about not letting them close our school down." He teaches them "We Shall Not Be Moved."

His reservations about the holiday don't prevent him from taking advantage of the long weekend, however, and, two weeks before the big budget hearings that will decide the fate of the school, Linda Jean and Barney pile Barney's children, Jason, 7, and Ramona, 5, in the aging red VW van and drive through the hot, rolling wine country to Calistoga to get their batteries recharged.

The hills are golden, the oaks are gnarled, the air is hot and dry. It's exhilarating to get out of the city. They play many games of 20 questions. He's impressed with how good the children are for their ages.

They camp out that night at the local state-run Napa Valley campground, which has a higher population density than Geneva Towers. That night, they resolve eventually to buy some land in the country so they can really get away.

Linda Jean makes up scary stories about the "Snappies," furry little creatures that make their nests high in the oak trees and only come down at night.

"They only eat selfish people," she says. "So you don't have to worry if you're not selfish. Plus, you can tell when they're coming, they snap three times, snap-snap-snap. The only trouble is, the snaps sound just like twigs snapping when someone is walking by."

At such a crowded campground, the night is filled with the sounds of snapping twigs as people walk by, so they cuddle together by the fire and giggle whenever they hear three snaps together, while Linda Jean teases us, "Uh, there's one now! No, sorry just someone walking by. Anyway, why are you worried, Ramona? You're not selfish, are you?"

"N-no, I don't think so," Monie answers, playing along.

The next day, they stop at a baroque German winery with leaded glass windows, heavy furniture and elaborate curly-cues along the edge of the steep roof. They decide to skip the required tour, pretending to be in one that's already finishing. A fat, white-haired, red-faced man in the tour gives them a look. Barney knows this look. They don't get it often in the city, but in the hinterlands, one expects to meet one's share of rednecks. "They weren't on the tour," the man says.

Barney smiles and shrugs his shoulders at the bartender, and he pours them their wine anyway.

"How come they don't have to go on the tour?" the man yells.

Without thinking, Barney sidles over to him. He leans his shoulder into him sharply and spits the words in his ear: "Maybe you should mind your own business, fella."

The man laughs out loud. "Now just who is it that's going to make me do something like that?"

"Try me, Jack," Barney stands his ground and glares in the man's face.

"Get the fuck out of my face, nigger-lover," he sneers and pushes Barney.

"Gentlemen," pleads the bartender.

Shit, Barney is wondering how he got into this, he's not exactly a street fighter, but this man is fat, and he can't back down now. He pushes him back.

Linda Jean tells him to forget it. Jason and Ramona look scared for their daddy. Boom! One punch and Barney is on the ground. He jumps to his feet, lands a glancing blow in the man's soft midsection, and the man decks Barney again, this time busting his lip. Linda Jean crouches over him and orders him to stop. She helps him up, and they return to their wine, ignoring the man who seems content to ignore them back.

The bartender pours Barney a tall one. "I used to think like you, but you know, it's not worth bucking the whole system."

Barney puts his arm around Linda Jean. He's loving her a lot at this moment. She keeps dabbing at his lip with a napkin. "Yes, it is," he says.

～

That afternoon, they splurge on a two-bedroom suite at one of the spas in Calistoga, renowned for its mineral baths. The spa they choose is rundown, a little seedy, but just the right atmosphere for their taste: neither medicinal nor athletic.

They leave Jason and Ramona by the pool and tell the lifeguard that they'll be in the spa if he needs them. They elect to have the full treatment, and go off to their respective sections, men's and women's. They've never done this before, though it's been recommended to them by friends.

Barney is nervous about what to do, what's appropriate, can he be nude, or what? A dark-eyed Mexican youth puts him at ease and directs him to one of the wooden dressing rooms with a curtain for a door. "Take your clothes off. I come get you." He hands Barney a towel. He strips to his underwear and waits.

"That too," says the boy as he returns, pointing to his underwear. He follows the boy into the bath area, steamy and sulfurous. He covers himself with a towel, until he sees other men naked. Then he relaxes. The boy leads him toward a huge, rectangular vat filled with brown stuff, which looks for all the world like shit. "Climb in there," he says. He looks at the boy oddly, but he does comply. He sinks to his knees in the muck, which is purported to be volcanic mud, and then lies all the way down. The attendant buries him so that nothing sticks up but his poor head, mangled from the fight.

At first, it's incredibly relaxing. Then suddenly, it's like being buried alive. Barney panics and climbs back out, unable to endure the full ten minutes. "I just can't sit still for that long," he pleads, apologizing to the attendant.

He does manage to handle the mineral bath, the steam, and the massage. When he finally emerges from the spa into the bright sun to meet Linda Jean, he feels completely rejuvenated, passionately in love with her, and sexy as hell. In spite of his mutilated face, he's proud of his manly show against the redneck back at the winery.

Linda Jean, on the other hand, seems distant. Since they have to retrieve the kids from the pool right away, it isn't until later that night when they're in bed in their own room that they get a chance to talk.

"What's up?" Barney asks, as soon as they get in the hot tub gurgling with sulfur-smelling mineral water. He's feeling so generally content after the two bottles of vintage chardonnay that they bought at the winery that he's not even annoyed to be once more the one to bringing up the "stuff."

"You could have gotten us killed back there," she says.

"What?" He's incredulous that she doesn't recognize his heroism.

"You don't know who that guy was. Maybe he's a KKK. Maybe he's got fifty buddies that could come after us."

"Come on, Linda Jean, you see anyone?"

"That's not the point. It's just reckless, Barney. This isn't liberal San Francisco and that there. You got to be more careful."

He looks away from her, besieged by a flash of horror. His sense of well-being suddenly crumples with the unstated accusation of racism. He knows this, he's accused others of it: a foolhardy attack against racism which endangers the very people it's supposed to protect is a form of racism itself, albeit unconscious.

"It's true, Linda Jean," he quickly admits, "I was being selfish. Snap-snap-snap." They both laugh.

"Really, though," he says, "I was thinking of myself, of the principle of the thing, and I suppose that is a bourgeois luxury."

"I was kind of proud of you, though," Linda Jean says as she cuddles up to him.

Now they feel closer than ever. Her body is soft and warm against his. They seem to fit together just right. The very perfection of the situation for dynamite sex arouses him – the relaxing treatment, the wine, the hot tub in the room, the reconciliation after an argument. It's one of those cosmic times, he thinks, as they start writhing together in the tub, sucking each other's' tongues.

But when they finally get out of the tub and start in on the bed, he's as limp as over-cooked spaghetti.

"It's okay," Linda Jean says, obviously disappointed. "Maybe it's all the hot water."

He tries everything, from rubbing Kama Sutra oil on his penis to fantasizing about a wild orgy where anything and everything goes. Nothing works. It's not okay. It feels awful. "Maybe things are just too perfect," he says, closer to tears than he even knows. He lies next to her, numb and cold as a cadaver.

He doesn't plan to say anything. It just slips out. "This wouldn't happen with Cali." He has no idea what makes him say this. He's not even thinking of her.

Linda Jean's shrinks away from him. Her whole body contracts with rage.

"Jeannie. I'm sorry," he says. "I didn't mean that. It's not even true. Oh, God, Jeannie, I swear."

Then he surprises himself again. Without warning, he starts crying. Bawling like a baby. He has no idea what's going on with him. He feels like he's losing control.

The tears do soften her. She sighs heavily and shakes her head. "I don't know what I'm going to do with you, Barney Blatz," she says with real exasperation.

Again, the words slip out as if his mind is no longer in charge of my voice. "Hit me," he says.

"What?" She looks at him as if he'd lost my mind.

"You're still mad at me. Hit me." He grabs her shoulders and shakes her. "Hit me on the ass. Do it."

She does it. She whacks him sharply on his left buttock. She laughs, weirdly. "Again!" he demands. She does it again, harder.

| 65 |

His penis stands up as if reaching out to her. "Again!" She hits him again and he rolls her over, climbs on top of her, and enters her wetness. They fuck like savage animals, grunting and slobbering, biting and clawing. They come together in short order.

He collapses next to her, shaking. He doesn't know what can of worms he's opened up. He turns his head away and goes to sleep without looking at her.

On the way back in the car you remember last summer when you and Linda Jean, with Jason and Ramona in tow, took off for the east for ten days to visit your families, five days apiece. You went to your parents' first, to the house on the lake in which you grew up, built in the twenties by your grandfather, a doctor and amateur sculptor, on land purchased by your great-grandfather after the Civil War, in which he served as a general.

Like the family that lived there, the house was a mishmash. It was originally styled ersatz French provincial, with angled planks in the stucco, a Mansard roof, and windows that opened like doors, but it was remodeled after that big fire in the late forties, a fire that still haunted you. The front still had a barn-shaped, four-sided roof, but the back had clapboard instead of shingles on the upper story and was shaped like a box. The windows were now picture-windows, which were much too modern for the rest of the design, and frequently killed disoriented birds who crash into their vastness, seeking a short-cut to the bird feeder out back.

You were not on the best of terms with your parents, your father in particular, a depressive, alcoholic old man now, with politics to the right of Ronald Reagan. But in recent years, you had silently agreed to be civil.

Your mother was a submissive woman, the essence of niceness built on a foundation of denial. Because it's in abominable taste, she hated prejudice, though she was not above wondering aloud – to you privately, of course – whether Linda Jean was "educated" enough for you.

Your father shared with many people who are saddled with traditional prejudices the propensity to make exceptions out of out-group members he actually met, like the black doctor he let into his practice, like Linda Jean. In fact, the two of them hit it off famously.

Neither of your parents was particularly shocked when you married her, having already been overloaded with shocks from you in the past, your arrests, your radicalism, your marriage to a Jew, Cynthia, whose "aggressiveness" your father couldn't stand.

One hot, muggy evening, you were eating on the porch, overlooking the orange twilight reflected in the glassy lake. To your mother's impotent dismay, your father was dressed only in his white boxer shorts, his big belly, as white as a bloated trout, hanging over the elastic. His crew-cut hair had been white since he was in his thirties.

You talked about the weather, inflation, overpopulation. Your father sipped his bourbon and tried to provoke you. He was the kind of alcoholic who didn't touch a drop until the sun crossed the yard-arm (to prove he wasn't an alcoholic) and then at 5 P.M. exactly began gulping a series of drinks that usually put him out by 7. But tonight, you insisted on roasting the chicken over charcoal, and it wasn't done until after 7, by which time your father was already several sheets to the wind.

As Linda Jean went to the kitchen fetch more corn-on-the cob, your father posted himself unsteadily at the butcher-block cart which holds the chicken. "Who'd like more meat?" he asked, waving the electric knife in the air.

Jason says, "I do!"

Your father ignored him. He lowered his voice. "How about a leg, Barney? You like dark meat."

Your first impulse was to leap for his throat, but you didn't do that kind of thing in your family. You flared your eyes at him in pure hatred. You watched in your mind's eye as his face is consumed in flame.

"Robert, really!" your mother scolded ineffectively.

"I'm sorry," he said. "She's a good woman, Barney."

Linda Jean returned with the corn and Jason, impatient, got up from the table and reached for the serving fork on the cart, surprising your father, who staggered backward with the knife in his hand. Regaining his balance, he brandished the blade at little Jason, pushing the button on the handle so the motor grinds and the twin blades slice the air. "Hey, watch out, boy!" he shouted. "You could get hurt."

Jason leapt back in terror and dropped the meat on the tile floor. You jumped up yourself and wrapped your arms around him. He was shaking, as white as a turnip. You flashed another look at your father.

Ten awkward minutes later, your father stomped out of the room. "I'm going to bed," he announced, to everyone's relief.

As soon as you hear the last stair creak, you opened up on him. "How can you live with that son-of-a-bitch?" you asked your mother.

Your mother was a small woman, with a round German-peasant face. "Oh, he didn't mean anything," she said. "He doesn't drink that much when you're not around."

"Oh, great, Mom, like it's our fault," you said.

"He's just not a people person," she said.

Your mouth dropped as Linda Jean joined this refrain. "Don't be too hard on him, Barney. You two are more alike than you know."

"Just what do you mean by that?" you fired back. "I don't go around terrorizing babies with knives."

"Jason's not a baby," Ramona said, on Jason's behalf, Jason himself being still in shock.

"He's still my baby," you said hugging him. He squirmed away. You continued, raising your voice at Linda Jean. "Don't you ever suggest that I'm like him, understand?"

"Okay," she agreed, lowering her eyes.

FIVE

My Lai

1.

The evening of the rally, the fog fails to come in, and the mid-July dusk is balmy. The rally is huge, wildly exceeding Barney's expectations, and he's giddy with excitement. He is the Leader. He can't believe this. He has always wanted to be popular, and now it seems he can do no wrong.

Linda Jean tries to warn him. "It's just a rally, Barney. It's not the revolution," she says as she sees him flitting about the various constituencies like a mad general.

They form a long picket line in front the decaying old school building that houses the administration offices and the auditorium where the board meets. "Building does not meet earthquake safety standards," says a sign on the door.

The Center has turned out in force. Latricia, their spokesperson before the board, her natural cut sharply, styled so it sits on her head like a helmet, is ecstatic. "We've won, Barney!" she beams at him.

It does feel like they've won. They've been spending the weeks before this meeting lobbying board members, and they have assurances from four out of the seven that they will vote to keep the center open.

Alice, the deep-voiced militant, overweight, sloppy, rough, and irrepressible, is leading the chants with her baby in a stroller. Her twins, along with the other Towers' children are upstairs in the childcare arrangement they organized in a room next to the auditorium. "Keep the center open!" she shouts into the bullhorn, a device Barney "liberated" from the Party in the course of the split.

Sue Ann, from the South, slow and solid, light-skinned with reddish permed hair, and Cali's buddy Charlene, dark, with a permanent scowl, are also taking leading roles, passing out flyers and picket signs, many of which were painted by the children in the school during the previous week.

The People's Temple has brought about a hundred supporters on two of their own Greyhound-style buses. Other churches and schools involved in the coalition, along with the teachers' union, account for another hundred or so people.

They march up the stairs and into the board room singing "We Shall Not Be Moved." They sing it over and over again, in defiance of the board president's gavel. Finally they decide to let the board conduct its business. It's a reflection of their power and their imminent victory that the board votes immediately to hear the motion first, put forward by the one black board member, to exclude Geneva Towers Children's Center from a previously adopted resolution calling for the closure of several sites.

Their first speaker is Barney Williams, Cali's son, probably the youngest person to ever address the board. "Don't close our school because I like to play in the doll corner," he says to wild applause.

They rehearsed each of their three child-speakers to say something different, but in the heat of the TV lights, Clarisse and Ronnie get nervous and just repeat what little Barney has said, "I like to play in the doll corner."

Then Latricia speaks, graciously thanking the board in advance for its rational approach to the problem.

Cali informs them in no uncertain terms, that "our center will not close."

Barney speaks next, delivering what he considers the piece de resistance: "Members of the Board of Education, I am pleased to inform you that we have met with the management of Geneva Towers Apartments, and they have agreed, in writing, to waive all rent for the facility, and to provide maintenance free of charge." They have kept this nugget secret to enhance the effect of the surprise. The crowd, their crowd, cheers tumultuously.

Dan White is their final speaker. He provides a well-reasoned summary which essentially states that since the board will save nothing by closing the center, they might as well keep it open.

Following their presentation, the board's legal adviser, a black man who talks as though his mouth were full of gravel, speaks. "It is not possible to reconsider this motion at this time. The resolution which this present motion seeks to amend was a subsection of the resolution which passed the budget for the entire school district. The only way to consider such a motion would be to rescind the vote on the budget resolution and that would be illegal because the deadline for approving the budget has already passed."

The board acts as if nothing has happened and moves onto the next agenda item, a surprise resolution to send emergency layoff notices to about 200 teachers.

"What happened?" Cali asks Barney frantically.

"I think we just got shafted." He runs up to talk to their staunchest ally, the black woman on the board. She tells him she's sorry, but she has done all she can.

He looks at Dan White, and he shakes his head and shrugs his shoulders.

Barney's spirits suddenly plummet from stratosphere to substrata. By the time he figures out that the only thing for them to do is to disrupt the meeting, the union president is making his own urgent plea for the board not to lay anybody off. It's too late to do anything. They trickle out of the meeting so disconsolate that no one notices that Barney's name is among the list of those to be laid off, even though he has nine years seniority with the district.

2.

Barney has been trying to avoid being alone with Cali, but here they are. She calls him at work because she's depressed. Linda Jean has to work at her other job, taking care of the doctor's house, so Barney rides the elevator up to Cali's to console her.

The first thing he notices is that she's changed her hair. She's washed out the tint and let it revert to a loose natural, softened and reddened by Jheri curl chemicals. It's a much better match for her increasing militancy. "You look great!" he tells her.

"I thought you'd like it," she sings. "It was supposed to make me feel better to change it, but it didn't."

"So *you're* depressed," he whines, slouching on her brown velour couch. "I'm fucking getting laid off."

"Did you call the union?"

"Sure. But they're pessimistic because my hiring date is listed as 1976, not 1971. They're not going to count five years I worked in the elementary schools. The union says they know I'm being singled out, but there isn't much they can do."

"Shit, Barney. Drag city. Here, have some of this." She pulls out a fat joint from a cigarette box on the fiberboard coffee table. She's dressed in her stretch tight jeans and a pink angora sweater with rhinestones that would look tacky on anyone else.

"I haven't done this shit in years," he says.

They smoke the joint. It doesn't do its trick of softening the edges around things. It does its other trick of jangling the connections between things, bristling the neck hairs, opening the black hole at the base of his spine. The nineteenth floor suddenly seems dangerously high off the ground.

Cali sits too close to him on the couch. She has

a funny, far-off, expectant look in her gray eyes, a dreamy smile. He moves away.

"Where's your hubby?" he asks.

"First off, he's not my hubby. I ain't worried about him. He's off on Temple business, you know. More and more people moving to Guyana. He wants us to go. I told him I'm thinking about it."

"You wouldn't go, would you?"

"I doubt it. Not now, anyway, with things so hot at the school."

"Oh yeah, that school."

Cali looks alarmed. "You're not giving up on the school, Barney, are you?"

He sighs. "You got any ideas about what to do next?"

"Yeah. I think if they try to close us down, we just stay open. We occupy the place, refuse to let it close. Parents can be the teachers for a while."

"Hmmm." He smiles. "Cali, I like how you think." She blushes.

He has a sudden urge to kiss her, followed by a just as sudden surge of terror, in which he sees those horrific flames darting out of her eye sockets again.

Right then, Mike storms in the door. "Cali! What's for dinner? I'm starved. Barney. What's up?" He narrows his eyes at Barney as if he can read his mind.

"Mike. We were just strategizing the next steps. But I got to be going now."

By the time he gets home, Linda Jean is waiting for him. "Where were you?" she asks, not without a suspicious tone in her voice.

"At Cali's. Strategizing."

She looks away, once more as if he'd kicked her in the kidneys.

3.

Barney makes still another decision to stay away from Cali and get close to Linda Jean. On the one hand, he feels burned by Linda Jean's suspicions about him when nothing is really going on. On the other hand, he does have feelings for Cali, and while some of those are based on the reality that she's a good person and they've been closely working together, some of them have more to do with her looks, her power, her sexiness, and he doesn't want to be caught in that sinkhole of being just another married man on the make. Male guilt is what it is. If he's going to live up to his promise of being a nonchauvinist male, he's going to have to put his commitment to Linda Jean ahead of his yearning for Cali. Besides, Cali is not free, and there is something about Mike that makes Barney think he wouldn't take kindly to being cuckolded by the likes of himself.

Consequently, he decides that the four of them should become friends. First, he has to persuade Linda Jean. After a few days of both of them moping about in stubborn silence following Cali's and Barney's "strategy" session, he hauls Linda Jean onto the frayed, tweed Hide-a-bed in the living room. The couch is next to the sliding glass door that opens out onto the balcony, which, like most balconies in the complex, is littered with Big Wheels, Tonka trucks, barbecue equipment, and dead plants. The valley stretches fifteen floors below, but the haze is such that you can hardly see the pastel stucco row houses. It's as if they are suspended in the clouds.

He holds both of Linda Jean's hands, assertively. "Let's talk," he says. She looks down. He sighs. "Look, I won't deny that I'm attracted to Cali. I won't even deny that I've been tempted to do something about it. But – and you just have to trust me here – I haven't. Every time it's come up, I've decided that that's not what I want, that what I want is for it to work between us. I don't want ours to become some middle-aged cliché of a marriage. I want us to keep going, to continue to get closer together no matter what gets in the way. Okay?"

She keeps her eyes downcast, her shoulders hunched over her pain, which he knows goes back further than his hurting her. "I don't know whether to believe you or not, Barney. I used to think you were different from other men, but I'm not so sure any more. You have a mean streak, too, you know. It scares me. But you know I love you no matter what, I'll always love you. It won't be that easy to get rid of me."

"Listen, Linda Jean, I don't *want* to get rid of you."

"I know, you say that now, and I think you believe that now. But after a while, something will come over you, this mean streak, this coldness, whatever it is, and I'll see it in your eyes and that there, that you don't want to be with me. It just kills me when I see it."

He squirms at the truth of what she's saying, but he can't admit it. "I think it's dangerous for you to try and read my mind, Jeannie. It may look like that to you, you know, but I think that's filtered through your own low opinion of yourself. Maybe it's myself I'm not liking when I look like that."

She looks me in the eye for the first time, albeit skeptically. "Maybe," she says with a slight smile.

"Anyway, what I'm thinking is that we should get to be friends, as a couple, with Cali and Mike. It will help the political work and hopefully it will defuse the jealousy business somewhat. What do you think?"

She's quiet for a minute. "You mean swing with them, like Al and Ruby?"

"Jeannie! Damn it, no! I mean just friends. Comrades. Treat them as part of our political base, you know? Remember, we used to have lots of friends like that when we were in the Party."

She sighs. "I suppose we could try it," she says.

On the second half of your vacation last summer, you visited Rochester, Pennsylvania, a grimy, working-class suburb of Pittsburgh, on the sludge-saturated Susquehanna River. The house where Linda Jean's mother, Estelle, lived with Linda Jean's brother, Wade, his 19 year-old son Bruce, and a half-witted family friend named Billy, was a clapboard Victorian, painted yellow with brown trim. The living room had a green couch covered with clear plastic, a 27-inch TV which was always on, and a shelf holding Bruce's weight-lifting trophies.

Wade was a small, thin man with glasses, who was injured in Korea, lived off his disability check, and spent most of his time on the couch in front of the TV, sipping vodka from a jar.

Estelle was a tall woman with clear skin, exceptionally good looking for someone in her seventies. She gushed over you in that embarrassing way that some, especially older, black people had that indicated she shared the prevailing view that whites were superior to blacks. Her lot in life was to complain about Wade's drinking, while she herself snuck sips of Keystone Beer from quarts she kept in the freezer.

You were struck by the similarities of your families, engendered by the commonality of alcohol.

On your first evening there, Estelle stuffed you with overcooked steaks in the yellow kitchen, and Linda Jean asked about her father. "You heard any news of Hudson?"

Estelle snapped, "Now don't you go speaking evil about your father. He's a good man who worked hard all his life. He'll be back just as soon as he settles his business in Alabama."

Linda Jean's tone sharpened to a frequency you had rarely heard from her. "Mom! He's been gone for six years! It's time you faced the fact that he's abandoned you. If you believe in that crap about the oil wells on his family's farm, you must believe in the tooth fairy!"

"I won't have you swearing in my house, Linda Jean."

"Swearing? You mean 'crap'? God, mother."

"Or using God's name in vain."

Wade shouted from the living room, "Is she defending that bastard again? Jesus, Mom!"

Estelle screamed with some hysteria creeping into her voice, "Stop all this swearing!"

You looked at Linda Jean, hopeful that she would move to defuse this confrontation, but instead she shouted back herself, "Mom, it's time you woke up! Don't you know about Felicia? Don't you know he raped her? Don't you know he's a god damn fucking child molester?" These words from her mouth were all the more potent, since she so rarely used them.

Estelle looked like she's been shot in the stomach with a 12- gauge shotgun. Her eyes were on fire, and she was huffing and puffing in short little breaths. She raised her hand to slap Linda Jean, but stopped herself. "You're lying!" she spit in a whisper that came from deep in her belly.

"I saw him," Linda Jean said quietly, with a trace of a smile on her face.

Wade staggered into the kitchen, his gait a combination of the effects of drinking and the shrapnel still lodged in his thigh. He just stared at Linda Jean. You couldn't tell whether his disbelief was for Linda Jean's words, or for the fact that she was saying them to their mother.

Estelle, fighting tears, finally said, "I won't listen to any more of this," and shuffled off to bed.

Wade let the subject drop. You listened while the two of them discussed what had happened to the people they grew up with, who had gone crazy, who died, which few had made it.

Later that night, in the bed Wade had given up for you (he slept on the couch), a rage that you didn't know you had bubbled up from the back of your throat. You told her,

"That was shitty, Linda Jean."

"You too, Barney? Is everyone against me? It had to come out, that's all."

"No it didn't. You just laid it on your mother so you could feel better yourself."

"That's not true," she said, tears flowing freely now. "I told her so she could face facts and go on with her life."

You knew you should let it go. You knew her intentions were essentially innocent, or at least unconscious. But you had lost control of your tongue again, and it said, "You take away some people's illusions you know, and you kill them. Is that what you're trying to do to your mother?"

"Barney!" she screamed. "How can you say that to me? I need your support, not your condemnation!" She shoved out her words between sobs.

You didn't answer, another escalation of cruelty. You stewed in silence on your side of the bed while she sobbed on hers.

In the night you heard a sleepless rooster crow. Then a long train clacking by on the nearby tracks. An insight trickled into your brain: it's her innocence you fell in love with – and her innocence that you hated most of all.

You sighed. You reached for her. "I'm sorry," you said softly. She sobbed harder, but she curled up in your arms.

4.

A few days after Linda Jean's and Barney's discussion on the couch, Cali and Mike come for dinner. Barney cooks: Boeuf Bourguignon, green noodles, spinach salad. A half-gallon of Gallo Hearty Burgundy, which they bought because they like it even though they can't remember if the farm workers are still boycotting this label or not.

Their apartment looks elegant too, even in this slum. A while ago they painted the walls royal blue and papered one wall in burgundy stripes. As in all the apartments, the kitchen area is separated from the living room area by a formica table built into an island formed by the stove connected to some plasterboard shelves. Linda Jean has sewn a special burgundy table cloth to fit this table. The light from the candles reflects off the window, mirroring the twinkling lights of the city below.

There is an awkwardness to the gathering, as if no one but Barney has any idea of what they are all doing here, so they are waiting for him to show his hand. But he doesn't really have anything in his hand, other than a sincere wish for them to all be closer, to put their petty jealousies aside and come together as human beings. They talk stiffly of the double-digit inflation currently sweeping the land, of the Bakke decision recently dealing a body blow to affirmative action programs.

Mike is a big man, muscular, dark, smooth-skinned, with a short natural. Barney finally decides to see if he can get him to talk about himself. Turns out he grew up outside of Pittsburgh less than ten miles from where Linda Jean grew up, and that they have acquaintances in common back there.

Barney asks him where he spent the war.

His eyes light up with the candlelight. "I was there, all right, man," he says. His voice is deep and resonant, delighting in his story. "I was right in the fucking middle of it, you know? I seen shit you wouldn't believe. My Lai, remember that? I was there. The killing, it didn't bother me really. I was surprised that it didn't, but it didn't. By that time I was used to seeing dead, mutilated bodies, whether they were big or little, in uniform or not, didn't make no difference. My Lai wasn't that different from any other battle, you know, some guys got a little carried away, that's all. Charlie came in all disguises. There wasn't no distinguishing civilians from soldiers. I didn't think about it. I just wanted to stay alive, man. I got out of it, though."

He gets quiet and stares into his wine glass.

"How'd you get out of it?" Barney asks.

"I really don't want to talk about it." There's a hostile edge in his voice that persuades Barney not to pursue it further.

He fills his glass again. "I haven't told too many people this story. After the massacre was over, I got the job of going around with a flame thrower and burning the evidence, you know, the gook bodies. One of my buddies, he was a good buddy too, a blood from backwoods Arkansas, he says 'C'mon, man, I got something to show you.' He drags me to the other side of the village, into to one of those grass sheds where they keep their pigs. He brushes away a pile of straw and pig shit, and there's this beautiful young gook chick of maybe 17 with her little breasts hanging out of those black pajamas they wear, you know, and she's dead as a coffin nail with a clean bullet wound in her head. My buddy, he starts ripping the rest of the goddamn clothes off her limp body. He's all excited. Then, believe it or not, man, the guy starts fucking her, just like that. I watch for a hot second, but he makes me so sick I switch on the flame-thrower and incinerate both of them. 'Now you two deserve each other,' I said out loud.

"That's what got me out of it. I decided what the fuck man, this shit was so fucked I'd rather be in jail, so I went to the CO and told him exactly what happened. Next thing I know I'm headed stateside with an honorable discharge. I still got the damn flame-thrower too, smuggled it out of there as a souvenir. How about you, man?"

Barney stares at the candle, dazed. His life seems so puny compared to this man's suffering. And yet, he's a killer. He glances into Mike's eyes and see flames, just the reflections of the candle flames, but for a second he sees the flames in the eye sockets of his dead friend's skull.

"Jesus, man, I can't follow that story," Barney says sheepishly. "I was the other kind of CO. A Conscientious Objector. As a Zen Buddhist. Worked in a mental hospital for a few months."

"You were smart."

"I guess. In a way I wished I had gone. I feel like I missed something somehow."

"Shit, you ain't missed nothing worth seeing man. Not a goddamn thing."

"I suppose it's survivor guilt or something."

"Tell you what. You take my experience; I'll take your guilt. Okay?" They laugh. Despite Mike's chilling story, the warmth in the room is palpable.

Cali helps Linda Jean with the dishes. Barney hears some rapport developing between them. "How are your kids doing, Cali?" Linda Jean asks.

"Oh they're doing so good at that school. I hate to think about them having to change. Barney knows all his ABC's and can write his name, and you can tell Darnell is going to catch up because he's so jealous."

Then Mike says, "Hey, you folks play bones?"

"Bones?" Barney asks stupidly.

"Dominoes."

"Yeah, we got some I think." Barney hasn't played in years, and all he remembers of the game is you play until your hand runs out. Mike shows them how to play scoring points, in multiples of five, and how to mark the score using x's and o's. They play on into the night until the wine is gone – and then the brandy – and they can't see the spots on the bones any more.

SIX

The Day After Labor Day

1.

"FOR IMMEDIATE RELEASE: The parents of Geneva Towers Children's Center announced today that despite notices from the school district, the school would not close...." So opens the press release that Latricia and Barney are trying to slap together, working on Labor Day night, the night before the district is scheduled to bring on its moving vans. They are sitting on her white leather sofa in her elegant apartment on the 20th floor of the A-Building, a haven of quiet away from the chaos of the center where the others are working, getting the center ready. The speckled gray generic linoleum tile is covered with egg-shell off-white, deep pile wall-to-wall carpeting. The walls are white with a touch of rose. Her coffee table and shelves are glass-on-chrome, but serious stuff, not cheap. On her wall hangs a chrome-framed geometric Mondrian print, 2 feet by 3 feet. On each end of the couch is a chrome floor lamp with a long, gracefully curving neck.

Latricia has butterscotch skin and a tight Jheri curl that is so sharply cut it fits on her head like a helmet. She's wearing a silky floral bathrobe and keeps touching Barney as she gestures, making him cringe, talking nonstop. On the one hand, he always likes seductiveness. On the other, He feels like his hands are full, and besides tomorrow is an event even more important than sex. When it rains, it pours, he thinks. This never happens to him. As far as he knows, no woman has ever come after him before, though maybe he wouldn't have noticed, being unable to believe it. Now there's two at once, maybe. He knew there was a reason he wanted to be a political leader.

"You know I've been talking to the People's Temple leaders," Latricia says, "and they're very interested in the Center. They've been wanting a base of operations in this part of the city for some time. What do you think?" She doesn't give him time to answer. "It seems like you and Jim Jones have a lot in common, at least philosophically. You're both communists. I remember you selling that newspaper door-to-door here. Jones doesn't advertise his communism like you used to, but that is what he's about."

"I don't know, Latricia, what about all this chicken gut business?" Jones has been accused in the press of faking cancer cures by pulling chicken guts out of tumors. "You're missing the forest for the trees, Barney. Sure, he uses some theatrics to get people interested, but the real question is, what does he do for people once he gets them in? You ought to see the senior homes and the childcare centers the Temple runs."

"And the beatings?" he asks, referring to another accusation in the press.

"I've never seen any. Even so, don't look for perfection. Just check it out and see if what Jones has going isn't programmatically miles ahead of everyone else. Isn't that what matters? If his operation can keep us safe through the coming period of fascism and nuclear wars, isn't that more important than whether his methods stand up to the scrutiny of the white liberals who will sign petitions all the way to the gas chambers? Check out their childcare centers with me anyway."

"Okay." She is wearing him down. He wants to get on with the press release. "I'll go look at their childcare centers, see if I like how they're run. Now, can we finish this?"

They do finally finish, and Barney goes down to the Center where the others are all gathered, drinking Bull. Barney types the press release and then one by one sends it on the thermal fax machine to the primary media outlets.

Cali and Linda Jean are trying to get the place in shape to continue the childcare program. Leonora, the teacher who married Linda Jean and Barney, a big woman, tough and full of good humor, is helping them and also straightening up the place in anticipation of the TV cameras they hope the release will attract. There are boxes all over, and they have to decide what will stay and what can go from the supplies the teachers have packed. They keep all the good toys, let them have the rest. Keep the new crayons, give them the broken ones. Keep the Legos, give them the cheap knock-offs. Keep the good puzzles, give them the ones with pieces missing. It's looking like for every box they decide to let go, they are keeping ten. Alice and Charlene are making posters to put on every floor of the apartment complex – there isn't time for a leaflet – requesting that people come to the center in the morning to persuade the movers to leave. "Don't let them close our center," the posters read. Sue Ann is trying to keep up with the overtired children (it's after 9 P.M.), including her own Dathan and Clarisse, Charlene's Rhonda, Cali's Barney, Darnell, and baby Keisha (now one-and-a-half) and Alice's twins, all of whom – except for the excessively quiet Rhonda – are generally working against the constructive efforts of the adults, scribbling on the posters, dumping out already sorted boxes, pulling down the blocks.

Despite the chaos, the atmosphere is festive. KDIA, the black radio station, seems to be playing all the political songs just for them: Marvin Gaye, "Save the Children"; Stevie Wonder, "Livin for the City"; the O'Jays, "The Rich and the Superrich." Taking a breather from work, they're hanging out in the small office. Cali spots the phone first. "I think I'll call my mother in Brooklyn," she says with an impish grin. They all realize the district will be disconnecting its phone tomorrow and consider the possibilities. They stand around laughing silently as they watch Cali become a child again. "Hi, Mama...Just fine, just fine.... It's midnight there? Sorry, I forgot.... Oh, yes I been takin' care of my babies. They're fine. Yes, Mama, I've been going to church..." This lie cracks them up, creating an uproar in the background. "Just friends, Mama. No, it's not a party."

"You guys are terrible!" she says after she hangs up, in mock disgust.

"Leonora, you want to call Guyana?" Barney suggests, thinking as far away as I can. He knows her son is in Jonestown.

"They don't have phones. Besides, I'm going down there in two weeks. I've had it with this school system, closing our school, laying us off."

"That's right, you guys are getting laid off," says Alice in her hoarse man's voice, a big boned woman, dark-skinned with straightened but unruly hair. "When's the big day?"

Barney glances at Leonora. "Tomorrow." Barney hasn't been thinking about it.

"Wow," say several people at once as though he'd said he was going to die.

"You can work for us then," says Latricia.

"Yeah, I suppose I could. Hard to live on nothing, though."

"We'll get a grant," says Latricia.

"Maybe," Barney says. "But let's not give up on the school district changing its mind."

"I do have some connections with the City," Cali says with an encore of her impish grin.

"Your Mr. White has been making himself a little scarce lately," Barney comments.

Charlene, a woman who never smiles, says to Barney, "You can be so sarcastic, Barney." It's not the first time he has detected her hostility toward him. There's an awkward moment, as the others notice too.

"Have you asked the Temple for a contribution?" Leonora asks.

"We haven't thought about what happens after tomorrow," he says. "I did tell Latricia I'd look into developing some kind of relationship with them."

"I'm selling my house and giving them the money," Leonora says. "I could divert some of it your way."

"Are you sure you want to do that?" Barney asks. "Sell your house, I mean? You trust Jones that much?"

"Sometimes, you just got to go with your faith, you know?"

Alice sneers. "I sure wouldn't give my money to no *white* man." She turns to Barney. "You people are always after our money." She says this without hostility. She often uses him as a foil for her anti-white feelings, good-naturedly enough so he actually feels good about it, as if it's a sign she trusts him.

But Linda Jean is uncomfortable with this turn of the conversation and, always the responsible one, says, "Let's get back to work."

As the group disperses, Leonora draws Barney aside. "You know Jones is doing the exactly the same thing you're trying to do here."

"Hmmm," Barney smiles at that thought. He has no end of respect for Leonora's judgment.

2.

September 5, 1978, the day after Labor Day, begins with a soft orange glow from the Oakland hills. Unlike most days, Barney has no difficulty getting out of bed. The adrenalin pumping through his system sharpens the senses and clarifies the mind, as cloudless as the sky.

When Linda Jean and Barney reach the center at 7 A.M. to open it for the day, there are already people milling about the entrance. The plan is to run a "normal" program with whatever children come and to have the allies from the Towers stand around as a vague threat to any movers that might show up. Meanwhile, they've called a press conference for 10 A.M. As Barney enters the front door which opens onto the large plaza between the two perpendicular towers, he declares, grandly, imagining himself as Fidel entering Batista's office: "This is now liberated territory."

The phone is already ringing. KCBS tapes an interview. The adrenalin loosens Barney's tongue which in other circumstances might be stuck. "We intend to occupy the center for as long as it takes until the school district changes its mind," he tells them.

Children trickle in for the first couple hours, as they normally do. By 9 o'clock, they have about half the normal enrollment, sixteen children, a bit disappointing, but certainly a more than adequate showing. Barney is of course the only teacher (Leonora being busy preparing to move to Guyana). He calls the children to the rug for circle time. He reads them "The Rosa Parks Story," written by himself, about the Montgomery Bus boycott. Children seem to understand about buses. They talk about their struggle. "What special day is it today?"

"Halloween," somebody says.

"Christmas."

"August."

Little Barney says, "They close our school."

"Aha. Give that man a million bucks. Why do they want to do that?"

"No money," shouts Darnell, drooling, not to be outdone by his brother.

"Right! And do they have the money?"

Silence. Latricia's son Ronnie finally says, "Money for war. Not for black people."

"Ten million bucks for Ronnie! Good answer." Some of the children get restless. "All right, Clarisse. Look at how nicely Dathan is sitting. Now. Do you know why they have money for war but not for black people?"

Ronnie pipes right in, "Black people too dark. They have to sit in the back of the bus because they too dirty."

"Um, not quite, Ronnie."

"'The law's unfair,'" Little Barney quotes from the story.

"That's good, Barney. They did pass a law, Proposition 13, which was unfair, and that's why they say they're closing our school. But are we going to let them do it?"

"*No!*" all the children scream together. This part they get.

Barney starts the song. "We shall not, we shall not be moved…"

He explains further: "Today, we're going to be on television. People all over the city will be watching us. How do we want them to see us?"

"Good," says Clarisse.

"That's right, Clarisse. We want to show them that the children of Geneva Towers Children's Center know how to act. What does that mean?"

"No fighting," says Ronnie.

"No running inside," says Little Barney.

"No spitting," says Darnell.

"You got the idea." Barney is nervous that the adult chaos will mirror itself among the children, and what the television people will pick up is how incompetent they are to run their own school. He bites his scruples and resorts to the kind of teaching he generally tries to avoid. "People who act nicely while the visitors are here will get a cookie. But, if you do act up, you'll sit on time-out all afternoon, got that?" He's taking no chances. Cali flies into the room. "They're here! The movers are here!"

"Oh shit," Barney says out loud, forgetting where he is.

"Ooooo," say the children.

"Shoot, I mean." He leaves the children where they are and rushes to the door. There's about twenty people from the Towers, plus a few Peoples' Temple supporters, including Mike, all standing in front of the door with their arms folded, glowering at two white men in blue coveralls, themselves looking bemused.

Barney gently elbows his way through the crowd to talk to the movers. "The people here don't want the center closed down," he explains.

"Hey, no problem, man," says one of the movers, a red-bearded man with a pot belly. "We get paid anyway. We'll just tell them we didn't want to start a riot."

"Just tell them the people wouldn't let you in."

"Great. Fine with us." The movers turn on their heels and return to their truck. The crowd applauds them. First victory of the day.

By the time Barney gets back inside the center, the children are all over the place, writing on the wall with crayons, spilling paint, riding the tricycles, and two TV stations have arrived with all their equipment. Fortunately, the press and the children are in separate rooms, though the rooms are joined by large open doorways. The parents – Cali, Latricia, Charlene, Alice, Sue Ann – are all just standing around in awe of the two celebrities, live-on-the scene reporters well known from the local news shows, one of them a weekend anchorman. Barney does his best to contain his fury. "Could you help with the children please?" he says to Charlene, his eyes flaring.

She flares her eyes right back at me and says, "I'm not your slave," loud enough for the news people to hear.

The others, who've heard this exchange, suddenly busy themselves talking with the press.

In desperation, Barney retrieves Linda Jean from the kitchen, where she is busily preparing spaghetti for the children's lunch. "We need some help with the kids."

"Where are all the others?" she asks.

"Busy with the news people."

Linda Jean clicks off the stove and enters the room where the children are. "All right, you guys," she says in a tone which is at once scolding and friendly. "It's time to come to the tables. Let me see who can sit down quietly by the count of three. 1...2...2½...2¾...3! Very good, you all made it." In no time, she has the children sitting nicely at the tables, playing with Legos, playdough, or coloring on paper. Once again, she has saved the day.

In the other room, a third TV station has arrived with its people, and the press conference is about to start without him. Latricia reads the press release they finished last night. She stands tall, dressed in a tailored beige pants suit. She finishes: "The parents are determined to occupy the center until the school district changes its mind. This is our center. This is our community. We will not close." The other parents applaud.

There are questions. "Isn't it true that all the children have been transferred to a nearby center?"

Barney answers, "That center is nearly a mile away, uphill, through some one of the roughest public housing projects in the city."

Another newsman asks, "How many of the children have stayed behind? It doesn't look like you have a full house here."

Barney answers, "About half the children came to this school today. We don't know how many went to the new school. Some parents may be waiting to see what happens."

A third reporter asks, "The district says it's short of money because of Proposition 13, and you people should be targeting Sacramento instead of them. They say their hands are tied."

Barney starts to answer, "We think they have the money..."

Latricia interrupts him. "Barney! Let the parents speak."

"...but you should hear from the parents," he smiles, aware he has once again made a mildly racist faux pas, but he's used to being chastised for this domineering habit and gives in good- naturedly.

Latricia speaks sharply, "Let *them* go to the state for money. We don't care where they get it. We see our job as demonstrating to the whole state that no matter what cutbacks they've perpetrated by passing their racist tax law, we are determined that this center will not be one of them. How many black people do you think benefitted from this so-called 'tax relief' measure? How many blacks are homeowners? Ten percent? Twenty percent? How many landlords will now reduce rents? Somebody's got to draw the line somewhere, and we're drawing it right here. We're just saying 'No, you can't do this.'" Again the other parents applaud. Latricia has been brilliant.

"What's the next step?" another reporter asks.

"Suppose the school district refuses to back down?"

Cali grabs the floor. "There is no next step. This is the last step. The parents will occupy this center until hell freezes over if necessary. This is our center. This is our community." She tries to take her line back from Latricia, but she is nervous, and her oratory falls flat.

The cameras pan around the center, take a few shots of cute children working intently with the play-dough, and begin to pack up their gear.

"What time will this be on?" Alice asks in her gruff voice.

"Probably 6 o'clock," says Channel 5.

"6 o'clock," echo the other two channels.

The rest of the day runs smoothly, powered by their elation at the mornings' victories with the movers and with the press. At 6 o'clock, they all crowd around the TV in Alice's messy apartment, flicking through the channels, looking for themselves. Alice's walls are painted dark brown with an eye-level strip of mirror tiles, numbers of which have fallen down. The formica table – just like Barney's and Linda Jean's – is covered with dishes full of breakfast's leftover Fruit Loops. Her dirty laundry is piled on the orangish (once orange, now brown) couch. She doesn't bother apologizing.

There is news of Carter meeting with Sadat at Camp David, news of another point increase in the cost-of-living index, up to 12%, news of a new detergent that can make your clothes whiter than white. There's news of some disgruntled people complaining that Jim Jones is keeping their relatives in

Jonestown against their will. Finally, there they are, on all three channels at just about the same time, each for about 15 seconds. Flicking rapidly back and forth, they see that one channel shows the children and remarks at our stubbornness, another has Barney being interrupted by Latricia, and the third shows most of Latricia's fine speech.

"Shit, is that all?" Alice complains.

"Hey, that's a lot," Barney says. "We did good. We're gonna win this."

His words are punctuated by a short group sigh which mixes people's various levels of hope and skepticism, and translates to a highly tentative "maybe."

PART TWO

SEVEN

Deer Creek

Even as you have reached the zenith of your political career (so far), a lurking fear settles into your life like an old friend. As a leader, you fear making a mistake and opening yourself up to attack. But they could attack you anyway. They already have. They have taken your job away. You can collect unemployment for a while, and you can tell lies about how much time your kids spend with you in order to get a large allotment of food stamps, but even surplus food won't fill that hollow in your belly where the fear lurks. It pisses you off that the system has such a hold over you, that it can mess with your mind simply by cutting off your livelihood, but that doesn't stop you from waking up in the middle of the night in a sweat surrounded by multiple images of skulls with flames flicking out of their hollow eye-sockets, followed by visions of terror that lurk in the shadows between dream and memory.

One of these dream-memories is of your first year teaching; you were trying to teach a roomful of black elementary children, and they were gradually getting away from you as you tried to hold a discussion about a fight two of them had outside on the schoolyard, but the children refused to take turns, and you felt them taking sides in the fight instead of looking for solutions. You wanted them to find their own solution, so they defied your authority in ways that had you half agreeing with them, which boxed you in so there was nothing you could do but give in to the chaos, as what had been a fight between two children threatened to escalate into a brawl between the two polarized halves of the class. Another image came from a memory you have of your first social contact with black people when you were eleven or so and your father invited a black ophthalmologist and his family to your home on the lake, a bold move on his part in those times, and how you took the family on a ride in your family's motorboat but you had no idea what to say and neither did anyone else. The silence grated on the ears in a bone-chilling, fingernails- on-the-blackboard kind of way. In another bold move, your father took this man into his practice – but as an associate, not a full partner, and the black family never returned to the house. The shrill silence conjured another image, when you were younger still, the silent black man who clucked at the horse pulling the hansom cab, clopping along the streets of Nassau with your vacationing family, your father, your mother, your sister, Pookie, sightseeing – but the sight you were seeing is of a shantytown of unbelievable – at least to your eight-year-old eyes – squalor; the hovels were made from corrugated tin and tarpaper, babies were screaming, your eyes stung from the smoke of the outside fires, the cooking smell mixed with that of the sewage, dark people in rags huddled in the darkness, the din of their crowding angry and frightful, while placid looks masked the faces of your family, and you thought: This couldn't possibly be real.

1.

The days following the center's official closing are heady indeed. There are a million things involved with running a school and Barney doesn't know what he's doing. After the first two days, Linda Jean and Cali both go back to work at their jobs, so Barney is on his own with Charlene, Sue Ann, Alice, and Eddie. Between them, they have to buy, cook, and serve breakfast and lunch, answer the phone – now listed in their name, Geneva Towers Children's Center, Inc. – maintain at least a semblance of paperwork, keep the place clean, collect fees so they can buy the food. After the second day, it's clear they're not going to get the school district back. The only pressure they have on the district is holding their furnishings, a cost they can easily write off. So they resign themselves to having to figure out all the steps it takes to get incorporated, independently licensed, and funded. Plus, they have to care for the children.

At first Barney has to do everything. There is a reason he never went in for administration. He hates telling people what to do, and he despises details. However, after two days of this, he resents even more the others not doing their share.

"Eddie. You seem to handle the children really well. Would you like to teach?"

"Sure!" he says, his eyes lighting up. He's a wiry man in his twenties with dark skin, long sideburns, and narrow features. Linda Jean thinks he's missing a screw, but he seems to really like the children.

He plays with them. He rides tricycles with them. He molds playdough with them. He paints with them. He does naturally just what the modern practitioner of the child-centered curriculum is exhorted to do by university-level Early Childhood Education programs.

Alice has an obvious aversion to children, and Charlene seems indifferent, so, without Barney having to say anything, they settle in the office and talk to who knows who on the phone. Sue Ann volunteers to do the cooking and cleaning. So, Barney is able to concentrate on handling the money such as there is, buying food, preparing sign-in sheets and emergency cards, researching the ins and outs of their legal status, buying insurance, recruiting a board of directors from the community, and doing a little teaching in his spare time. His evenings he spends writing proposals, a skill he has to learn from scratch. He's never been so busy, but he has a great sense of purpose and gleans a fair share of manic energy from the aura of victory that the continuing existence of the center reflects.

Someone from Supervisor Harvey Milk's office drops a hint to Cali that the center might be eligible for CETA funds, from a city-administered federal program aimed at the chronically unemployed.

On the first Friday of the occupation, they decide to take a "field trip" downtown. They pile fifteen children and five adults including Barney into his aging VW van. Cali has talked Dan White into joining her in a meeting with the superintendent of schools, a technocrat from New York with a preference for efficiency over humanity, and they plan to demonstrate while the three of them talk.

Despite their having blanketed the media with press releases, only the radical radio station, KPFA, shows up. Barney tapes an interview with them.

At Alice's insistence, they march around the inside of the entire administration building, banging on pots and pans at bemused secretaries before they finally settle down in front of the superintendent's office on the third floor.

Barney convinces them to wait quietly for a while, he hopes until the meeting is over. He's uncomfortable in this role of trying to cool the parents' militancy, but he doesn't want to give the Superintendent an excuse to end the meeting.

But after twenty minutes, Alice is restless and wants the children to make some noise again. With Charlene's support, she starts the children singing "We Shall Not Be Moved" again along with the pot banging.

Thinking quickly, Barney decides the children need toileting, so he leads them down the stairs to the bathroom. By the time they return, the meeting is over. Cali speaks to them. "They wouldn't budge," she says.

White is dressed in his best suit for the meeting and seems nervous around the children and parents. He makes some slightly incoherent remarks to the effect that "we have to be realistic, but don't give up yet."

They renew the noisemaking with increased vigor, and Barney's all for it now. White stands by briefly but is clearly uncomfortable in this milieu. He moves on.

A Mr. O'Brian from the Superintendent's office, a red faced fellow Barney knows as the hit man, approaches him, yelling, "Blatz! You better cut this stuff out or I'll call the police and have you arrested."

It would not be the first time. "Go ahead," Barney says to him.

They march around some more, daring arrest, and ease out the door just as the cops show up. They continue the parade down Van Ness Avenue, a broad thoroughfare known for its car dealerships, which passes through the Civic Center. Cali marches with them. They pass the Symphony Hall, a brand-new structure with a rounded wall of glass panels that seem to hang in the air, and the neoclassical Opera House and Art Museum. Barney reminds Alice, "The land where they built that new Symphony Hall? The school district sold it to the city for one dollar. One dollar! There's always money for the amusements of the rich."

At City Hall, they jam the children through the revolving doors three at a time. Clarisse hollers, afraid of being trapped. The pot-banging really echoes off the dome. Their rag-tag crew sounds like an army of hundreds. They go up the sweeping marble stairway and enter the mahogany-paneled Mayor's office. "We want to see the Mayor!" Alice demands of the elderly receptionist. "We won't leave until we see him."

"Just a minute," the receptionist says. She smiles at the children. She disappears through a door behind her desk and appears moments later with Mayor

George Moscone himself, a big man with a rumpled suit and a large open-mouthed smile.

They're so shocked to actually get to see him, they don't know what to say. He, on the other hand, seems fully at ease shaking hands with the children. Or rather, he puts his hand out to shake, and the children 'give him five,' much to his amusement.

"We want them to keep our school open, Mr. Mayor," Cali finally says.

"Of course you do. I've heard about you. You're the ones who took over your childcare center. Good work. Keep it up."

They're shocked again by such support. "Will you help us get some funding?" Cali asks him.

He looks at her with a wry grin. "Don't I know you?"

Cali blushes. "I work here, in the Supervisors' secretarial pool."

"Ah," he says. "I'll do what I can. Apply for CETA funds."

"Okay, we will," Barney says. "Thanks."

Alice kicks me. "Don't let him off that easy," she whispers. "Get something in writing!"

"Can we get something in writing?" Barney stammers.

"Get me something in writing first," says the Mayor. "Submit your proposal. I'll support it." He disappears into his office.

"Don't forget now," Alice hollers after him.

2.

One of the fringe benefits of having been laid off is that Barney can now withdraw his retirement money from the state fund. He's amassed over $10,000, and they decide to use the money to buy some land in the country. He puts together a consortium of buyers, all of whom will put up with an equivalent share: his old friend Bob who went to Cal with him and is now a carpenter; a political comrade Rennie, a Jamaican, also a carpenter, and his white American wife Sue.

Linda Jean and Barney spend their autumn weekends driving around the region checking out the possibilities. At first they try Mendocino and Monterrey Counties, figuring the farther away from the Bay Area, the cheaper.

There is nothing quite like Northern California for variety of natural beauty. Seascapes, mountains, redwoods, lagoons, wild rivers, all blessed with an exquisite climate, especially in this Indian Summer time. Native American Summer, Linda Jean and Barney joke.

With directions from local realtors (they apparently don't take them seriously enough to accompany them), they check out a hundred acres near Ukiah, an old logging town where the smog from the burning sawdust of the lumber mills still stings the eyes. There's a *yurt*, a Mongolian tent-cabin popular with hippies, on the land, but no apparent source of water. They check out an apple orchard in Sebastopol one week; the next week a barren hill near Aptos which has been raped of its trees.

On the way home from Aptos, which is south of Santa Cruz, in the late afternoon, Linda Jean and Barney are tired and discouraged. They don't speak for over an hour, a not uncommon experience, but one which irritates Barney just now. "You know, I get pretty tired of our silences," he says. "I'm really tired of always being the one to break them. It's like you're afraid to talk to me or something. It's going to do us in, unless you start talking to me."

"What do you mean, 'do us in'?" she asks, an injured whine in her voice.

Her tone infuriates him. "Christ, Linda Jean. Don't be so goddamn thin-skinned. You have to fight to keep a relationship going, you know? What I mean is, if you don't get over your fear of talking to me, I am going to leave you, got it?"

"Oh," she whimpers. This speech does not inspire her to instant loquaciousness. It occurs to him that this is the first time he has directly threatened to leave.

They fall silent again. The van putts laboriously toward the summit on Highway 17 through the Santa Cruz Mountains. Each curve unveils another panoramic vista of redwood-forested valleys. The sky fades to orange behind them. Barney gets an idea. "It's so beautiful. Why don't we spend the night near here and look for land in this area in the morning? I know we've assumed it's too expensive, but we ought to check it out."

"Barney, you know tomorrow's Sunday, and I have to work."

"Oh, come on, Linda Jean. We'll stop and call them. The doctor won't mind. He probably just keeps you on for old time's sake anyway now that his kids are grown."

"The whole family will be there tomorrow. They're expecting me."

"You should quit that job anyway. You have a job with the school district. With a few college units, you could be a teacher, you know. I don't like the idea of you being anybody's maid, no matter how nice they are."

"It's not like I'm their maid, Barney, you know that. I've been with them twenty years. *I* raised their kids. They've been more like a family to me than my own family ever was."

"Yeah, right. What do they call you?"

"What do you mean, what do they call me? They call me Linda Jean, you know that."

"And what do you call them, the parents I mean?"

She sighs. "Dr. and Mrs. Grossman," she says, sinking into her seat.

"Aha! Precisely what I mean." He flushes with victory.

"Just what will we do for money if I was to quit? They pay me cash up front, remember? Tax free money for almost no work. It's not as though you were working and that there."

"That's a low blow," he bristles. "Like it's my fault."

"I didn't mean it was your fault, Barney."

He pulls the van up to a phone booth by the side

of the road. "Call them. Tell them you'll come in the evening tomorrow to clean up if they need you."

She pokes out her lips and clenches her teeth. Obviously against her will, she gets out of the van and goes to the phone.

Barney's anger surges while he waits for her. Why the hell doesn't she stand up to me? he thinks. Why doesn't she just tell me no?

When she returns, she seems happy again as she tells him, "It's fine. They were wanting to go out for dinner anyway."

"Okay. Let's go to Big Basin then." They take the next turn off west toward the ocean, and wind through ever more rugged terrain, primeval forests clinging to cliffs as steep as canyon walls. The beauty of their setting rubs off on them and erases the bad feelings that crackled between them just minutes ago. There's also the mutual excitement of doing something – anything – spontaneously.

They stop in the one-street town of Boulder Creek, a kind of boutiquery of the old west, with redwood burl shops and serious hardware stores banked up against tony restaurants with names like the "Wildwood Cafe." They pick up some steaks and Korbel at a super market-cum-general store and wind the rest of the way out of town to Big Basin State Park. The campground is practically empty, thanks to the season.

They find a site in the palpable darkness beneath a tree which is as big around as their van would be stood up on its rear bumper and older than the Spanish presence in California.

The back of the van includes a bed Barney made with plywood and 2x4s, and he generally carries a full line of camping equipment – just in case. You never know when you'll need to retreat to the hills. They go to sleep friends again, though they have only papered over their differences.

In the morning, a young realtor in Boulder Creek takes them in his 4x4 truck back into the hills on old dirt logging roads to show them a ten acre site with redwoods and meadows, horsetail ferns, and wooded cliffs, the ponderous silence broken by a perky little creek, Deer Creek, which bisects the property, dribbling its way through a king-sized bed of giant granite boulders. Biggest surprise of all: it's actually affordable and only 90 minutes out of the city.

They fall in love at first sight and rush back to town to report their success to their partners, arrange for them to see it, and click the real-estate deal-making machinery into motion.

The following weekend, with the selling owner's permission, their partnership camps out on the land in the natural campsite beneath a grove of skinny redwoods surrounding a massive stump overlooking the creek. They've brought along Darryl, Jason, and Ramona, and Rennie and Sue have brought along their children Rosalie and Victor, who are around the same ages as Jason and Ramona. Though the children explore the far reaches of the land together, they don't click with each other very well, perhaps because their parents want them to so much.

Linda Jean cooks up a spread of barbecue chicken and potato salad and Bob leads the way for Barney and Rennie to follow him into a drunken stupor, downing Bud after Bud.

Linda Jean's son Darryl, his hair cropped close to his head now, tries his hand at fishing with a makeshift line on a stick. Despite their skepticism based on the shallowness of the creek, he actually catches a couple of undersized perch, which they cook up and eat anyway.

Late that night, when all the others are asleep, Barney finds himself confessing to Rennie his attraction to Cali. Barney has long admired Rennie for living nonmonogamously without apparent adverse consequences. He is Harvard-educated and brilliant, which enhances Barney's awe for him. They are seated cross-legged on neighboring boulders in the middle of the gurgling creek. They catch glimpses through the trees of a sky more crowded with stars than the city is with people. The air smells as sweet as it might have centuries ago.

"Women are programmed to make the nest, and men are programmed to spread the seed," he says, his island accent so thick Barney can barely understand him sometimes. "You can't fight nature, man." He's a compactly built man, muscular, with caramel skin and freckles, a medium-length natural with long sideburns. "There's something special about a long-term commitment," he continues, "a kind of resonance that develops between you, but you can't let it trap you, man. You'll resent it, you'll resent her. I'd advise you to go ahead. Go for what you want. Women may grumble about it at first, they may feel threatened, but they expect it of us. In some ways it frees them not to be so, so sort of mindlessly enamored of us. It forces them to be more independent, which they really need, you know?"

"That sounds like sexist rationalization to me, Rennie," Barney says, resisting the degree to which he likes what he's hearing.

"Barney, do you think women will still like us if we let them roll over us with their accusations of male chauvinism for everything we do? The great biological contention between us is what makes sex so fucking interesting, man."

Consciously, Barney dismisses what he says, but on some level, he senses that his monogamous resolve is quietly unraveling. Why should it be such a big fucking deal? he asks himself.

Returning to the city in the van the next day, however, he's feeling especially close to Linda Jean, as all five of them bask in the glow of a thrilling new endeavor, the development of "a place in the country," untouched by the ravages of a runaway civilization teetering on the brink of imminent collapse.

EIGHT

Follow the Drinking Gourd

1.

They assemble an impressive Board of Directors: Cali as president, Charlene as vice-president (Cali insists), Latricia as Secretary, Barney as treasurer. They dig up two local ministers, one black, one white. They also tap Reggie "Wreck" Johnson, the Towers' recreation director, and a Mr. Brewster, representing the Towers' management (a brilliant coup on Cali's part). Latricia brings with her two men from People's Temple: one, a white man named Larry Cordell Barney recognizes as the slimy type in dark glasses with no eyebrows who interviewed them when they went to the church; the other, a handsome black man named Jay. They hear a rumor through Wreck that Cora Jimenez, the tenant's association head, is pissed they didn't ask her, but that's what she gets for opposing them when Sylvia Conners came to their parent meeting. Dan White agrees to let them use his name but doesn't show at the meetings. At their first meeting, they agree to have a fund-raising party.

And what a party it is, too! "Take me to the next phase," is how they bill it, after a current hit song by the Isley Brothers. They invite all their allies from the fight with the school district. They invite all two thousand Towers' residents, Linda Jean and Barney personally shoving a flier under all five hundred apartment doors. Alice's sometime boyfriend has an excellent band which sounds like the Temptations and performs that group's songs along with its own originals – and plays for free. They hold the dance in one of the Towers' big meeting rooms, which, by midnight is wall-to-wall boogie. By three, the joint is still jumping, but Barney isn't. He's pretty wasted. The room is as dark as the far side of the moon and smokier than Cali's fire. He staggers into Cali, off in a dark corner smoking a joint. "Great party," he says.

"Want some?"

"Sure."

She puts the lit end of the joint in her mouth, and points at the other end for Barney to put in his mouth. Looking around guiltily, he does as she indicates, and she blows him a lungful of smoke. Then their lips touch and linger a little too long.

"Yeah," he says. "You're going to get me in trouble."

"I certainly hope so," she drawls.

He hastens away from her to look for Linda Jean. Fortunately, she hasn't witnessed this vignette.

2.

Jay, who doesn't use his last name, seems to be a high muckymuck in that part of the Temple hierarchy that hasn't emigrated to Guyana (Barney is told that Jones' wife Marceline left last week). He is an impressive man, clearly intelligent, and flexible in his thinking. He communicates a sophisticated awareness that this movement goes way beyond Jim Jones and his charisma, the latter being merely one tool useful for bringing people together. He's tall, chocolate-skinned, with invitingly warm eyes behind tortoise shell glasses. Talking to him and Latricia, Barney is increasingly attracted to the idea of the Temple taking over the arduous job of administering the center. He might even affiliate himself as closely as might be necessary for them to pay him as head teacher.

So Barney is ready to be convinced, even converted, as Jay gives him and Latricia a tour of the Temple's largest childcare facility, located in a converted Victorian on Broderick Street in the Fillmore.

The facility is impressive. It's bright, well-equipped, with a wonderful hand-constructed wooden climbing structure in the back yard with bridges and tunnels and ship's prows and spiral slides.

In fact, Barney has only one problem with the place. It's 11 A.M. and, although he's told there are twenty-five children in attendance today, the school is as quiet as a graveyard. "It's so quiet," he says to Jay. "Where are all the children?"

"We're not one of your loosey-goosey centers," he says. "We believe in discipline."

Barney follows him into the front room where the children are assembled. They are seated in a perfect circle, with their legs crossed, listening to a story about Harriet Tubman.

There have been times in Barney's life when he would have been impressed. As a teacher, he has flip-flopped over the years on the question of discipline. When he first started teaching, he was full of the idealism of the free-school movement: *Summerhill*, Herb Kohl, Jonathan Kozol. But the children he was teaching were so unused to such freedom that they quickly took it – and Barney – to the limit. His first few months were so chaotic – there were fights all over the place, hardly any work getting done – the administration was threatening to fire him. Finally, a ten-year- old boy came at him in front of the class brandishing a broken bottle. Suddenly his instinct for survival as a teacher eclipsed all his ideals. He grabbed the little bastard and whacked his ass good with a ruler right then and there. The class cheered. Their days of freedom were over. From then on, he regulated everything so carefully that "misbehavior" became unthinkable, even though he never had to hit a child again. On the one hand, he was glad for having prevailed. On the other hand, what was he teaching? He was almost as oppressive as the worst of the racists.

When he discovered preschool teaching, he realized that at least for the younger ones, he could give them the skills they would need to liberate themselves, like thinking, questioning, speaking their minds. For one thing, the ratio of children to adults in preschool is 8 to 1, compared to 30 to 1 in the elementary program. It's a possible job. He began to think of his job as fifty percent oppression, fifty percent liberation.

As time passes, he begins dreaming of increasing the ratio of liberation. But he's been too caught up in the day-to-day struggles at Geneva Towers to do much in this area since the takeover.

When the Harriet Tubman story is over, the teacher, a long- haired, hippy-looking white woman with cold eyes, tells the children, "Harriet Tubman leading her people north to freedom is exactly what our Father, Jim Jones is doing for us, leading us to freedom in Guyana."

She directs them in a song, "Follow the Drinking Gourd," which they sing perfectly on key with adult harmonies. She asks, "What is the 'drinking gourd'?

A prim white girl in an ankle-length dress stands and recites, "It's a bunch of stars we call the Big Dipper that's always in the North."

"Good, Dawn. And what is the Underground Railroad?"

Barney thinks of his class. He'd be getting all kinds of answers about trains, BART, the new local subway.

A black boy stands erect as a soldier. "The Underground Railroad was a network of safehouses which the slaves used to escape to freedom in the north."

Barney watches while the teacher dismisses the children in perfect lines of eight to work in the painting area, the number center, the science area, each supervised by a staff member well trained in classroom control techniques.

On their way out, the three of them, Jay, Latricia, and Barney, talk in the entryway. "What do you think?" Jay asks.

"Your program is too rigid," Barney says. "Children this age need more freedom."

"You forget, we are training them to be soldiers in the revolution. We don't have time for petty bourgeois freedom," Jay says as nicely as he can.

"I guess we disagree about this." Barney smiles. They shake hands.

In the car on the way home, Latricia asks him, "Does this mean you now oppose the Temple's taking over the center?" There's an edge to her voice.

"I don't know. It depends on how much control they want. Couldn't they just give us the money like a foundation would and let us run it our way?"

"I don't think they do things that way, Barney. I think if you take their money, you take their program."

"I'm not quite that desperate, yet." He smiles.

She looks away, without returning his smile. "It's not just your show, Barney."

"I know," he says. "I know."

3.

Keeping their options open, Barney finishes off the proposal to the city for CETA funds, and everyone they talk to tells them what a good chance they have. They get letters from White, Milk, their state legislators, the Childcare Switchboard, various ministers, and neighborhood luminaries.

There's one hitch. The law requires that CETA funds be "supplementary rather than sustaining," meaning, in plain English, that they have to find someone else to fund the salary of a person to supervise the CETA people (Barney as the obvious candidate).

On the way home from work, he meets Cali in the elevator and tells her the problem.

"Let me talk to Maurice," she says. Him and me is getting real tight, and he knows all the ropes."

"Maurice?"

"Harvey Milk's aide."

Without thinking, Barney follows her home. A charged silence falls between them as Barney notices where they are alone in her apartment, sitting on her brown velour couch. She looks at him wistfully, expectantly.

He suddenly wants her badly. "Cali..." he starts, but an image of Linda Jean's face with that injured look on it stops him cold.

He gets up to leave. "Good, Cali, you follow through with Milk. I'll talk to you later." He zips on out of there as if his life depended on it.

That evening, Linda Jean and Barney have dinner with Leonora Jackson. He cooks up a mean coq au vin, served with wild rice.

"I brought you some money," Leonora says as soon as she's in the door. "I sold the house. I told the Temple I wanted the money to go to the school. They said they 'weren't ready' to give you all of it, but they came up with some. 'Tell him it's a down payment,' Jay told me. Have you been talking to him or something?" She hands a roll of hundred dollar bills. "Fifteen hundred. The Temple wanted it all in cash and I figured that would be good for you too, you know? Maybe you won't have to pay taxes on it or something."

"Leonora, this is great." Barney hugs her. "When are you leaving?"

"The day after tomorrow." Her bulk jiggles with excitement.

"No shit? Well, this'll be like the last supper then. God, we'll miss you."

They reminisce about colleagues and former students. Of their fellow teachers, how many have gone north to grow marijuana, how many have strung themselves out on cocaine; these times are not kind to teachers. With the students, they make predictions. In twenty years, who will be doctors and lawyers? Who will be gay? Who will be pimps and prostitutes? Who will be the solid working stiffs: the carpenters, the bus drivers, the secretaries, the teachers?

4.

Just to make sure nothing goes wrong, Barney decides to invite Dan White and his wife Mary Ann to have dinner with Linda Jean, Cali, and himself at Jack's, a "very San Francisco" restaurant in the financial district, where the power brokers meet. It's not his usual type of hang-out, but if he's going to play the political game in a way that might actually be successful, they have to make some compromises.

The place is brightly lit, walnut paneled, with no-nonsense decor. The waiters are all over seventy and wear tuxes. They don't take reservations, so they have to wait in line. They were all smart enough to dress up, Barney wears his black velour jacket with tan slacks – but he never thought to wear a tie. The restaurant requires ties. They make him choose one from a selection of the three ugliest ties he has ever seen. He picks a narrow brown number with abstract yellow triangles and circles. He looks much worse with it on than off, but rules are rules.

Dan and Mary Ann arrive a few minutes after Linda Jean and Barney. Dan is in an affable, punchy mood. "I hate this place," he jokes. "San Francisco is bought and sold here, cut up in little pieces." He does however shake hands with columnist Herb Caen and Assemblyman Willie Brown, seated at their regular table in the back.

Mary Ann is bubbly, perky, the kind of woman who was "Miss Personality" in high school. She has brown permed hair, a soft smile, blue eyes. She talks to Barney and Linda Jean as if they'd known her all their lives. "Dan's such a kid," she says while he's off shaking hands. "He says he hates it, but he is really so thrilled around all these famous people."

Linda Jean asks her how she likes life in the spotlight. "You'd think it would be exciting, but to tell the truth, it's a strain. Especially without the money to keep up appearances. They've got you over a barrel when they pay you $9,500 per year for this job and expect you to rub elbows with millionaires on a daily basis."

As White returns to the table, still brimming with ebullience, Barney looks at Cali and wonders what their relationship really is. Cali, dressed in a violet jump suit, gives no sign. Neither does White. And Cali and Mary Ann seem cordial enough to indicate that Mary Ann isn't the least bit suspicious.

White orders a scotch. "I don't actually drink. But this is a special occasion." Linda Jean and Barney order Korbel on the rocks, Mary Ann a glass of white wine, Cali a manhattan. When the drinks arrive, White poses a toast: "to your success," he says. "I admire you, Barney," he continues. "You're a real hero to people in the Towers, isn't that right, Cali?"

Cali looks at him skeptically. "I suppose."

"But you're the one who saved Cali's children, Dan," Barney reminds him.

"Ah, yes, my one moment of glory. The one time I felt equal to my Dad. He was a hero too, you know. He was also a fireman, got a citation from the mayor when he saved a kid from committing suicide. I've always felt I had to live up to that. And I did in that fire, but it wasn't enough to match his feat. Somehow I've got to surpass him. I have to save the whole city."

"That's okay," Linda Jean says, "Barney thinks he has to save the whole world." This remark annoys him, because she shares his compulsion in this regard yet won't cop to it.

Linda Jean and Barney order rack of lamb, a two-person meal that symbolically solidifies them as a couple in front of Cali, a deliberate move on Barney's part. The others all order steaks. Like many fancier restaurants, the service is slow, so they order more drinks.

"What is it about men?" Mary Ann asks. "Why can't they just be satisfied saving their own families, or at least keeping them above water? Honestly, you're all so insecure. Always having to prove yourselves." She smiles as she speaks, keeping the tone of this discussion light.

"Really," says Cali. "Mike's the same way with his People's Temple business."

Dan darkens the tone. "Does it occur to you that saving our families might require more than just earning a decent living?"

"Yes, but you could start there," Mary Ann snaps, and then softens it with, "I'm not saying give up your dreams. Just pay a little more attention to the practicalities of everyday life. Am I right, girls?"

Linda Jean and Cali both nod their heads.

Barney welcomes the opportunity to strengthen his bond with White. He likes the guy, for some reason. Maybe because he was a fireman. "Dan and I both see a threat that you women don't seem to see," Barney says. "We have different views of the threat, and different solutions, but I think we both sense that this society we live in is falling apart and that the situation is an emergency that calls for emergency measures, even heroism if necessary."

"That's right, Barney," White enthuses, taking a gulp of his third scotch. "Take the perversity that's running rampant in our streets. Do you girls really think your families can survive in an atmosphere of unbridled sodomy?"

"Whoa, there, Dan," Barney stiffens indignantly, the volume of his voice increasing with his own brandy intake. "If you're saying what I think you're saying, I think you better stop."

"C'mon, Barney," White lowers his voice. "I mean I like Harvey a lot, but if we let the queers take over the city, they're going to turn our own children into queers. The human race could die out, you know."

"Dan," Barney says sharply. "I won't tolerate that kind of prejudiced talk at this table. I'm afraid you're seriously misinformed about gay people."

"Just who are you calling misinformed, buddy, huh?" He grips the arms of his chair and sits up. "I know that word. People are always calling me misinformed. What they mean is stupid. I'm sick of people implying I'm stupid just because I never went to college."

"Not stupid, Dan, it's just that some people who talk like that are simply scared of their own homosexuality," Barney says without thinking, grinning broadly at his own nerve.

White's face turns pink, then red, then purple. He stands up seething at Barney. Barney sees flames of rage in the hollow of White's eyes and stands up himself, prepared to meet his challenge. The tension crackles through the silence in the restaurant, as the other diners stop their own conversations to stare at them.

Linda Jean kicks Barney. "Barney!" she remonstrates sharply. "Apologize!"

"Dan," Mary Ann whines.

Cali frowns at both of them.

Linda Jean bores her eyes into Barney. Barney laughs. "Okay, sorry, Dan. I was just kidding. Let's not embarrass the ladies any more, okay?" He sits down.

Dan also deflates and sits down, a shadow of humiliation crossing his face. Mary Ann grips his hand. "It's the booze," he mutters. "I'm not used to it. I've been under stress lately. You're a good man, Barney. I respect a man who'll fight for his ideas, no matter how harebrained." He laughs.

Barney laughs too. The food finally comes. They spend the rest of the dinner rebuilding their rapport. The tension between them doesn't dissipate entirely, but in some subtle way, it feels to Barney as if their near-fight has brought them closer. They discuss the strategy of using community block grant funds to finance his salary, so he could supervise the CETA workers. Feeling important, Barney pays the check out of center funds. When they are outside in the rain preparing to separate, Dan even gives Barney a gentle hug.

NINE

The Bank of America

1.

"I can't account for White," says the sparkly Harvey Milk to Cali and Barney in the cluttered back room of his camera shop. "You're going to have to deliver him, Cali." He's a sloppy, fairly fat man, his clothes are disheveled, and the whole place smells of the body odor of hyperactivity, but his energy is infectious.

"I understand," Cali says. "White has to support us on this, I mean, it's his district and everything."

They have arduously hammered out the proposal which enables federal community block grant funds to be used to pay a head teacher for Geneva Towers Children's Center, Inc., thus freeing up their eligibility for CETA funds.

Milk says, "We could use some help with this Briggs thing out your way." Barney knows that he's referring to Prop. 6, a proposed constitutional amendment, authored by the archreactionary State Senator John Briggs, to ban gay people from teaching in the public schools.

"Sure, I'll take some fliers," Barney says uneasily, uncertain how the issue will play in the homophobic black community. Unsure of himself, too, a refugee from a homophobic faction of the left.

But they leave the meeting with Milk, once again, certain of victory, a feeling they should have learned by now to distrust. They celebrate with a beer at the Elephant Walk, a popular gay bar on Castro Street.

"I used to hate queers, you know?" Cali says under her breath. "But shit, they get a raw deal, too."

"Harvey is a hard man not to like," Barney says. Barney too is shedding his prejudices, but he's not about to cop to them to Cali. There's something of the mentor in his relationship with Cali. He doesn't want to reinforce her biases by admitting his own.

Changing the subject, she says, "I think Mike's going to Guyana soon."

Barney is not sure how to take this. "How do you feel about that, Cali?" he asks in his best psychologese.

"I don't know. I know I'm not going with him. I don't want to compete with Jim Jones any more. We've been together two years. I guess it's over between us." She says this into her stein of Anchor Steam.

"I'm sorry. I like Mike."

"Yeah, well. That's the way it goes." She gives him her best grin-and-bear-it smile. It's clear she's in pain. Her pain touches Barney.

Three days later, Cali, Linda Jean, and Barney go to the Board of Supervisors meeting to witness the vote. On the way, Cali tells them, "White's a little soft. He's pissed that we talked to Milk, can you believe it? He also told me that Cora Jimenez had been to see him, arguing against him supporting us. But I'm sure he'll come through. He couldn't be that petty."

But when they enter the chamber, the meeting is already underway and Dan White is not there! They can't believe this. Most votes on this split board come down 6-5 with White as the swing vote. Which side he ends up on is unpredictable.

The three of them scurry around the mahogany-paneled hearing room politicking with various aides, trying to get the vote postponed. They are not successful. The funding for too many other projects depends on this measure passing. The vote on their amendment comes down 5-5, which means it fails. The main measure passes, giving their $12,000 to some competing group.

They also then vote on the CETA funds, with the name of Geneva Towers Children's Center having been taken off the list as ineligible.

Cali is furious at White. She spends the next several days calling him at his home, his office, his schlocky french fried potato stand at Pier 39, a new waterfront tourist development near Fisherman's Wharf, but he eludes her. She's at the point three days later of going to his house, when Barney announces to her that he'd gotten a letter that morning from the Bank of America promising the center a donation of $8,500, a quarter of what they asked for, but hey.

The irony of the largest capitalist institution in the world funding their little piece of liberated territory is not lost on him.

The next day, Cali quits her City Hall job and Barney puts her, Charlene (at Cali's insistence again), and Eddie on the payroll as teaching assistants at five dollars an hour, and Barney as head teacher at eight dollars an hour. They're in business!

2.

That night he can't sleep at all, he's so excited. Ever since he read *Summerhill* 15 years ago, he has had a fantasy of running his own school. He'd forgotten all about it, but now that the situation has fallen into his lap, he can't get it out of his mind. This school will be revolutionary, a liberation school. They will rebuild it from the bottom up. There will be no more oppression of children. No more lines, no more asking to go to the bathroom, no more "time-outs", no more hands-folded perfect silence criss-cross apple sauce. They will treat the children with every bit as much respect as they would if they were adults. He practices speeches in his head to Cali, Charlene, and Eddie.

He tries to share some of his excitement with Linda Jean, but she's skeptical. "You really just want the kids to run wild?"

"They won't, Linda Jean, you'll see. They'll return the respect we give them."

"Sure, Barney. It's not like we live in a perfect society and that there. Even in Jonestown, they seem to use a lot of corporal punishment. Some of these poor black children come to school with a lot of anger. You give them too much freedom, and they'll be acting out their anger all over the place."

"Good. A healthy thing for them to do. Let them. Let this be a place where young people can have their emotions instead of sitting on them all the time."

As he suspects, Cali and Eddie go for the idea, with Charlene hesitant. What they decide to do, over Charlene's objections, is divide up the children into three groups of six, with each of them responsible for one group, Eddie in the morning, Charlene in the afternoon.

It doesn't work very well at first. Cali, who has no experience teaching, is completely inconsistent, first letting her group do just as it pleases, and then when they start getting too wild, she screams at them to shut up. Barney's group doesn't do much better. His idea is to basically follow them around while they play. But of course, they are confused by their new freedom and try to test its limits. Dathan in Barney's group goes straight for the blocks and pulls them all down. One of the twins comes over from Cali's group and starts throwing the blocks. A block hits Clarisse on the temple, and she screams as if she's close to death. Ronnie decides he wants to paint, and Barney is pleased as he watches him get the paints and brushes out by himself. Then, while Barney's dealing with Clarisse, Ronnie starts painting the wall.

Eddie seems to handle things just fine, however. The withdrawn Rhonda is in his group, and she seems to come out of her shell when she isn't afraid of being criticized. Eddie works with her, little Barney, and the other twin in the doll house, playing the father while Rhonda plays the mother, little Barney plays the baby, a role he enjoys, and the twin plays big sister. It's sweet to watch them, Eddie is so unself-conscious. He gets peals of laughter from little Barney by putting him over his knee and pretending to spank him by clapping his hands behind his butt. The twin and then Rhonda both squeal, "Spank me! Spank me!"

When Latricia comes in to pick up Ronnie about 3, the place is in total shambles. The blocks are still all over the floor, the paint is still on the wall, and the Legos are strewn all over the rug. Barney had planned to clean up some during nap, but of course no one wants to take a nap. "What's going on?" she asks. "Looks like an earthquake hit the place."

"We're just trying to give the children a little more freedom," Barney says.

3.

One night Barney tells Linda Jean he's going to a meeting and instead has dinner with his ex-wife Cynthia. They've had their ups and downs since the divorce, but they've tried to stay friends for the sake of Jason and Ramona. There've been moments recently when he's even wondered whether he should have left her in the first place.

They eat in a new Thai restaurant on Mission Street. The walls are painted very blue. Cynthia's long, straight, brown hair is now short and curly. She's a small woman with dark eyebrows like Ramona's. In fact it's been said that Ramona looks more like Cynthia than Cynthia ever did.

"Linda Jean and I are having some problems," he tells her.

"What a surprise, Barney," she says with a hint of sarcasm. "You mean you seem to be confronting the same issues over and over again? Pushing each other's buttons?"

"Something like that,"

"I think that's called 'marriage,' but I'm no expert on how to handle it," she reminds him. She's been married and divorced once again since she and Barney split up. "Are you sure you don't just want to be 25 again?"

"Maybe that is part of it. But mostly I just need someone I can really talk to. Like I used to be able to with you. Linda Jean, I don't know, it's like she's afraid of me or something."

"Well, Barney, it's tough. It sounds a little like you are saying, 'my wife doesn't understand me,' but I don't mean to denigrate the feelings, or is that a bad choice of words? Minimize the feelings. I know it hurts. I feel for you.

"I'm not sure we did talk that much," she continues. "It seems to me those agonizing silences were a problem with us, too."

"Yeah, but with us it was me perpetrating them and now it's her."

"Out of the frying pan. Welcome to the other side of the problem."

"For instance," Barney says, "Linda Jean and I couldn't be having this conversation."

"Of course not. Then you wouldn't be having the silences. We didn't have this kind of conversation back then either. It's easier to talk when you're not 'involved.'"

"I suppose. There's just so much fear between people."

She says, "I read on a bumper sticker once, you know that's where I get my best insights, 'Do what you fear, watch it disappear.' I think that says it all, complete with the bad diction. Watch *what* disappear? Your mind?"

Barney laps up this rapport greedily. When they get back to her house, to the red Victorian they bought together six years ago, he kisses her hard. "I'd love to sleep with you again," he says.

"That might be fun," she says. "But not while you're still married."

4.

A few evenings later, there's a board meeting at the center. Barney is expecting it to be routine, a formality where they vote to accept the money from Bank of America.

As soon as he counts noses, he begins to worry. There's Latricia, Larry the white slimy guy, Jay with the tortoise shell glasses, and Mike, all from People's Temple. And then there's Barney, Cali, Charlene, Linda Jean, and Eddie. None of their more honorary board members show, no preachers, no management reps. Luckily, they've established a policy of letting whoever shows up at a meeting vote.

"This looks like an ambush," Barney whispers to Cali.

Cali starts the meeting with a cold stare at Mike. "We need a resolution to accept the money from the Bank of America. Any objections?"

Latricia speaks right up. "We have an alternative proposal. Last night we were able to get the board of People's Temple to agree to take over management of the center. This would mean then that Jay would be in overall charge of hiring a staff."

Barney's count of the votes tells him that it depends on how Charlene and Mike go.

"Well, something as important as this should have a full debate," Barney says, full of disingenuousness. He wouldn't call for this if he thought he had the votes.

"Barney," Latricia says. "Let's face it. You've lost control of the situation. You want to run the center as if it were in the white middle-class suburbs, not the heart of the ghetto."

Barney strikes back. "Are you implying that education is somehow different in the ghetto? That ghetto children aren't just as smart as white middle-class children?"

"I am implying that black families are different from wishy-washy white liberal families. We believe in disciplining our children, not letting them run the show," Latricia says.

Cali speaks up. "As I understand it, what we're trying to do, Latricia, is teach freedom, liberation, revolution. And that means teaching children to think for themselves, make their own choices. It may be chaotic at first, but they'll learn."

"Sister," says Jay, "I'm afraid we just disagree here."

"Can we vote on my proposal?" Latricia asks.

"I'd like to see it tabled until the full board can meet," Barney says.

"All those in favor of tabling this discussion?" Cali asks.

The vote is 3-4, in favor of tabling, with Mike and Charlene abstaining. Jay, Larry, and Latricia all glare at Mike. Mike laughs. "Jesus, you all put me in a tough spot," he says. They all laugh, easing the tension.

Cali gives Charlene the eye. "Charlene, don't you want to vote?" she asks pointedly.

"I don't like your chaos, Barney. And the Temple seems like it has more to offer than the Bank of America. But I suppose we need to talk more. I'll vote to table."

Whew, Barney thinks.

"In that case," Mike says to Cali and Barney, keeping his tone light with a folksy dialect, "I reckon I'll vote with the Temple, since you guys have already won."

"This round," says Jay, quietly.

After two days of whining to the absent board members about a coup d'état by the People's Temple folks, Barney is ready for another meeting. His cause has been aided by the bad publicity the Temple's been getting. On the other hand, he hasn't counted on them organizing against him.

All his people are at the meeting. The two reverends, Wreck, and Brewster, from Tower's management. Cali's been leaning on Charlene, and says she's won her over mainly by warning her that she'll lose her job if the Temple takes over. But Latricia's been busy too, inviting Alice, Sue Ann, and three other parents to the meeting. Who knows what she's said to them. He knows the discipline issue is working against them, and the past few days have not been any less chaotic.

Cali moves the meeting quickly to a vote, figuring most people's minds are made up. Barney's side wins, but it's damn close, 7-6, with several abstentions, including Charlene, Brewster, and one of the preachers. Mike shyly votes with the Temple. The estrangement between him and Cali is palpable. Alice and Sue Ann come through for Barney and Cali, but all three of the other parents go with the Temple.

Whew, again, he thinks.

The meeting breaks up without hard feelings, or so Barney thinks. Jay comes over and shakes his hand. "Congratulations," he says. Then he looks Barney in the eye in a chilling way. "I hope you don't turn out to be real sorry about this."

Barney wonders what he means, but he doesn't ask.

It's not completely true that you don't know your feelings. You do know fear. Fear has been with you it seems since your birth and has wrapped itself around your every experience. Not only fear, but fear of fear, sometimes called anxiety, the constant little fear that seems to keep the big fear at bay. Your image of fear seems to sharpen as you grow older. In the middle of the night you wake up to see a white face in the midst of a raging fire, surely the fires of hell, flames darting out of its vacuous eye-sockets like the tongues of snakes. The face in the fire burns ever so slowly from white into black. The fireman of your mind jumps into the picture with a heavy-duty fire extinguisher that blasts clouds of thick white smoke at the fire and quickly suffocates it, leaving a shadow on the black face with the hollow eyes, dead, as Mike would say, as a coffin nail.

TEN

Halloween

1.

"Not all witches are bad," Cali tells the children at circle time, her gray eyes sparkling. "There's different kinds of witches. Did you ever see the 'Wizard of Oz?' 'The Wiz?'"

Halloween is in the air, and Cali takes to the day like a true San Franciscan. She is into it. She's determined to make the entire center a scary house. She covers the walls with cottony spiderwebs, egg-carton spiders, and Kleenex ghosts. She buys out Woolworth's of its plastic vampire bats, inflatable skeletons, and hackled black cats.

She pumps the children on what they want to be. Dathan, with his sad, narrow face, answers, "Superman."

"Everyone wants to be Superman," Cali says. "What about something different? See how different you can be."

"A roach," Dathan says. The children crack up.

"That's good, Dathan. That's scary. We'll do it. Who else has something different they want to be?"

Her own son Darnell, drooling as usual, says, "I want to be the Monster of Geneva Towers."

"We can do that," Cali says.

"I want to be a robot," says little Barney, not to be out done by his brother, rolling his big eyes.

"That could be original, Barney," Cali says. "How about you, Rhonda?"

"Invisible."

Cali chuckles. "That might be tough, Rhonda. How about an animal? You're famous for loving animals."

"Zizzer-Zazzer-Zuzz."

"From the Dr. Seuss book. Red hair, pink-and-white checked body, tail. Okay, we can do that."

Both Barney and Cali have been working on originality with the children. It's tough at this age. They all want to be Smurfs and GI Joes, what they see on TV. They develop a movement activity where each child gets to lead a movement, and they encourage the children to come up with unique movements, like waggling the tongue, or screwing up the face.

Cali decides to go all-out and get the parents to refuse to buy the ready-made costumes. She makes Barney go to great lengths to rent a Betamax to show both "The Wizard of Oz" and "The Wiz" on videotape.

They also show the Disney version of "The Legend of Sleepy Hollow," narrated by Bing Crosby, every day for a week. In this story, Brom Bones gets rid of Ichabod Crane, his rival for the charms of the beautiful Katrina, by driving him paranoid on Halloween night.

"What are you going to be, Barney?" Cali asks suggestively. "Don Juan? Casanova?" All this collaboration has made them closer than ever, and she flirts with him shamelessly.

"I'm going to be the Headless Horseman, from Sleepy Hollow," Barney says in his spookiest voice, "and drive your other suitors mad." He cackles.

"That's good," she says, "I'm going to be a witch."

"That's not very original," Barney says.

"A good witch. I'm going to wave my wand and make people happy."

"Hey, I'm the one with the wand," Barney says, thrusting his hand in his pocket to accentuate the bulge in his pants. "That's my job."

"Barney!" she scolds. This banter takes place right over the children's heads as they sit cross-legged in a circle on the rug.

On Halloween itself, the fall day dresses up in its summer costume. The sun shines like a giant pumpkin. Barney wears his black velour suit, a black turtleneck jersey stretched to cover his head, with two eye-holes cut between the shoulder seams. He carries a head-sized pumpkin on his arm.

Cali's dressed in a black leather miniskirt, a black lace camisole, a black crocheted shawl, black fishnet pantyhose, and black patent leather shoes with stiletto heels. She carries a broom, and tops herself off with a black pointy cap.

The children and their parents are decked out, too. Clarisse, with all the braids, is dressed as Michael Jackson's scarecrow in "The Wiz," and her brother Dathan is a roach after all, his extra set of legs made by a shirt tied around his middle, dyed brown, the sleeves stuffed with newspaper. Their mother Sue Ann has draped herself in yellow crepe paper and made a mask from yellow construction paper to become the cowardly lion, a character which fits her shy yet dauntless personality. Darnell is the Monster of Geneva Towers in green long underwear and a surplus gas mask, and little Barney is a combination tin man and robot in a cardboard tube covered with aluminum foil. Rhonda is Zizzer-zazzer-zuz in a red wig and wrapped in pink-and-white checked butcher paper. The other assistant teacher, the dark, lanky Eddie is dressed in street clothes, his only costume being a white Santa Claus beard that he has colored blue with powdered tempura. "Bluebeard," he identifies himself. Alice's twins, Tenisha and Ronisha, both of whom wear their hair short and natural, are dressed in white and black reciprocal commas, painted on butcher paper, "yin and yang," Alice explains with greater cleverness than Barney expects from her. Alice herself has painted her face with zebra stripes, wears a dashiki, and carries an authentic-looking spear and shield she borrowed from her cousin who runs an Afro shop. "Shaka Zulu," she identifies herself in her warrior voice. "The blood who almost freed South Africa a hundred years ago. And you better watch your ass, white boy," she threatens, in fun, flourishing her spear at Barney.

They parade the children through the hall, take them down to the dark, dank, subbasement near the abandoned garage where the Monster of Geneva Towers allegedly lives, to give them a scare. Easily intimidated, Clarisse starts into screaming so much they have to cut their visit short. Then they march around the block.

At the far end of the Tower's block-square yard, they come to a grove of poplar trees. Cali hesitates. "There's blackbirds in those trees," she says.

"So?" Barney says. "You think this is an Alfred Hitchcock movie?"

They continue past the trees. Suddenly, the birds do attack, dozens of them. They swoop down from the trees and peck everyone on the top of the head, children and adults. The children scream and run.

Cali shrieks at the birds, flailing her broom. "Get out of here! Stop it! Git!"

Something strikes Barney as both hilarious and touching in the vigor with which Cali repels the black-bird attack. The first two lines of a poem pop into his head.

> Wisp of a witch who lives in the sky,
> Banishes the blackbirds with a bat
> of her eye.

Oh-oh, he thinks. Writing her poetry.

They return to the center to have an unsuccessful apple bobbing contest. The children's mouths are too small to grab the apples with their teeth. Cali's worm trick works better. She holds out a black plastic bag full of cooked spaghetti and challenges the children, "Anyone brave enough to stick their hand in my worm bag will get a piece of apple." Little Barney, filled with trust for his own mother, accepts the challenge and the others follow, except for Clarisse, who starts to cry again. Cali gives her a piece of apple anyway.

Eddie gives the children naptime nightmares by showing his "dead finger," his own finger of course made to look dead by talcum powder, and stuck up through a hole in a small, cotton lined box.

Barney has worked it out so Cali and he have the same shift, 9-4, and they leave the center together, with Charlene in charge.

Even at 4, the day is unseasonably warm. "It's such a beautiful day," Cali says. "I feel like going to the beach."

"Let's go," Barney says, without thinking. They drive in his van to Baker's each, out past the Golden Gate Bridge, without saying much. He knows there's an extra bubble of warmth for her in his heart, but he's trying not to think about it. Mike leaving for Guyana soon might have something to do with it. But there's more to it than that. Somewhere in the course of this day, around the time he made up the poem, some rubberband of resistance inside him snapped, and he decided to go for it with her.

The beach is nearly deserted. They take off their shoes in the van. As Cali slips off her pantyhose, he catches a glimpse of her black lace panties.

Once their toes are digging in the sand, he grabs her hand and pulls her toward the water. "C'mon, Cali, let's go for a swim."

"No!" she screams as her feet touch the icy surf. The jack o'lantern sun grows reddish in the west.

He puts his arms around her. Fuck it, he thinks. He kisses her lightly on the lips. The surf rolls languidly in and out in the background. She kisses him back. They kiss long and hard. Their tongues reach out to each other.

"Shit," he says into her ear as they hug. "Now what are we going to do?"

"Shh," she shushes, touching his mouth with her finger. "I'm quite sure we can handle it."

He's not. But he doesn't say anything. They kiss some more. Seagulls screech at them derisively. Embarrassed, the sun turns redder.

2.

Many kisses later, he walks into his and Linda Jean's apartment with his feet two inches off the ground. I can do this, he thinks. Why not? My love for Cali in no way diminishes my love for Linda Jean. In fact, it enhances it. He sweeps Linda Jean into his arms and kisses her sloppily and hungrily, pawing her all over. She is dressed in a patchwork clown suit from her own school party.

"What's gotten into you?" she asks, pleased.

Better you should ask what have I gotten into, he thinks, but never mind. "You've been on my mind all day," he lies, the first of a long line of such. "Let's do it."

This 'it,' as Linda Jean seems to understand, is not the classical 'it,' but rather a pronoun standing for 'getting ready for Halloween.' They've planned this evening in some detail. It was Barney's idea some weeks ago that they go out on the town dressed as each other.

They start off with a Korbel on the rocks and a few tokes of thai stick (a renewed habit, scored through Cali), the latter of which brings on a bad case of munchies, which they satisfy by stuffing themselves with their – or Barney's – favorite snacks: tree-ripened olives, marinated artichoke hearts, Italian salami, smoked gouda, pickled herring on Ak Mak crackers.

Meanwhile, the doorbell is ringing like crazy with belligerent trick-or-treaters, shouting, "We know you're in there," or "We'll knock your door down!" Linda Jean and Barney just smile at each other benignly. "We gave at the office," he keeps reminding her. They need have nothing more to do with any pint-sized imps this night.

By unspoken agreement, they get off into erotically dressing each other. First, they remove each other's clothes. Barney already turned up the heat so they can fiddle around naked for a while. They kiss a few times to get the juices flowing, but they don't give into their mutual urge to ravish each other just yet, as they don't want to spoil themselves for the lascivious plans they have for later – or, Barney doesn't anyway, him being the one with physical limitations on how many times 'it' can be done.

Yin and yang, they apply the pancake makeup to each other's' faces, pinkish-gray to hers, mahogany-brown to his. They similarly make up their necks and wrists, having decided to glove their hands. From a tube, she squeezes out a length of scar tissue above her left eye, while he smears on more make-up above his eye to cover up his scar.

She holds out a pair of her burgundy nylon panties for him to hop into and pulls them up against his
tumescent member. He holds a pair of his white jockey
shorts for her. She snaps him into a corset she's gotten from somewhere, a "merry-widow" she calls it. It
includes a bra which she stuffs with more of her crum-
pled panties. Barney helps her into one of his tighter
t-shirts, which reads "Another Teacher for Peace" and
minimizes her already minimal breasts. Over that
she puts on a blue oxford-cloth, button-down shirt,
a wide, red paisley tie, and his same old black velour
three-piece suit, the trousers of which she rolls and
pins. With her help Barney puts on her lavender silk
wrap-around dress, so they reciprocate the costumes
they wore to the People's Temple a couple of months
ago. He shivers as he slips into her black fish-net stock-
ings, their pattern identical to that of Cali's pantyhose.
On his feet, he wears some Goodwill pumps with
two-inch heels; on her feet, she wears his suede wal-
labies, stuffed with newspaper, over black sweat socks.

On their heads, they wear wigs, Barney's a short
afro, hers a sandy mop combed Jimmy Carter style, the
way Barney wears his. He wears her favorite gold-ring
earrings. She applies lip gloss to his lips, eyebrow
pencil to his eyebrows. He takes off his wire-rimmed
glasses, and she puts on an old pair of his, from which
they've removed the lenses. They stare at themselves
in the full-length mirror, amazed at how accurately
they resemble each other.

Without having planned it, they take on each other's ways. Barney becomes stubborn. Linda Jean becomes brash and arrogant, the way Barney can sometimes be. Their voices have about the same pitch anyway, but they do use each other's expressions. "...and that there," is one of hers that he usurps, while she mimics his habitual hip talk with sprinklings of "like," "you know," and "man."

3.

Linda Jean drives, as she normally wouldn't. They finally find a parking place as close to Castro Street as they can, which means below Mission Street, twelve blocks away, but he is passive about it (as Linda Jean would be), while Linda Jean (as Barney) curses other drivers and rehearses her impatience. Walking slowly – it takes him a while to master the heels – they reach the closed off section of Castro, near Market Street, by the newly restored Castro Theater, an oriental masterpiece of tile and arabesque. The first people they come to are the lookyloos, dressed in street clothes, lining the sidewalk to enjoy the show. They get sympathetic nods for their costumes, a few, "Hey, right on!"s.

The street itself is jammed with revelers, mostly dancing to the ersatz Motown sound of Pride and Joy, a local group (white) of adequate if unexceptional skill. It's rumored the famous Sylvester will play later. There are innumerable drag queens, or perhaps once-a-year straight types like Barney, in fabulous sequined gowns, some of them wired electrically, living light shows with multicolored lights that blink in time with the music. Several people are still recycling their Nixon masks. There's an oil sheik with a fistful of dollars in one hand and a gas pump handle in the other. From their vantage point they can see at least three people dressed as penises, all erect, one of them at least twelve feet high with a sign on it reading "Double Digit Inflation."

Linda Jean and Barney plunge into the crush of bodies. In the first ten seconds, he feels a hand on his balls and a pinch on his butt. "So this is what it's like," he says. It doesn't feel good, but he makes every effort to acquiesce to the helplessness of violated privacy. "I guess we have to think of this crowd as having one big body."

He closes his eyes and tries to live up to this challenge. Something else happens instead. For just a moment, he can't remember who he is. The terror courses through him like a flash-fire. He thinks of Cali too, which confuses him, because as Linda Jean, he can feel her jealousy, and it's one of those primal fears, like the fear of losing a parent when you are very young.

He looks around. One of the fearful masks, a plain white mask with large, hollow eye-sockets, leers at him. A cowboy looks at him with utter disgust, and Barney senses that he sees him as black. That makes him miss Linda Jean terribly and he squeezes her hand, but it's not her hand, it's the hand of an evidently gay man, an androgynous clown in white-face who smiles seductively at his squeeze. "Sorry," he mumbles, shuffling away. He doesn't see Linda Jean anywhere. Suddenly he realizes that in fact the masks are the real faces and the real faces are masks. The Nixon really is Nixon. What's he doing here, Barney thinks. The cats really are cats. The draculas, frankensteins, and werewolves really are draculas, frankensteins and werewolves, and they're after him, because they think he's black. The penises are really penises. Really? What would a twelve foot penis feel like, he wonders, and laughs at himself, which almost brings him around again, but just then, for no apparent reason, the crowd surges away from the stage, toward Market Street, and someone steps hard on his foot. Pinwheels of panic go off in his brain. "We're going to be trampled," he yells aloud. Dizzily he calls, "Linda Jean!" then in confusion he calls his own name, "Barney!" and he feels like he's about to run amok through the crowd except he can't move, he can't breathe, he's about to faint, and then he sees her behind him and throws his arms around her, and with tears in his eyes, he tells her, "Let's get the fuck out of here."

Somehow, they maneuver their way back toward the sidewalk and away from the crowd, where they hear people talking, "Did you see Briggs?" someone asks. Apparently the reactionary state senator who wants gay teachers fired had the nerve to show up on the periphery of the crowd, and would have started a riot if he hadn't gotten out of there in a hurry. They continue toward the car, holding hands, calm reasserting itself in his being as he focuses on this simple goal, which he keeps chanting ominously to Linda Jean, "Let's just get to the car. Let's just get to the car."

Once there, he slumps in the passenger seat and holds his head in his hands until the wave of panic subsides. "I thought I'd lost you," he says with tears in his voice. "Barney!" she grabs his shoulders and speaks into his face, her voice calm and steady. "It's all right. It's just Halloween. You got scared, but there's nothing to be afraid of. I'm here. I'll always be here."

He returns her gaze. Her eyes reassure him. "Okay," he says. She's broken the spell. "Thanks," he says. They hold each other.

"What would you do without me?" she laughs.

He laughs too and then reverts to his role. "Well, Barney," he says. "Are you ready for the next phase and that there?"

"I guess so, man," she says.

4.

Xanadu is in the lower Haight, also called Hayes Valley, near where the prostitutes roam unmolested (except by consent), a beautiful Victorian mansion, with a ten-foot wrought-iron grill surrounding the front, gold leaf on the spikes. The house is painted Barney's favorite color, burgundy, trimmed with black, with gold accents on the gingerbread. This is their first time here – indeed, at any such establishment – and they're both a little nervous, though Barney is fairly sure that his anxiety is closer to excitement whereas Linda Jean's is closer to dread, in spite of their role reversal. There's an edge to his excitement too, a residue from the panic attack. Still, he passively waits for her to announce their arrival into the intercom. She keeps looking at him funny as they stand in front of the gate, but she finally does get it, presses the button, and responds to the "Yes?" with "Barney and Linda Jean Blatz. We have a reservation."

A small, skinny black man with an earring in his left ear and a many-colored robe like the Biblical Joseph's looks them over through the bars and then opens the gate. He smiles not at all at their sartorial joke.

"Fifty dollars, please," he says. Barney nods his head at Linda Jean for her to pay him out of his wallet.

Inside, the place is painstakingly restored, from the polished brass doorknobs, to the painted leather wainscoting waist-high along the wall, to the gleaming redwood banister along the stairs.

A heavy-set peroxide blonde dressed in a fuchsia nightie and matching bikini panties, her huge nipples easily visible, greets them in the foyer, under an elaborate crystal chandelier. "Welcome to Xanadu. Aren't you a cute couple. How can I tell you apart?" She giggles. "Never mind. My name is Sarona. Let me show you around."

In the parlor, which has violet brocade wallpaper and a crackling fire in the marble fireplace, two couples are dancing to Donna Summer's "Love to

Love You Baby," a song replete with orgasmic groans. Although this event has been billed as a costume party, Barney and Linda Jean are the only ones wearing much of anything at all. One of the couples greets them with big smiles. The man is wearing only a leather harness of some kind on his chest and a thong around his penis. He has black curly hair, a goatee, bright blue eyes. His female partner is small with a short blonde mop of hair, dressed in see-through champagne-colored bra and panties. They are both wearing Lone Ranger masks.

Another couple, both fat and dressed in nude body suits, is monopolizing the elaborate hors d'oeuvre table.

"Help yourself to the whore's ovaries," Sarona giggles. Barney dips a tortilla chip into the fresh salsa. Linda Jean spreads liver pate' on a Triscuit. "We have one fundamental rule here," Sarona continues, "summed up in one word: Ask. Don't assume that just because someone is here they want to have sex with you. They probably do, but you have to ask first, even to touch." She shows them the next room, where there's a giant projection TV showing a porno movie, "Sodom and Gomorrah." Barney recognizes it from the scene of the contortionist giving himself a blow-job. She leads them upstairs. "Upstairs are the party rooms. No one's up here yet, I don't think. Oh, one couple." She shows us two huge rooms both carpeted by four-inch thick, satin-covered foam. In a corner of one of the rooms, a couple is fucking.

"Let me show you the basement." They follow her. "This is the dungeon, not everyone's cup of tea." In a small, dark room, there are stocks, a cross on the wall with wrist and ankle straps, whips and collars hanging on hooks, a leather sling chair hung from the ceiling with chains. "Next is the pool room," she says moving on. She points out an idle pool table. "And everyone's favorite, the hot tub." The tub itself is huge, perhaps fifteen feet in diameter. Inside it are about a half- dozen people, some embracing, some soaking. "That's your grand tour. You're on your own now, but whatever you do, enjoy yourself. That's what this place is for."

They decide to return to the parlor to warm themselves up with some dancing. As soon as they start in on the floor, the curly- headed masked man taps Linda Jean on the shoulder and asks, "May I cut in?"

She shrugs and goes off to dance with his blonde partner.

"I'm Bill," he says to Barney in a hoarse whisper. "What's your name?"

"Ahh, Linda Jean," Barney answers, not really prepared for this, but somehow committed to see where it leads.

"I think you're really hot," he says.

Barney blushes, but no one can see, thanks to the makeup. The thought occurs to him that the guy doesn't know he's male, but he knows their makeup job isn't *that* good. They dance through the entire Earth, Wind, and Fire album. Then Percy Sledge comes on, "If a man loves a woman," and Bill is all up on him, rubbing and hunching, and he resists at first but then he thinks what the hell, it's Halloween.

"Come with me," he orders, and he pulls Barney by the hand downstairs and into the dungeon. Oh-oh, he thinks, he's definitely not ready for this, but instead of getting out the whips, Bill produces a small leather bag that's been hanging from his harness and brings forth a pocket mirror, a razor blade, a rolled-up hundred dollar bill, and a small fold of paper. He opens the paper and forms four lines of white powder on the surface of the mirror. He sucks one into his nose with the rolled up c-note. An old druggie, Barney is still a virgin with this stuff, so he just copies what Bill does. After they each do two more lines, his heart is pumping like a Texas oil well and he's ready for anything. Bill is all over him again, but Barney is like playdough in his hands. He kisses him on the mouth, he thrusts in his tongue, he rubs his hands all over Barney's "breasts," his ass, his "clit," and he's burning up. He roughly shoves Barney over to the sling chair and throws him down in it. He tears off the pantyhose, rips his panties out from under his corset, and goes down on his throbbing "pussy" with his mouth. Barney runs his fingers through Bill's hair and moans. He comes up for air, straddles Barney at his waist, sticks his cock in Barney's mouth. Barney nearly pukes, but he's seen *that* movie too, so he knows it's possible to open your throat, and he does this. Then he feels Bill's hands on his "vagina," greasing it up with Vaseline from somewhere, then he feels his fingers, then his cock all up inside him – ouch, this really hurts at first – while he strokes Barney's humongous "clit" with his hand, and screaming into the night, they both come at the same time, Bill inside Barney, Barney all over his silk dress.

"Whew," is about all Barney can think of to say. Bill suddenly repels him. But then Barney's no longer the choice cherry he was for Bill either. They exchange pleasantries, "Thanks, man," he says, and Barney says, "Yeah, maybe later."

As they stand there dumbly, the wave of panic returns. It felt awfully good, Barney thinks. Will he ever be satisfied by a woman again? Who the fuck is he anyway? A man? A woman? Black? White? Gay? Straight? Real? Unreal? If he does it with a woman now will that make him a lesbian? He looks all around the inside of his brain to find a familiar vantage from which to proceed with his life, but it's like trying to climb a cliff when there's no toehold, or more like what it must have been like for Dorothy swept away by the tornado, dizzily grasping at the swirling winds.

Without saying anything, Bill rescues him from his confusion by offering him another line of coke. The ritual of sucking this powder up his nose brings him back to reality, and they finish off the gram. Then he goes back upstairs, and Barney heads for the hot tub, hoping to wash away the dirty feeling.

Linda Jean is in the hot tub by herself with a sullen look on her face. She looks at Barney's wild-eyed disheveled self with a mixture of hurt and disgust. Barney decides the masquerade is over. He removes his gloves, throws off his wig and the rest of his clothes, and climbs in the tub beside her. He finds a jet to straddle and let it massage his balls, his ass, his lower spine.

"You having fun?" she sneers at him.

"Yeah," he says. "You?"

"I didn't know you were *that* way," she hisses.

"Hey, it's only fun. What's the big deal?" He uses the chlorinated water to wash off his make-up. "You haven't found anyone here you like?"

"Yeah, you," she says, throwing her arms around Barney.

He pushes her away. "Linda Jean, if you wanted to just fool with me we could have stayed home. The whole point is to do something different, you know?" She gets that devastated look on her face and it's Barney's turn to be disgusted, so he gets out of the tub and goes all the way upstairs to look for some more action, not completely unaware that a certain meanness has crept back in with his reawakened masculinity.

There's a woman spread-eagled on the floor with five men on her, so that she has one cock on each hand, one on each breast, one in her mouth. Her pussy is free, so Barney volunteers himself to dive in and suck it. It tastes like several different flavors of sperm.

Bill and his partner come along, and he orders her to suck Barney's cock. Barney is surprised that it's raring to go again, and after a while he leaves off the first woman and starts into fucking Bill's cute blonde partner, while Bill cheers him on.

He senses Linda Jean nearby, and then she clears her throat to make sure he notices her. "Come on, let's fuck," Barney hears her say and catches her out of the corner of his eye grabbing the small black man with the earring who let them in and pulling him on top of her. She makes exaggerated grunts and groans, Barney is sure, for his benefit. For her benefit, Barney slows down what he's doing to Bill's partner, whose name turns out to be Candy, and watches Linda Jean with a devilish smile on his face. He knows she wants him to be jealous, but he's just not. For one thing, her little man, contrary to stereotype, has a dick even smaller than Barney's own pea-shooter.

On the way home, the silence between them resounds like the echo from the Grand Canyon. They've switched clothes again so Barney is wearing his suit and Linda Jean her soiled silk wrap. Barney's back in the driver's seat. Linda Jean is slouched in her seat as far from him as she can be without falling out of the van. Her chin pokes out aggressively. He sighs, wishing they could recapture the fun they had switching roles, so she'd be the one to bridge the abyss between them. He waits her out all the way home, up the elevator, into their bed. She turns her back to him, apparently satisfied to go to sleep with them as alienated from each other as they've ever been.

"All right, Linda Jean, out with it," Barney says simply.

"There's nothing to say," she says stubbornly. "You know what's wrong."

"No, I don't. You agreed to go with me to that place. You must've known what it would be like."

"What really hurts, Barney Blatz, and you know it, is that you wouldn't make love to *me*."

"Linda Jean, I make love to you every night of the week..."

"You do not!" she interrupts, seething.

"Well, lots of times, as much as you want, almost, anyway. The whole point was for us to share some variety, you know?"

"You could have made love to me once, and then gone and had your fun with your...your buddy. Or at least after *him*. Before *her*. And you didn't have to *enjoy* her so much."

"Look, Linda Jean, if you didn't want to try this 'swinging' stuff you shouldn't have agreed to do it, you know? I mean men are different than women. There's a biological limit to how many times we can do it, to how long we can stay hard. Women can do it forever. The whole idea of this was to keep things out in the open so we wouldn't have to sneak around like most couples do, you know? To use these trysts with other partners to enhance our own sex life. Wasn't it fun for you to have a black partner for a change?"

It's her turn to sigh. "Not particularly. I didn't know the guy. I have to feel something for someone to enjoy sex."

This shuts him up, her reminding him of his 'affect deficit' or whatever the shrinks would call it. A shivery thought occurs to him, maybe he can consider betraying Linda Jean with Cali because he has no feelings.

It's Barney's turn to be silent, but this time Linda Jean does bridge the gap. "I hadn't thought about your limits as a man," she says, softly. She turns toward him. "I can't help it, I just get so jealous." She moves in close.

He puts his arms around her. Surprisingly, he finds himself hard again. He rubs up on her and slips it in. She is very wet. Generally, he's a once-a-night kind of guy, but tonight he breaks his all-time record with three orgasms. Maybe it's the fight with Linda Jean, maybe it's the cocaine, maybe it's the thrill of breaking the same-sex taboo, maybe it's this wondrous thing about to begin with Cali. He slips in and out of sleep all night, floating on a violet cloud of bliss.

ELEVEN

Elephants

1.

Linda Jean collects elephants of all sizes, shapes, and materials – ceramic, wood, cloth, ivory – and the morning after Halloween it feels to Barney as if she's gone and stolen a live one from the zoo and coaxed it into sitting on his head. In the desert, so that his head sinks two feet into the sand. He doesn't remember ever having felt this awful. When he tries to get out of bed, the elephant panics and tramples his body over and over, trumpeting his bellow into his ear with his snotty trunk.

Somehow, he gets to the children's center. He hides out in the office as long as he can. When Cali comes in, dressed in thigh-length cutoffs, braless, in a see-through white blouse, she finds him sitting at the desk. She sneaks him a kiss on the mouth and then rubs his face in her crotch while running her fingers through his hair. He's getting the message, today's the day, but is it ever not. In addition to his physical debilitation, he's feeling as morally bankrupt as Nixon on his worst day. Somewhere between the blissful night and the halocaustic morning, it dawned on him that his grand plan of indulging in a delicious affair with Cali while hanging onto Linda Jean wasn't going to work – yet he was powerless to stop what he'd already started.

"Is my Booboo a little hungover?" Cali coos. "I've got just the cure for that later." After automotoning through the day, his spirits still somewhere below the liquid magma inside the earth, he follows Cali to her apartment and slumps on her couch, sulking.

Cali sidles next to him and strokes his face. "What'sa matter, Booboo?" He guesses he's stuck with this pet name.

"I don't know. I'm depressed. I guess I feel guilty about Linda Jean."

She jumps up from the couch and storms into the kitchen area. "God damn you, Barney Blatz!" she spits at him with no little venom. Knowing he deserves this retort, he says nothing, stares at his shoes. Finally he says, "Cali, I don't know much, but I do know one thing." He pauses for dramatic effect. "It's all fucked up, babe. It's *all* fucked up."

Helplessly, in total confusion, he moves to leave. He tries to kiss her anyway, at least to keep his options open, but she coldly turns away her mouth and offers her cheek.

By the time Linda Jean comes home all bubbly and affectionate in a way that makes him nauseous, like he's duty bound to respond even if he doesn't feel it, he's changed his mind again and finds himself wishing he hadn't left Cali's, that he'd gone for it, that he'd made love to her. He announces to Linda

Jean that he's going out to buy some beer and drives down to the 7-11 to use the phone.

He dials Cali's number: it's busy. He buys the beer, dials the number again. Still busy. He waits in the car for 15 minutes and tries again. Still busy. On the way home, he stops by her door and knocks. No answer. Oh, well, he thinks, I can fix things up with her in the morning. He gives up and returns home.

The next day, Cali doesn't come to work, and she doesn't call or send little Barney and Darnell, either. Barney calls her house about a dozen times, and the one time the line isn't busy, there's an answer without a voice, and when he says "Hello, Cali?" There's a click.

He asks Eddie to work overtime in her place. It's a chance to observe him teaching. Barney is a little disturbed as he watches Eddie break a long-standing taboo of riding the tricycles inside, and then make a game out of crashing them. "Eddie," Barney has to say, "You'll tear up the bikes that way." But otherwise, he decides that Eddie is okay.

At one point while Barney is working in the office, he watches Eddie leave the children and take Rhonda outside the center into the hall. This seems rather odd, and Barney confronts him about it when he returns a few minutes later.

"Sue Ann had just finished washing the floor in the kid's bathroom," he explains. "I was just taking her across the hall to use the grown-ups' bathroom."

Barney checks the children's bathroom, and the floor is indeed wet.

"Next time let Sue Ann or me know you're leaving so we can watch the rest of the children. The children have to be supervised at all times, Eddie."

"Okay, Barney."

Barney tries Cali's number at fifteen minute intervals throughout the day. It's either busy or there's no answer. He's thinking if he can only see her and apologize, everything will be all right again. He can think of little else. When Charlene comes in, he asks her, "Charlene, have you seen Cali?"

Charlene is tall, skinny, high-strung, her skin medium-dark, her hair in a loose perm. She would be pretty if she ever smiled.

In answer to Barney's question, she does execute a kind of smile, but it's not a nice smile, it's a thin, crooked, sneer of a smile as if she knows more than she's letting on. "No, I ain't seen her, Barney."

"Did you talk to her or anything?" he asks, little shards of desperation leaking around the edges of his voice.

"I don't know what she's up to, Barney."

Around lunch time, he goes to knock on her door. No answer, and he doesn't hear anything either. When he's off at four, he goes back again, this time banging harder than discretion would advise. He does hear some little mouselike noises inside, even a click which could be her peeking out the peephole, but she doesn't open the door. "Cali!" he shouts. "Come on, open up!" He's unable to disguise the whine in his voice.

That evening, he keeps sneaking out to call, not even caring what Linda Jean thinks. If she even notices his behavior, she gives him no sign.

The next day, Cali continues avoiding him, and Barney sends her a telegram:

CALI I LOVE YOU STOP BARNEY

There, he's said it. He writes her a letter too, and sends it special delivery, with a return envelope also stamped special delivery.

Dear Cali,

I am really, really sorry for how I acted the other day. By avoiding me you have only shown me how much I care for you, how badly I need you to be in my life. I am willing to sacrifice just about anything for you, even my marriage, if necessary. However, I am also your friend, no matter what, so please stop treating me like your worst enemy.

Love, B.

That afternoon, out of sheer sexual frustration, Barney pays a visit to Latricia. He's hopeful that their political clash hasn't negated her feelings for him. Her apartment is empty, and the painters are repainting. He asks in the office, and they tell him that she moved to Guyana.

After two more days of agony, he finally gets a letter back from Cali.

Dear Barney,

If you only knew how this has been for me! I do have feelings for you, I do, I do. I can't stand to be separated from you any longer either. We do have to take up our friendship at least where we left off. You bring out the best in me. I'm so proud of what we've been able to do with the school and everything. If it's going to happen between us (and I don't think it will), it will happen. I can't wait to continue seeing you again.

Your friend, Cali.

He reads over her letter at least a dozen times before he realizes that it is what in high school they used to call a "Dear John" letter.

2.

Election Day, November 7th, comes and goes, marking a great victory for the gay community. The Briggs Initiative, calling for the firing of homosexual teachers, fails to pass by a 2-1 margin statewide. In spite of how recently Barney converted to the cause, he shares a piece of the jubilation.

Linda Jean and Barney make a cameo appearance at Castro Camera where the victory party is taking place to congratulate Harvey Milk. Harvey is ecstatic, drunk, and talks about running for mayor.

Three days later, Cali calls him, as she never does anymore, with the news that Dan White has resigned from his seat on the Board of Supervisors. She's all excited, because she heard the news directly from the mayor who called her up to get her opinion about who he should appoint in White's place.

The mayor called her? Barney's heart flutters. The mayor has a reputation for liking young black women, and he can't see any other reason for him calling her; she's not that important a force in the community.

But White's resignation is good news for the children's center because maybe they can get someone in there who will really do the center some good.

"I told him to appoint you," she says.

"You're kidding."

"Why not?"

He's flattered, but he hardly thinks the mayor would go along with her recommendation. Who is he? He's nobody. Or less.

A silence gathers like a flock of birds on the phone line. Cali and Barney have been tiptoeing around each other ever since their exchange of letters. They've both been cordial but cool, protective of their feelings. Barney has been wandering around in a demoralized daze, unable to believe that he had her in his hot little clutches and just let her go.

"So. How are you?" He risks into the empty receiver.

"I'm all right."

He blurts it out. "I want it back, Cali. What we had. What we almost had."

"I don't know, Barney. It seems too complicated.

What about Linda Jean? I don't want to be no damn homewrecker."

It's late afternoon, cold and gray, that dangerous time of day between his coming home from work and Linda Jean's coming home from work.

"You want me to come over?" He asks.

"I've got company. I just wanted to tell you about the mayor."

He's alarmed at the sharp pang in his chest that her words induce. Who? Man or woman? That it might be a man fills him with murderous rage. He thinks of the .25 automatic he keeps under the mattress. Shit, he thinks. I don't even believe in jealousy.

"Hokay, babe," he signs off, swallowing bile.

3.

One afternoon, while Barney's relaxing after work, Mike Davis drops by the apartment with worry etched in his large, dark face.

"I think Cali has another lover," Mike says, looking down at the floor.

"Really?" He does everything in his power to suppress his blush. "What makes you think so?"

"She's been acting funny. She writes letters in secret. She never wrote a letter before in her life."

"Do you have some idea who it might be?" he asks nervously, crossing his fingers behind his back.

"Dan White."

"Dan White? You're kidding." Barney happens to know they're feuding at the moment. But maybe it's best to let Mike think it is White, rather than himself. "I suppose it's possible." As he says the words, he starts to believe them. "But Mike, I thought you were leaving for Guyana anyway. Why do you care so much?"

"Guyana? Who told you that?"

"Cali."

"She did? Well, it's true, I've been thinking about it. But I need to know the truth about her and White, and how long it might have been going on. Will you help me?"

"What do you want me to do?"

"Follow her with me. Tonight. She says there's some committee meeting she has to go to. I'll watch her get on the bus from the window, then we'll follow the bus. I used to do some intelligence work in Nam. I know how to do it."

Barney hates this kind of shit, but he's afraid if he doesn't go along with Mike, he'll get suspicious. It's just as well if they prove to themselves that nothing is going on. "Okay," he says, "give me a call when she leaves."

Mike calls at about 6:30, and Barney goes up to Cali's apartment to watch her catch the bus. As soon as she gets on, Barney and Mike take the elevator downstairs, hop in Barney's van, and follow the route of the 25 Bryant to a block away from the Hall of Justice on 7th Street, where they watch her transfer to the 19 Polk toward City Hall. From the front of the library across the plaza, they watch her wait at the entrance to City Hall and then get in a beat up yellow Fiat.

"That's not White's car, not even his type of car," Barney says. "He drives a blue Buick sedan."

"Who the hell is it then?"

Barney shrugs his shoulders. "Let's go," he says, suddenly overcome with curiosity himself.

They follow at a safe distance down Polk Street until they see the Fiat park. They watch the two of them – Cali and her mysterious escort – get out of the car and enter a popular "fern" bar, called Henry Africa's, perhaps the place that pioneered the genre, still unable to identify her companion.

Casual as anything, Barney parks the van and takes the first sortie past the window to see what he can see. Peering in a gap in the fog on the glass from all the heavy breathing inside, he sees exactly who it is, surrounded by a small mob of admirers. "Holy shit!" he swears, almost loud enough for them to hear him. He runs back a block to where Mike is waiting. "You won't believe this Mike!"

"What? What?"

"It's the mayor."

"Moscone?"

"The very one."

"Holy shit!"

"That's exactly what I said."

He looks at Barney matter-of-factly. "I'll kill him," he says, calmly. He balls his fists and starts toward Henry Africa's.

Barney's first thought is, what a good idea, I'll help. But then he says, placing himself in Mike's path, "Mike, you're upset. Let's go have a drink and talk this over."

"Get the fuck out of my way, Barney. I know what I have to do." He gives Barney a shove.

With uncharacteristic bravado, Barney continues his challenge. He looks Mike in the eye. He shoves him back, gently. "Get in the car, Mike! I won't let you do anything you'll regret later." He looks like he's about to grab Barney's skinny body and throw him into the street. Then he suddenly wilts. "Maybe you're right. All right. Let's have a drink first."

They drive about three blocks to Tommy's Joynt on Van Ness, another "very San Francisco" bar that serves buffalo stew and 92 brands of beer, and has a ceiling hung with all the junk you can think of: an ox-drawn plough, model bi-planes, old-timey beer ads, mounted buffalo heads, antique ice cream makers, and so forth. They settle in a booth and order two double brandies.

Mike stares at the table. Barney has never seen him look so down. Finally, he says, "Barney, for some damn reason, I trust you. What do you think I should do? Seems to me I got three choices. Kill him, kill her, or fuck the whole thing and go to Guyana."

"Why choose, Mike? You could kill both of them and then go to Guyana."

He chuckles. "Now there's an idea. Seriously, what do you think I should do?"

"Mike, I don't know, man. I don't know what I'm doing myself more than half the time. But jealousy is a dead-end street, you know? It is the fucking mayor. If you had a chance to fuck, say, Donna Summer or someone like that, wouldn't you jump at it?"

"That's different, man, I'm a man."

"Why should it be any different for a man? That's bullshit, Mike, and you know it. We don't even know for sure if she's fucking him."

"Yeah, right," he says skeptically. "Fuck it, man. I know what to do. Let it go. We haven't been getting along that well anyway. I guess this is the sign I've been waiting for. I'm going to take your advice, man. I'm going to Guyana. Like, tomorrow. I miss my people. Yeah." He beams at Barney, ecstatic in his resolve. "Thanks, man. You saved my life. I owe you one." He gives Barney's hand a soul shake, hooking his thumb, rubbing his palm, grasping Barney's fingers in his, then tapping Barney's fist with his fist. Barney reciprocates the whole maneuver awkwardly.

Barney is not aware of having advised him to go to Guyana, but he decides to take the credit, rather than argue details.

4.

Linda Jean and Barney are lying in bed, watching TV, engaged in one of their periodic silences, but this time he knows he's the one perpetrating it, and he has no desire to break it himself or for her to break it. He's feeling deeply and darkly distant, his little heart convulsing in pain over Cali, exacerbated by the new information about her and the mayor – isn't he a married man, too? What about wrecking *his* home, to say nothing of his political career? But there's no way he can talk about his feelings, not to Linda Jean, not to Cali, not to anyone.

On the news, there is a lot of hoopla about Congressman Leo Ryan flying to Guyana to investigate Jonestown. Linda Jean finally speaks, "You think Jim Jones is crazy?"

"I don't know," Barney answers curtly. Jim Jones is the last person on his mind. "How can you know anything?" There's an aspect of his tone that reverberates beyond the boundaries of this discussion.

Stubbornly, she continues, "You think the boy is his?" She's talking about John Victor Stoen, the subject of a custody battle that is motivating Ryan's investigative junket.

"Probably. You know these preachers."

"So you think it's a cult that ought to be busted up or a progressive movement that's being hounded?"

Barney is not really interested in this question right now. "We both know they're a little weird, but no weirder than the U.S. government. They're powerful, and they're radical. Since when has the government left anyone like that alone?"

"But the boy is only six years old. Shouldn't he be with his mother? What if it were Jason?"

"You mean suppose Cynthia had tried to keep him from seeing us because of our involvement with the Party? That's the parallel, isn't it? We'd fight her, wouldn't we?"

"It's different, though. You're not in separate countries, thousands of miles away, and that there. The bond with the mother is different, too."

"Bullshit!" He feels his face turning hot, in spite of his powerful urge to withdraw from her and go to sleep. "One of the good things Jones has done is disrupt bourgeois family relationships. Utopian, provocative, adventurist maybe, but a good idea."

"You mean if it was me fighting for Darryl you'd side with Jones?"

"Darryl's old enough to make up his own mind."

"What if he weren't? What if he were six?"

"God, Linda Jean, it's late. I don't know. If Jones were the father? You wish. That's a lot of hypotheses. I suppose I would support Jones, I don't know."

"What? You wouldn't be jealous?"

"I'm not a jealous person, Linda Jean."

There's a pregnant pause. "That's because you don't love me."

"Christ, Linda Jean. Don't do this."

"It's true, isn't it? You don't, do you?"

"We were talking hypothetically, remember? I'm not a jealous person because I believe it's possible for people to love more than one person, that's all."

"Oh, really? And who else do you love, Barney Blatz?"

"Linda Jean, stop this."

"It's that heifer Cali, isn't it? I know there's something going on. You may think I'm stupid, Barney Blatz, but I know what I know."

He stifles an urge to squeeze his thumbs into her trachea. "You don't know anything!" he spits at her, all of a sudden ready to cry.

"Let me hear you deny it then."

He sighs. "There's nothing going on between Cali and me, fuck you, and I'm going to sleep."

"Don't say that to me!"

"What, fuck you? Fuck you, fuck you, fuck you, fuck you, and if you don't give up your irrational fears of Cali, then I'll make something happen between us just so you'll have something to be jealous about. Okay? Now, good night!"

That finally shuts her up, and they sleep with a chasm between them as deep and wide as the San Francisco Bay.

The next morning, they receive a letter from Leonora Jackson from Guyana.

I'm having the time of my life down here in the tropics. It's hot, but then I'm a Loosianna girl, and it's not that much hotter than back home. The work is hard, but you really feel like you're working *for* something, for the good of the whole commune. I work in the kitchen, and you know how I love to cook, so it's almost like it isn't work. I also teach in the school, of course, but what I teach is so different from back there you wouldn't believe it. I teach Co-operation. I teach Struggle. I teach Communism. I'm not supposed to use that last word, for fear of pushing the wrong buttons, but – you old commies, you – I know you'll understand.

I hear they are still lying about us all over the papers. This is no surprise. You know how they lie about Russia and Cuba and all. And about black people, especially those making it on their own steam (we are mostly black down here). What is surprising is how many otherwise progressive people seem to believe what they are saying about us, about how we're a "cult," and people are down here against their will. Please do what you can to counteract their lies. Tell everyone we know that I love it down here, that my son loves it down here, that we've never been so happy, that this experiment is really *working!* I know it's hard to believe, we who've been fighting for progressive causes are so used to failing that when we do succeed, it's like there must be something wrong.

Anyway, I miss you both and love you very much. Give my best to Darryl, Jason, and Ramona. Tell everyone I'd rather die than return to the U.S., and if that should happen, Linda Jean, I want you to have my collection of elephants that I have stored at my mother's (Mrs. Shirley Beaumont, 2946 Bayou Rd., New Orleans, LA 70119). It's nowhere near as good as yours, but the two together will be impressive – like the two of you. Love, Leonora

This letter with its eerie final paragraph makes Linda Jean and Barney forget about last night's argument, and after they both read it, they give each other a hug to ward off the chill.

For reasons you can't explain, the fear that lurks in the shadows of your life is intensifying, threatening the ability of your anxiety to hold it in place. Like the anxiety, the fear has no particular object. Perhaps "fear of losing control" describes it. What it has, this fear, are physiological consequences, chief among them sleeplessness. At midnight, you'll have palpitations of the heart. At two in the morning, hyperventilation. At four, you'll turn over and look at the inert lump of the sleeping Linda Jean, and you'll be filled with a revulsion at the core of your being, a hatred, really, and a concomitant fear that you can no longer control your feelings or the ramifications of them. Coldly, you consider killing her. You consider killing yourself. You are gratified that you can still respond to both these considerations with a resounding "No!" But you wonder how long you can resist. You seem to have gotten yourself caught in the worst of both worlds. Linda Jean thinks you are having an affair, and you suppose she is right, an affair of the heart, if not the body. You certainly want the body. You almost had it. But your guilt got in the way. But now that it doesn't look like you can have her, you want her all the more. You can't get her off your mind.

You know Linda Jean does not deserve this. She has been nothing but good to you, and loves you more than perhaps anyone ever has. Yet you can't take it in. You are unworthy of such love, you even suspect that her love for you has more to do with her own needs than you, that she has idealized you. Perhaps the same way you feel toward Cali.

In the small of your back is a knot of coldness. A snarl of ice. A singularity inside of a black hole, infinitely dark, infinitely cold. Like a black hole, it feels as if it could suck you inside itself.

Years ago you dubbed it, this entity, the "unconscience," that irresistible force that continuously pushes you to do the thing you know is wrong. Stay up too late, procrastinate, sleep too late, take too many drugs, drink too much, betray, or try to betray, your wife...

TWELVE

An American Tragedy

1.

On Monday, November 15, the day Congressman Leo Ryan arrives in Guyana, Dan White announces that he made a mistake when he resigned, and he wants his seat on the Board of Supervisors back.

Cali drags Barney to a press conference on the City Hall steps, facing the fountain which, like government itself, isn't working. The long, rectangular reflecting pool surrounding the fountain is empty of water and strewn with yogurt containers and wrappers from Peanut Butter Cups and Twinkies. The gnarled sycamore trees landscaping the plaza are barren of leaves – "paranoia" trees Barney named them in his druggier days, with their stubby, octopus limbs raising knobby fists to the sky. The morning is chill, damp, the air is drouzzling, as if the clouds have sunk all the way down to street level. The neoclassical government buildings surrounding the plaza give off an air of ruin.

There's a half dozen participants in the press conference, twice as many press people, all waiting for the three TV cameras to set up. A man in wide bell bottoms and top hat, shirtless in a tuxedo tailcoat, hair down to his shoulders, long beard, no shoes circulates a petition calling for the legalization of marijuana.

The first speaker is a woman named Goldie Judge, White's original campaign manager, a very light-skinned black woman with short reddish hair who looks remarkably like Cali but chunkier. She gives a chilling indictment of White for his hypocrisy in failing to support a pay raise for the supervisors, and then resigning ostensibly because the pay is too low.

Looking impressive in a charcoal gray pants suit, Cali speaks to the rolling cameras like an old pro. "Dan White started out as an honest man, a man of the people, but the big boys from downtown, from the chamber of commerce and the Police Officer's Association have gotten to him."

Suddenly a man in dark glasses, a snap-brim hat hiding his forehead, shouts, "That's a lie, Cali, and you know it!" It's White himself, of course, incognito at his own denunciation.

Cali is taken aback. She stumbles for words. "It's true, Dan. You sold out. I'm sorry."

He glares at her with the purest hatred for a moment and then huffs into City Hall.

On the way home in the van, the tension crackles between Barney and Cali as they try to converse. "White looked angry," Barney understates.

"Yes, he is pissed at me," she says.

"I hope he doesn't...oh, I don't know, retaliate or something."

"Don't worry. I know him. He's the type that will go

home and beat up his wife, and then he'll be fine. He really doesn't like politics anyway. He'll be relieved if Moscone doesn't reappoint him. He's only protesting now because downtown is pressuring him. They feel he owes them, and they desperately need his vote."

"You're probably right," Barney says. Then he tells her about Leonora's letter from Jonestown and asks her whether she's heard from Mike, who's been in Jonestown for about a week.

"Yeah, I got a strange letter from him yesterday. It was kind of creepy, because he kept saying over and over how much he liked it there, working in the fields 14 hours a day and all, and how he loved the heat, and how much he liked rice. Now I know damn well he hates physical work. He used to say it always reminded him of slavery whenever he would sweat while working. He absolutely hates rice and can't stand the heat. I got the feeling he was almost writing in code, like the Temple people would be reading his letter but wouldn't catch the sarcasm."

Barney reassures her. "Living so isolated in the jungle must do odd things to people, but Mike's a survivor. I'm sure he'll do fine."

Silence. They stop at a red light. Barney makes a fool of himself. Feeling desperate, he grabs her. "Cali," he whines. He tries to kiss her.

"Barney! Down boy! Stop it!" she squeals.

He lets her go and looks away in shame. He wants to tell her that he knows about her and the mayor, but he's afraid of alienating her further.

"It's too late, Barney." Then she says, "I might have gone for it if your approach had been a little bit different."

He sulks, stares into the speedometer. "I yam what I yam," he tries to joke.

"I know," she says, not without sympathy.

2.

As the weekend approaches, Barney is suffocating. He has to get out of town by himself. At least without Linda Jean. He doesn't even ask her. He just tells her he's going down to Deer Creek. He calls his partner Bob, and they head down the road in the early morning rain, putting away three or four beers apiece before they get to the dirt road leading from the highway to their new property.

The road is a mess. They get stuck three times and are totally covered with mud by the time they get the chains on. Even then, there's a big untraversable mudslide a half-mile shy of their place. They hike in the rest of the way, at one point sinking up to their knees in what had once been the road. They question the wisdom of their buying such a place. "I wish we had waited till now to make an offer on the place," Barney says, guiltily, being the inept negotiator for their side who eventually agreed to a higher price than his judgment told him the place was worth. "We probably could have saved $5,000."

Bob is a carpenter who can read newspapers in eleven languages. He's a drunk, a compulsive gambler, a chain smoker, a hermit after two failed marriages, and among the sweetest souls Barney had known in his life. They are neither of them aces when it comes to feelings, but Barney has to talk to someone, and by the time they get to rest from their slog through the mud, sitting in their raingear on adjacent boulders in the middle of the raging stream, he's ready to pour his heart out as copiously as the sky is discharging its rain. The tops of the redwoods are hidden in the clouds.

"I'm in love with another woman, Bob," he begins.

"Oh-oh," he says. "Does Linda Jean know?"

"She suspects. She doesn't know for sure."

"Who's the woman?"

"Her name's Cali. She was like my main partner in taking over the childcare center. She's gorgeous."

"Married?"

"Sort of, but her old man's in Jonestown."

"At least he's not in the way. But it's just lust, you know, Barney. It's probably not worth it."

"Lust? How can you say that?" Barney bristles.

"Because only lust would be strong enough for you to risk hurting Linda Jean like that."

"It's not just lust, man," Barney contends. "We've got real feelings for each other. We've been a powerful team together. There's something about her power I've got to have."

"So, you're like doing it and everything?"

Barney blushes. "Not exactly. We almost did, but then she got cold feet, or I fucked it up by mentioning my guilt over Linda Jean."

"So it's not going to happen then. You're in luck. You didn't fuck it up. You saved your marriage. Congratulations."

"You don't understand. It's worse now. I can't keep my mind off her. I've got to have her. I will have her."

"Wasn't it Marx that said 'I don't want to be a member of a club that would have me for a member?' Groucho, I mean."

Barney laughs. "I suppose there is something to that."

"You have my complete sympathy, man," Bob says. "I've been in love a few times. What a pain in the ass."

Barney feels better. He decides maybe Bob is right. It's not worth it. He'll recommit to Linda Jean. Forget Cali, who isn't exactly coming through for him anyway. They slog back to the van, heat some Dinty Moore canned beef stew on the propane stove, and sleep in the back on the same bed, with the rain peppering the roof. Barney feels close to him. He wants to tell him about Halloween and his experience with that man. He wants to tell him he wouldn't mind diddling around with him. But he doesn't have the nerve.

3.

As Barney gets home Sunday evening, he's missing Linda Jean a lot, and he's anxious to tell her about his decision to recommit to her. He yells for her around the apartment. She isn't home. It shouldn't be any big deal, he's sure she'll be home shortly, but it feels awful, symbolic, ominously out of proportion.

The headline to the Sunday paper lying casually on the formica kitchen table reads: "REP. RYAN SHOT." Oh-oh, he thinks.

He scours the paper for details. Ryan and four others were shot dead by Peoples' Temple members as they were boarding the plane to leave Guyana with fewer than a dozen defectors from Jonestown. Wounded, among others, Michael O'Brian, a reporter for the *Examiner*, son of the school district administrator who threatened to have Barney arrested.

He calls Cali. "Isn't it awful?" she says, shrilly, clearly spooked.

"I hope Mike will be all right," he says.

"Yeah. Me too."

Linda Jean shows up within an hour and he hugs her tightly. "Where were you?" he demands, whining.

"I was just at my sisters," she explains, looking at him funny.

"I missed you."

"Good!" she says, sincerely pleased.

"I'm scared for Leonora and Mike. And Latricia."

"Latricia? You didn't tell me she'd gone down there, too," she says.

"I guess it slipped my mind."

4.

That night they're in bed, cuddling, feeling all cozy and close, watching an old movie on UHF, "A Place in the Sun," Liz Taylor, Montgomery Clift, based on the Dreiser novel, *An American Tragedy*. Clift, the hero, is about to take a fateful boat ride with his pregnant girl-friend, a young Shelly Winters, when Barney notices he has a throbbing erection. He begins biting Linda Jean's ear, stroking her cheek. She sighs and turns toward him, welcoming his advances. They kiss, en-twining their tongues. He massages her breast, gen-tly pinches her nipple. She rubs her foot on his calf, runs her fingers down his chest, squeezes his balls. He nibbles on her neck, licks her shoulder blades, sucks her breasts, slides his tongue, slowly, down her belly, reams her navel, skirts the edges of her pubic hair, slip-ping his body down, down, down between her legs. He licks the insides of her thighs. She moans. He touches his tongue to her labia. She shudders. Snakelike, he darts his tongue at her engorged clitoris. She jumps. With her hands, she pulls his head toward her. She's drenched with sweet-tasting juices. He squeezes both her breasts at once and buries his head deep in her wetness. She screams. Then she suddenly stops writh-ing and freezes in mid-thrust.

"Barney!" she calls his name sharply, as if he's done something terribly wrong.

He pokes his head up.

"Listen!" she commands.

Still perched between her legs as if ready to re-sume the action just as soon as this annoying inter-ruption is over, he hears the gratingly self-important voice of the TV announcer: "...initial reports indicate that Jonestown residents drank from vats of poi-soned Kool-Aid. At this time, it is unknown whether such action was voluntary or forced, though guards at Jonestown are known to have been armed. Cult leader Jim Jones himself also appears to be dead from a bullet wound to the head. Stay tuned for more information as we receive it. Now back to our movie."

"What the fuck?" he says. "What happened? I missed the first part."

"They're dead, Barney," she says shrilly, quaveringly.

He sucks in his breath. An icy feeling begins in the small of his back as if a hole has opened up there and his insides are trickling out.

"What do you mean? Who's dead?"

"Hundreds of them. At Jonestown. They committed suicide." She's gagging as if she can't believe her own words.

They switch around the channels starving for more information.

"Maybe it's not everyone," he says.

Linda Jean comes apart. She dissolves into hysterical sobs.

He doesn't. He's dizzy and queasy for a moment, and then he doesn't feel a thing. Nothing. The scariest feeling of all.

Linda Jean clings to him, trembling, as they lie in the bed unable to sleep. Every now and then they look at each other in disbelief, shake their heads. Close to dawn, he pushes her away and drifts off. He dreams that he's there, in Jonestown, drinking down the cyanide-laced Kool-Aid. He goes into violent convulsions and wake up covered with sweat.

The morning paper has the body count at 400.

Linda Jean and Barney, along with the rest of San Francisco, are too stunned to speak.

The Towers are sunk in an eerie quiet. Hardly a person lives here who doesn't at least know someone who knows someone who was in Jonestown and is now, presumably, dead.

He goes to the center. Eddie has opened it as usual, but there are only a few children. "Isn't it terrible?" is all Eddie can say.

Alice brings in her twins but can't decide whether to leave them or not. "See how you people are?" she jokes at Barney, as is her wont, to use him as her white devil. "This wouldn't have happened if Jones was black."

"Yeah, like Idi Amin. Remember him?" But he actually hasn't thought of the racial angle. A new wave of hopelessness washes over him, before he gets a chance to counter it with numbness.

Not surprisingly, Cali doesn't come in to work. When he finally gets the nerve to call her, she is hysterical. He visits her that afternoon to console her. He holds her while she cries.

By Friday, 380 "missing" bodies are found underneath those of the others, bringing the total count of the dead to 780. Leonora Jackson and her son Charles, Latricia Lewis and her son Ronald Rodgers, are on the first published list of the dead. But not Michael Davis. It will be weeks, however, before all the bodies are identified.

There's a report that a group of survivors are in the Bay Area, calling themselves White Knight, with the mission of wreaking revenge on the Temple's detractors.

All Barney can think about is how the place must smell.

FOURTEEN

Thanksgiving

1.

On the Tuesday following Jonestown, as Barney rides the elevator to work, he watches the numbers jump from 12 to 14 – there is no 13 – and he wonders if luck can be so easily fooled. There is, after all, a 13th floor; it is simply numbered "14."

Waiting for him in the office is a distinguished looking black man with salt-and-pepper hair and a full mustache, dressed in a sport coat and turtleneck. He introduces himself as Inspector Williams of the Police Department.

"Weren't you involved in that Officers for Justice suit against the police department a few years ago?" Barney asks.

"I was. You have a good memory."

Barney does a quick flip-flop. His initial instinctive revulsion for the police is mitigated by this man's progressive reputation. He relaxes. "What can I do for you?"

"I'm with the sex crimes unit now," he says, and Barney bristles right back up again. "You have an employee here named Eddie McRay?"

"Yes."

"A parent named Charlene Johnson with a child named Rhonda Parker?"

"Yes. Charlene...Ms. Johnson is also an employee."

"The child claims that Mr. McRay sexually molested her. We're conducting an investigation."

Barney says nothing. He feels as if he's just stepped in a hole in the ice of a frozen lake.

"Do you have any records on Mr. McRay's performance? Any background?"

Barney lowers his eyes with guilt that they have neither. "Not really. We're a pretty new school, a kind of grass-roots, shoe-string operation."

"I know you took over from the school district," Williams says. "I remember reading about that. McRay has some priors. Nothing sexual. Petty theft. Grand theft auto. Nothing too heavy."

"I don't know what to say. He's very reliable, and he plays well with the children."

"Maybe a little too well."

"What does Rhonda say happened?"

"She says he would take her across the hall. You have a staff bathroom there?" Barney nods. "Says he did it several times, stuck his penis in her mouth, her vagina, her rectum. One time you were here."

"Oh God. I do remember him taking her over there. I questioned him about it, because he'd left the other children unsupervised. His excuse was that the floor was wet in the children's bathroom. Which it was."

"Well, I'm sorry about this. I've already questioned Mr. McRay. If I were you, I would suspend him until our investigation is complete. We're waiting on the lab report on the semen samples. Probably tomorrow morning. In the future, I'd advise you to do closer checks on people you hire."

After Williams leaves, Barney calls Eddie into the office. Eddie looks scared. "Under the circumstances," Barney tells him, "I can't let you work here until this business is cleared up."

"I didn't do nothing, Barney. I didn't do nothing," he whimpers.

"Then you can come back when the investigation is over," he says, but Barney has already convicted him in his mind. He looks so seedy and disgusting and pathetic, he wonders why he didn't notice this before.

Barney takes over for Eddie with the children, and they play about twenty consecutive rounds of a game with origins in the plague years that seems particularly appropriate right now:

> Ring around the rosy,
> A pocket full of posies,
> Ashes, ashes,
> We all fall DOWN.

Charlene comes in to the center about two, naptime. Barney is sitting next to Dathan, who is squirming sleeplessly on his cot. Barney is half-dozing off himself, not eager to feel anything at all. One look tells him not to tangle with her. A second look tells him he has no choice.

"Where's Eddie?" she says, tensely, as if it's taking everything she's got to contain herself. "I'm gonna kill him."

"Take it easy, Charlene," Barney says.

"Don't tell me to take it easy," she says, raising her voice.

"When did you find out?" He's hopeful that getting her to talk will ease the pressure.

"Yesterday. Where the fuck is he, Barney? You protecting him?"

"I suspended him pending the outcome of the investigation."

She mocks him. "'You suspended him pending the outcome of the investigation.' God, I hate white people. Are you calling Rhonda a liar?"

"No, Charlene. What happened to her was horrible, and if Eddie's guilty, I hope they throw the book at him."

"She says you were here one time."

"Maybe. He did act kind of suspicious once, but I didn't think.... Well, I just never imagined..."

"Oh, 'you didn't think...you never imagined...' she pushes his shoulders with her hands, as if trying to knock him out of the child-sized chair. "It's your fault, motherfucker," she shouts. She slams him again on the shoulders. All the children are waking up now and watching this drama intently.

Barney stands up from the chair, careful to make no retaliatory move. He doesn't want this to escalate. "Charlene. Get hold of yourself," he says. "I'm really sorry about what happened. I'm sorry if you think I'm responsible."

She sneers, "Yeah, well, you're sorry all right. You're one sorry motherfucker." She puts her hands on her hips. The worst is over, he thinks. "I just came to tell you I'm pulling Rhonda out of the center, and quitting my job here."

"I'm sorry," he says, not at all sorry right at that moment.

"Yeah, you're sorry all right."

She turns her back to him and storms out. Barney is left then to run the center without Cali, Eddie, or Charlene. Sue Ann is the only one left, and she comes in for an hour at noontime to fix lunch and clean up.

After the children leave, Barney balances the checkbook to see if they have enough money to hire someone else. It's been awhile since he's done this task, and he discovers that if he were to be paid for the month of December, the center would have a negative balance.

He sits at the desk for a long time, unable to move. He stares out the window at the gray sky and watches it turn darker and darker until there's no light left in it at all.

2.

The next day is Wednesday, November 22, Linda Jean's and Barney's wedding anniversary, as well as the fifteenth anniversary of the Kennedy assassination. They chose the day originally as a bit of macabre humor, the idea being that at least they wouldn't forget the date. They hadn't anticipated the recent escalation of the macabre. That the woman who performed the ceremony is now dead, rotting away in the jungle with her 700 comrades, doesn't add to their sense of jubilation.

The thought fleetingly brushes Barney's consciousness: maybe the marriage is dead too.

They sit across from each other on leather armchairs in The House of Prime Rib, a fancy restaurant by their standards, picking away at these two huge slabs of red meat, and dissect the tragedy, as hundreds of others no doubt are doing in this city at the same time. "I just wish I could find a shred of dignity to the whole thing, you know," Barney says. "I mean, they must have had some perverse notion of Christian sacrifice, but it all seems so sleazy."

"You can't say what happened, Barney. Maybe the CIA really was involved. It wouldn't be the first time."

"I'm sure they were in some way. But I don't think even the CIA would tell parents to squirt cyanide into their children's mouths to kill them. Maybe if they'd waited until the soldiers did come to attack them, I'd be more sympathetic. You got to hand it to them for being willing to die for a cause. But think of how much more powerful it might have been if they'd stayed here and invaded a nuclear test site or something."

"Maybe Jones just went crazy, I don't know," Linda Jean says.

"What happens to people?" There's a desperate tremolo to his voice. "What would make Jones do something like that? Or Eddie? Not that the crimes are comparable. Except it feels like they are. It feels almost as bad for someone to rape a child as to urge or force 700 people to drink poison. The banality of evil. You can only take so much horror before your system goes on overload and you can't feel anything at all anymore."

"Mmm," says Linda Jean, as if she isn't understanding anything he's saying, as if she were thinking about something else.

Suddenly he notices a tall, skinny, medium-dark skinned woman in a shadowy corner of the room, across a sea of white faces. "Oh-oh," he says, "do you see who I see?"

"Where?"

"In the corner."

"Another black person. Hurray."

"Linda Jean! That's Charlene! She's following me."

Linda Jean laughs. "Barney, it looks a little like her, but it isn't her. You're just paranoid."

"Are you sure?"

"Positive."

He believes her, but a spiny glob of fear has suckered itself like a sea urchin to the small of his back.

On the way back to the car, he notices at the bus stop a dark-skinned, long-faced black man with side-burns.

"Look, Linda Jean."

"What?"

"It's Eddie! Now *he's* following me."

She stops walking and stands in front of him. "Barney!" she says in that same firm-but-loving voice she uses so well with children. "That isn't Eddie. No one is following you. Times are crazy enough. Don't you go crazy on me, okay?"

He stares into her eyes uncertain whether or not to trust her judgment or his own. The echo of her voice has a certainty to it that makes him choose to trust her, for now.

"Okay," he says, putting his arm around her.

By the time they get home, he's feeling close to her. "Shall I carry you across the threshold for our anniversary?" he says at the door.

"Sure!" she says, leaping into his arms. She is heavy. "Don't drop me!"

He struggles to lift her through the door, and then he does drop her, gently, on purpose, and falls on top of her. "Sorry," he says, and he kisses her hard on the mouth. "Happy anniversary," he says.

When they return to their feet, his eyes fall on a mélange of materials on the formica table. Linda Jean has been making a model turkey for her school children to copy. She's traced her hand with a marker on brown construction paper, splaying her fingers to make the tail, while her thumb forms the head. She's colored the head red and glued multi-colored feathers to the tail with a giant big squeeze bottle of Elmer's glue.

He gives her a devilish look and says, "Don't you love peeling the glue off your fingers after it dries?"

"Barney! That's strange. I thought I was the only one who got turned on by that."

"I knew it! It's the way you like to pick my blackheads too. I have a fantasy of covering my whole body with that glue." They look at each other and smile. "It's funny about me and my fantasies," he says. "I tend to fulfill them."

"Oh, Barney. I love how our minds work alike. Let's try it. Let's glue ourselves together."

He kisses her. They retreat to the bedroom, glue bottle in hand. They undress each other. They put a big towel down on the bed. Giggling, they lie down on the towel on their sides and embrace, facing each other. Barney squeezes the bottle of sticky white cream first on her breasts and his chest, then he runs a thick bead of it all up and down their bodies, avoiding the hairy places. "God, we're weird," he says.

"I know," she says. "It looks like sperm."

He keeps squeezing the bottle until it's empty.

"Now I know you'll never leave me," she says, laughing.

They lie as still as they can, intermittently kissing, waiting for the glue to dry. Their skin starts to itch. Barney gets hard and puts his thing inside her, but they don't move, for fear of breaking the bond between them.

After about half an hour, he says, "I think it's time."

"Okay," she says, an inordinate sadness in her voice.

He slowly pulls away from her. The strands of glue stretch between them in gossamer filaments. It feels as if their skin is coming off. She peels off grapefruit-sized membranes from his chest. The skin underneath feels raw. She looks at him wistfully; her eyes fill with tears. The poignancy of the moment penetrates even his thick skin, symbolically thinner now with the peeling away of this faux epidermis. He peels the membranes from her skin. They try to identify the shapes. "Texas," he names one squarish piece from her breast.

One of the pieces she pulls off him is roundish with two holes. "Look," she says. "A skull. A death's head." It chills them both.

When they're finally done, they rub their raw, skinless bodies together. He feels closer to her than he has for a long time, but there's something about this experience that disturbs him, as if it were a dress rehearsal for an excruciating mutual flaying in the not-too-distant future.

3.

Thanksgiving. Barney and Linda Jean are not exactly overcome with the holiday spirit, but they do manage to gather their immediate family – themselves, Darryl, Jason, and Ramona – to eviscerate a turkey.

Barney usually cooks on holidays like this, but today he doesn't feel like doing much of anything, so he hangs out with Jason and Ramona watching Charlie Brown on TV. At around three, Linda Jean gets it in her head that the kids need to go outside, and there's a certain way she comes on about this that forces Barney to swallow his objections, some way he defers to her on matters regarding the children, not for the usual sexist reasons but because he feels like he already messed up with them by leaving their mother.

He also really wants them to be able to hang out with the Tower's children, even though he can see they are afraid. They'd be afraid no matter what color the children were, being basically shy kids, but the fact that the neighborhood kids are black gives a taint of racism to their fear, and this, too, has him guiltily going along with Linda Jean's strident wishes.

It's not that easy going out to play here. The children have to take the elevator 15 floors down. Barney offers to go with them, but Linda Jean says sharply, "They've got to learn to fend for themselves around here someday, Barney," and he supposes she's right, though they are only seven and five years old. So, he lets them go, bundled in their second-hand coats, nervously holding hands.

Half an hour later, they're knocking frantically at the door, along with another child, Shawn, a sweet, slow boy of twelve whose mother is a friend of Barney and Linda Jean. "The other kids were beating up on Jason, so I brought them home," Shawn says. I can see tears streaking down Jason's face and some terror in Ramona's bright eyes.

"Did you fight back, Jason?" Linda Jean says to him sharply.

Jason loses it and starts bawling helplessly. Barney's heart leaps out to him.

Linda Jean screeches, "Jason! Stop all that crying. You're no baby. Toughen up!"

Barney can see him fighting the tears and failing, which brings on more tears. Barney wants to hug him, but he thinks, too, she's right somehow that he has to toughen up.

Darryl joins in. "I can see you need to learn how to fight, Jason. Show me what that boy did to you."

This actually distracts Jason from his pain and, laughing and crying, he punches Darryl in the stomach. "C'mon, Jason, harder. Hit me," Darryl yells.

"Were you scared, Monie?" Barney asks, kneeling down to her level. She looks at Linda Jean to gauge her reaction. "Yes," she says. "Those kids are mean."

"They just don't know you well enough yet," he tells her. "They'll get used to you, and you'll get used to them." He knows there's something wrong with how they are handling this. There's something they' missing here about letting them have their feelings, but Barney doesn't feel confident enough to stand up to Linda Jean about it, which is ironic, considering he usually defines the problem in their marriage as her inability to stand up to him.

Then she softens toward Jason in that endearing way she has, gives him a big hug, and says, "You know when I'm rough on you it's because I care about you, don't you?" Barney can see him wanting to cry all over again but stifling the tears. "C'mon and eat now. Barney, you sit at the head of the table."

"Linda Jean, please. I don't want this role."

"C'mon, Barney, aren't you the man of the house?"

"Aren't we supposed to have an equal relationship here?" he counters.

"It's Thanksgiving. Can't we be a real family for once?"

Barney feels sort of stupid fighting for her equality, so he gives in. Again.

"I don't want to make too much out of this holiday business, but we might as well see if we can find anything to be thankful about," Barney says. "Who wants to go first?"

Darryl answers, "I'll go. I'm damn thankful that I wasn't in Jonestown."

"Hear, hear," Barney says. "For real."

"I'm thankful there's no school today," Jason says.

"Already Jason?" Barney says. "You aren't supposed to turn off school until at least the third grade. I guess you're precocious. Monie?"

"I'm thankful that it's almost Christmas."

"Oh? Why Christmas?" Barney says.

"Because at Christmas you get presents and everyone's nice to each other and it snows."

We laugh. "I hate to disappoint you, Monie, but it doesn't snow here," Barney tells her.

"Oh yes it does!" she says with absolute certainty. "It has to snow so Santa can come on his sleigh!"

"O-kay, Mone," Barney says. "Okay."

It's Linda Jean's turn. "I'm just thankful that our family's together. What about you, Barney?"

"Me, I'm thankful that since so many horrendous things have happened this year, it just isn't possible for one more bad thing to happen."

What did it mean, Jonestown, you wondered. "Don't follow leaders" was an obvious answer. Rely on your own thinking. That's easy to say. But you were caught in some kind of limbo between consensual reality and individual freedom. If the consensus could no longer be trusted, you had to make up your own reality as you went along. In this, you were absolutely free. You could take nothing for granted. You had to start over, from the beginning. In the middle of the night, you kept trying to do this, but you kept getting more and more confused, and then more and more frightened. Consensual reality said you stay with your wife. Individual freedom argued that you go for Cali. Consensual reality was held in place by rigid anxiety; individual freedom unleashed the power of raw terror. With Jonestown, you understood that something has ended, but on the other side of that something was a vacuum so vast and so cold that you couldn't even contemplate it without swooning with panic.

And what about Eddie? You looked at the children in the center and imagined what it would be like to molest them. Even imagining this made you anxious, and you look around furtively, as if someone might see your thoughts. You see how it could happen. You would have had to be in a space where an arctic freeze enveloped your heart, but such a state was not unfamiliar to you. You decided, for the time being, to make no moves, to make no decisions, to wait and see what happened next.

4.

By the Sunday after Thanksgiving, a certain calm has settled over Barney, as if the bottom had finally been reached
and there was nowhere to go but up. He and Linda Jean
spend the morning in bed, reading the comics, avoiding
the Jonestown news, which is now old news. The body
count is up to 912, the entire estimated population of
Jonestown. Mike Davis is still not on the list.

Jason and Ramona spend the morning playing
Pong on the Commodore computer Barney had given
them last Christmas. There is something profoundly
reassuring in the blip-blip sound that faintly emerges
from the children's bedroom.

For early dinner, they have turkey soup that Linda
Jean made and turkey curry that Barney made. Barney
then drives the children back to their mom's.

Barney and Linda Jean retire early, a little bit hopeful that tomorrow life will return to something like
normal.

At about midnight, the phone rings. "Who is this,"
Barney answers angrily.

"Hi, Barney. Sorry to call so late. It's Dan."

"Dan?"

"Dan White."

"What is it, Dan?"

"I heard from a reporter that Moscone is not going
to re-appoint me tomorrow."

"I thought that was obvious, Dan. It's politics."

"I know. But I heard it from a *reporter*. The motherfucker didn't have the decency to tell me in person!"

Only with this uncharacteristic epithet does Barney hear the alcohol in his voice.

"So, what are you going to do, Dan, shoot him?"

"Funny you should say that. I've been thinking about it."

"Really, Dan? I was kidding you know."

"Were you? You know he deserves it. Both he and Harvey. Maybe some others too. Did you see the papers today? 912 people! You know the mayor and his minions have been protecting Jones all these years. Someone has to stop this drift toward the utter bankruptcy of socialist liberal degeneracy."

"It's after midnight, Dan. I need to get some sleep. Shoot the bastards if you think it will help. Now, good night."

"Maybe I will, Barney, maybe I will. Good night, and thanks. You're a good man, Barney Blatz." Click.

Barney stares at the dead receiver for a few seconds with an uneasy feeling. No, he couldn't be that stupid.

He returns to bed. "Who was that?" Linda Jean asks.

"Dan White."

"Really?"

"He's pissed at Moscone for not reappointing him or even calling him to tell him in person. I told him to shoot the guy."

"Really?"

"I was kidding, of course. I hope he understood that."

"Yeah. Me too." Barney bristles slightly at her tone, as if she was implying that he was being reckless with his words again. But he doesn't say anything.

FIFTEEN

No More Pie

1.

There's a bumper sticker that reads "Time is nature's way of keeping everything from happening at once," but this November, it isn't working. Monday morning, November 27th, Barney is at the center by himself, fighting off exhaustion, trying to keep it together with the kids. He's abandoned his attempts to foster freedom and resorted to the old authoritarian methods which are hard on the children but so much easier on him. And fortunately, enrollment is low, probably in part because of the rumors of Eddie's molestation of Rhonda – the semen tests were positive, he was arrested on the Friday after Thanksgiving. There are only a dozen children in attendance today.

He's conducting an extended circle time, because it's easy and uses up time. For a week now, everything he looks at gives off emanations of death, even the children, as if death were an intrinsic quality of matter that radiates from it visibly, palpably, like the waves of heat given off by blacktop melting in the sun.

He reads the children "Hansel and Gretel," a story in which children get away with murder.

Even the songs they sing have a morbid cast. "I know an old lady who swallowed a fly, perhaps she'll die." "Ladybug, ladybug, fly away home." "Oh my, no more pie," a call-and-response song of successive disasters ending in a train wreck. It's this last song they're singing when the phone rings.

> ...The car's too slow,
> I fell and stubbed my toe.
> My toe got a pain,
> I got to catch a train.
> The train had a wreck,
> I nearly broke my neck.
> Oh, my,
> No more pie.

"Hello?"

There's nothing but snuffling on the other end.

"Hello!" he shouts into the phone.

"It's Cali," says a nearly inaudible voice.

"Cali! Could you come into work? I can't do this myself."

"You haven't heard?"

"Heard what?"

"Dan White."

"What about him?" His patience is wearing thin.

"He shot the mayor and Harvey Milk this morning."

"What?" He nearly drops the phone. "Oh, Cali!" He doesn't know what to say. "Are they all right?"

"They're both...dead."

"Oh my God."

That shivery feeling again, like the hole in his back has opened up all the way through and his guts are slithering out like snakes.

"Can you come over?" Cali sounds no older than six.

"Of course. I'll close the school. Let me call the parents."

He goes down the list calling parents while the children are doing who cares what in the classroom. He gets all but four. Two have disconnected phones. Two have no answers.

While waiting for the parents to come, he brings the children back to the rug, but he doesn't enforce any of the usual rules. He can't seem to care whether they criss-cross applesauce their legs nicely or not. He tries to talk to them.

"A terrible thing has happened," he begins.

"Again?" says the narrow-faced Dathan.

"Again. Someone has shot the mayor."

"Dr. Martin Luther King was shot," says Dathan.

"That's true, Dathan."

"My uncle was shot," says Clarisse, her hair fixed in a dozen pig-tails.

"My auntie died in Jonestown," says one of the twins as if she were sharing her trip to Disneyland.

"Where do you go when you die?" Dathan asks.

"Heaven if you're good, Hell if you're bad," answers Clarisse.

"It's not quite that simple," Barney tries to explain. "To tell you the truth, nobody has any idea what happens to you when you die." As he says these words, he has trouble believing them. Could this be true? With all our incredible scientific knowledge about the origin of the galaxies and the structure of DNA, nobody knows anything about something as simple and commonplace as death? A shudder passes through him as he tries to accept this ignorance.

"Nobody know?" asks Dathan again, incredulous himself.

"Nobody knows," Barney says.

The children all look at each other as if Barney's fear is scaring them. Should he make something up to reassure them, he wonders.

The phone rings again. Linda Jean. "You heard?" she asks.

"Yeah, Cali told me," he says without thinking.

"Cali."

He ignores the hurt sound of her voice. "What do I say to the children, Linda Jean? I can't seem to say anything without scaring them."

Her voice sounds annoyed. "Don't say anything. They won't understand anyway. They don't need to hear about all this killing."

"Don't you think they hear about it anyway? Don't you think they pick up things from the grown-ups? Wouldn't it be scarier for them not to talk about it?" He can't believe they're having an argument at a time like this.

"Let them be children as long as possible, Barney."

By the time he gets back to the children, all of them have been picked up but the four whose parents he couldn't reach. He takes them around to all of their apartments, finds one mother home, leave notes for the others. He has no choice but to wait.

He listens to the radio for the details. It seems that White snuck in through a basement window in order to get his ex- policeman's .38 past the metal detector. He met the mayor in his cozy inner office, and then blew his brains out with four shots. He ran out a private door and down the hall to his own office, right next to Milk's, where he reloaded. When Harvey came in to greet him, White filled *his* skull with five slugs, spattering his brains, Barney imagines, all over the sylvan photo-mural, the bloody flecks blending with the colors of the New England autumn.

Even though there were witnesses who saw everything but the actual shootings themselves, even though Dan White turned himself in a half hour later, a Fresno TV station reported receiving a call from a man in San Francisco who claimed credit for the killings in the name of "White Knight," the avengers of Peoples' Temple.

Barney lets the children take a long nap that afternoon. The last child is finally picked up at five o'clock. Barney is dying to get out of the place.

He rushes to Cali's. He's feeling desperate for solace, and she's the only one who can give it to him. Her hair is disheveled. She's dressed in her grungy blue quilted housecoat without sash or buttons. Her eyes are bloodshot. She collapses in his arms. They crumple together on the couch. The room is dark. The lights from the street cast an eerie glow through the fog. They cling to each other as if that were the only way to keep from slipping into the abyss, as one might grasp a tree trunk in a landslide to avoid being swept over the cliff.

Every now and then, Cali convulses with sobs. When she cries like that, tears well up in his own eyes, and for what seems like the first time in weeks, he is able to feel something, not his own grief yet maybe but some of hers at least.

"It's my fault, don't you see?" she says.

"No, Sweetie. That's silly."

"He called me last night. He begged for my support. He groveled. Then he started talking crazy about Jonestown, about getting even with Moscone and the other bastards responsible for killing Mike. I hung up on him."

"You really aren't responsible, Cali. How could you have known?" Barney can't help wondering whether or not she and White were ever lovers, and whether he knew about her and Moscone, but now is not the time to ask. "He called me last night too. He must've called everyone in town. I told him to shoot the guy if he thought that would help. I was kidding, of course. But maybe White didn't understand that."

"Oh, Barney," she says and burrows into him more closely.

After a while, as if coming up for air, she pulls away from him slightly to look at him in the face. She smiles. "Barney Blatz. What am I going to do with you?" she says. She tweaks his nose. She kisses him on the lips. "There's no one I'd rather be with," she says.

"Me too," he says. He returns her kiss. Their tongues meet. It seems like odd timing for this to be happening, but here it is happening, and with all those ancient associations between sex and death, maybe it isn't so odd. Soon they are rubbing all up on each other. He lets his hand slip inside her housecoat. She's wearing nothing under it. He squeezes her small breasts, pinches her nipples gently. Her breathing gets faster. He rubs his hands all over her taut, slender body.

She runs her hands up his shirt and pulls at his chest hairs. He pulls the shirt off. He pulls her robe off her shoulders and presses his chest into hers, rubbing their nipples together. He squeezes her buttocks, lets his fingers graze the top of her thighs, circling ever closer to her triangle of hair. She opens her legs for him. She's incredibly wet.

"Where are your kids?" Barney suddenly remembers.

"I took them to my mother's. Don't worry."

He thinks maybe he wants to slow things down, but she is working on his belt. It's a complicated buckle and he has to help her. Soon, they are lying together naked, melting into each other. Finally, he thinks. He bites her neck under her ear, and her body writhes under him. "Um, shouldn't I use something?" he asks.

"Don't insult me," she says.

Still, he wants it to last. He sucks her breasts, he slides down between her legs, sucks her navel.

Suddenly, the door to her apartment flies open with a crash. The cold wind rushes in from the hall. They freeze in place. "Cali!" shouts a gruff male voice. Mike! Jesus!

They jump up and try to cover themselves.

"Cali!" he shouts again. He switches on the light. His eyes are wild. His hair stands up in nappy spikes, as if uncombed for weeks. It's his turn to freeze. He stares at them open-mouthed.

"Mike!" Cali squeals in her little girl voice. "My God! I thought you were dead." She throws on her robe.

He doesn't say a word, nor grant Barney as much as a look. He grabs Cali by the arm and pulls her into the bedroom. Whack! He hits her. She screams. He hits her again.

"Mike!" Barney yells to distract him as he finishes dressing. "If this has something to do with me, I'm leaving now."

Cali runs out of the bedroom still in her robe, and out the door of the apartment. Barney runs after her. She runs toward the stairs. By the time Barney gets to the dark pissy stairwell, she's gone. He calls her name, "Cali!" No answer.

With a blast of wind, he has a vision of himself dead on these stairs. One floor below Cali's, he re-enters the hallway and goes for the elevator. When it comes, it's full. In the back is Mike, still wild-eyed. Barney considers letting the elevator go, thinks better of it, gets on. He doesn't want Mike to know how scared he is.

Mike stinks of the craziness of the past week. "I'm glad you're back, Mike," Barney says. "We really had given up on you."

He says nothing. He looks at Barney without recognition of the cordiality they once had, with a rage that seems limitless and chills him like dry ice stuffed into that hole at the base of his spine.

2.

When Barney gets home, the apartment is dark and unearthly quiet. "Linda Jean?" he calls. No answer. He checks the time, about eight in the evening. He's relieved she isn't home. He doesn't even turn on the lights. He sits in a chair and shakes.

Anxious for diversion, he reaches for the Chronicle sprawled all over the kitchen table. In the dim light, the headline reads "Egypt-Israel accord near," having been printed before the murders. Around the edges of the front page, Barney sees that Linda Jean has written something. He switches on the light. "Wouldn't it be lovely to cruise down the freeway and crash into neverneverland. This life is too hard."

Oh-oh, he thinks. He looks out the window for her car. It's not in her usual parking place. He calls around to try and find her. He checks her sister's, the Grossman's where she works, Darryl at the gas station. No one has seen her. He doesn't tell them about her note for fear of alarming them.

For one terrible instant, he hopes that she is dead. But then he thinks, no, I don't mean that, that's just my horrific despair talking. What he really wants is for her to be alive so that they can separate with no regrets.

He decides if she's not back by ten, he'll call the police. He pours himself a big glass of Korbel and sits in the dark. She comes in the door at five minutes to ten. She's drunk.

Her eyes are wild too, reminiscent of Mike's. "You went to *her* didn't you? How could you?" She starts hitting him.

He grabs her and restrains her arms with his arms. "You don't have to worry about her," he says. "Mike's back."

This sobers her up some. "He is? He's alive?"

"He's alive."

"Oh," she says.

He considers waiting until morning to confront her about the note. But he doesn't. "What the fuck is this?" he says. He shows her the newspaper.

"Oh. You weren't supposed to see that. I just wrote it, that's all. I was just sitting here waiting for you, waiting, and waiting, and I wrote it, that's all. You know I'd never do anything like that. I'm afraid of the dark."

"Yeah, right. I wasn't supposed to see it. That's why you left it out on the kitchen table like that." He knows he's being cruel, he knows he has no real right to be this mean, but he can't seem to help it. It does piss him off that she would threaten suicide this way.

"Barney." She starts to cry.

He softens. "I'm really not worth it, you know," he tells her.

She looks up at him. She laughs through her tears. "That's for sure," she says with a tone that actually frightens him.

SIXTEEN

Cloud Nine

1.

For a while, Barney sees Mike everywhere. He sees him in the elevator. He sees him hanging out with the streetcorner men in front of the Towers, the men who drink Night Train and Thunderbird out of paper bags and sell tiny ziplock Baggies of bad marijuana to customers passing in cars. He sees him when he brings Darnell and little Barney to the center. Even though Mike doesn't look at him, Barney gets the strangest feeling that he's watching him. He's combed his hair, but his eyes still give off an eerie light, as if he's experiencing something that no one else can perceive.

Sometimes Barney sees him with Larry Cordell and Jay in Jay's huge bronze '69 Cadillac, parked in the visitor's lot. He's dying to know what they're talking about. Are these the enforcers known as "White Knight" who are rumored to be plotting the deaths of the enemies of People's Temple? Would they consider Barney one of those enemies?

He doubts it. He doubts the existence of such a conspiracy. No one's been killed yet, and his suspicion is that these three, like the other survivors, are simply clinging to each other, still in shock, still wondering what the hell happened to this movement that meant everything to them. And yet, his heart pirouettes dizzily when he sees them, and he avoids them whenever he can.

Which means he avoids Cali too. He doesn't pressure her to come in to work, since the center has no money anyway. Though it is painful, and he can even feel some of the pain through the coldness which seems to have enveloped him, he's considering giving up on her. But the more he considers it, the more he finds her on his mind. He can't help thinking that she is the woman he wants to be with, perhaps the woman that he has wanted all his life.

He's developed a proposal to the state to get funding for the center, and he does need to get Cali's signature as chair of the Board of Directors. One evening after the children have left the center, he calls to make sure she's alone and then pays her a visit. He's surprised at how fast his heart is beating as he waits for her to answer the door.

"Hey, Barney-barn-barn, wha's happening?" She's dressed in her tight jeans with the polka dot halter top, and she's flying. The record player blares the Temptations' "Cloud Nine:"

> You can be what you want to be.
> A thousand miles from reality, reality,
> reality...

"I just need your signature, Cali," he says. He hates being around loaded people when he's not loaded himself.

"All business, today, huh, Booboo? You weren't like this the last time you were here." She puts her hand on his shoulder and bumps him with her hip. "Come on in and get high with me."

"Not now, Cali. Where's your hubby, anyway?" He glances out the window toward the corner, but low clouds obscure the street.

"That weirdo. I keep telling you he's not my husband. God knows what he's up to. He hangs out with those Temple creeps and his old buddies from his fencing days. I'd throw him out if he wasn't so violent. He's strange since he got back."

"Yeah, well, who wouldn't be? How did he survive the thing anyway?"

"He was in Georgetown with the Temple basketball team. He was one of the guys that shot that guy, Ryan." She says this as if she were telling him about what happened on "As the World Turns." "He did go back to Jonestown when he heard what happened. That's when he says he started losing it. Can I borrow $20?"

He was one of the guys that shot that guy Ryan – her phrase echoes in his mind. "I really need to go, Cali. Could you just sign this thing?"

"Pul-eeeze? I'll pay you back."

He guesses he doesn't want her to think he doesn't trust her, so, feeling foolish, he gives her the money.

"I'll be right back. Don't go away, hear? Keep your eye on the babies?"

She flies out the door, leaving him with his document still unsigned. He checks in the bedroom and sees Darnell, Barney, and the baby Keisha mesmerized by Wily Coyote forever chasing the Roadrunner. They don't even look at him.

"You'll never guess where I got this," Cali says when she returns, waving a tiny fold of paper in his face. "Wreck. Can you believe it? That old straight-arrow jock? He's dealing now."

"No shit? God, he's always seemed like such a model citizen, someone the youth could really look up to."

"Hey, now they *really* look up to him," she says as she flutters about her kitchen area, preparing the cocaine. "See, to smoke it you gotta turn it into rock, you know?" she explains like a hip Julia Child. "You dissolve it in water in a spoon, add a little baking soda, cook it until it crystallizes."

She puts the clear crystals on the brass screen of a glass pipe with a bubble in the stem. She heats the pipe bowl with a Bic lighter, sucks on the stem to fill the bubble with smoke, and then inhales the smoke.

"I've only snorted this stuff before myself," he apologizes.

"You're in for a treat then, my boy. Okay, pull until you fill up the bubble with smoke. Easy! You're burning it!"

It takes him awhile to get the hang of it, but he finally does get a hefty cloudful into his lungs. The cloud goes straight to his brain while his heart runs laps around his rib cage. His whole body goes numb like a Novocained tooth at the dentist's, only suddenly, as if an evil dentist, instead of using Novocain, has decided to snap his spine. And yet, it's all light, it's all easy, he's feeling no pain. All is right with the universe and he's at the center of it. "Hey, Cal, where ya been hiding this stuff? I feel like climbing a mountain. Hey, I know. Want to climb down the front of the Towers?" He stands up, goes to the window. "Just kidding, Babe. I can't see your hubby out there with his knot of compadres. You know I been seeing him everywhere?"

"He has his eye on you, Barn-barn, are you surprised? He is jealous. He needs to be. My feelings for him are nothing like they are for you."

"Oh, Cali, I..." he stammers, moved. "I sure wish he weren't around."

"Aw, Barney, you old chicken, you're nothing but a dirty old man."

This stings, puncturing his euphoria. "What do you mean by that?"

"Just that you won't go to the wall for me. Supposing I wanted Mike out of my life. Would you help me?"

A big "No!" echoes through his brain with a flash of terror that brings him down some more. He sighs, a great ontological sigh. He equivocates. "Is that what you want? You want to get rid of Mike-mike and hang with me?"

"No, because you won't take Mike on – and I wouldn't want you to, anyway. I value your life more than I want to share it. I don't know what he's capable of at this point any more than you do. I'm scared to death of him half the time myself. He's only beat me up that once, but he balls up his fists all the time. Still, I can't just turn him out now, not after what he's been through. Can you imagine seeing 900 people you thought were your best friends lying dead in a heap like that? He's hooked into me."

Barney sighs again. How far is he willing to go for her? "I'm not going to let him stand in my way," he says boldly yet uncertain just how he's going to stop him. He starts to move in on her, ready to kiss her, to make love to her, but his fear stops him. Instead, he asks her, "Did you ever sleep with White?"

"That's been on your mind all this time, Booboo? It's funny. We actually tried once. In the early days. But he couldn't do it. He's like you, said he felt guilty about his wife."

"How about Moscone?"

"Shit, Barney, you have to know everything? Once. In the back of his little car. At the beach."

"Oh." He's more hurt than he'd ever admit. He wonders if he'll ever have his chance.

In the next few minutes, their tongues freeze up again, and their psychic elevators sink to the basement. A leaden cloud of gloom sinks in where the white cloud puffed so breezily moments before, so heavy, so empty, the inside of a vacuum cleaner. If the coke shines in your brain like the stars, the aftertaste sucks up the light like the frigid emptiness of interstellar space. More,

more, screams the old cerebellum, so they smoke some more, but it seems like each puff gets you slightly less high and each aftertaste brings you down a little bit further, and you can see that this freebasing is a losing proposition which is, as a whole, actually boring.

When Mike comes in, luckily they're sitting three feet apart from each other on the couch. He glares at Barney anyway. His hair is combed, his clothes are clean, his jeans are pressed, but his eyes still gleam. "Barney. 'Sup," he says. "Time for you to go now."

Barney glances at Cali. She nods her head. "Okay," he says.

He leaves with an uneasy feeling in his stomach, like it's not what he wants to do. As soon as he gets home, he realizes that he left the papers there, and he has to go back.

He retrieves the .25 automatic he keeps under the mattress, a tiny gun which probably wouldn't hurt anyone unless you emptied it into his temple, and slips it into his back pocket. He rides the elevator back up and rings Cali's bell. She looks at him questioningly as she answers the door.

Mike stands up from the couch as he sees Barney, but not out of politeness. "You're back?" he asks, his voice crackling with hostility.

"I'm back," Barney says, sitting on the couch and putting his feet up defiantly on the fiberboard coffee table.

"Barney, man, I don't think you understand. I don't want you hanging around my woman no more."

"*Your* woman? Maybe we should ask *her* whose woman she is. I think she's her own woman."

Mike stares at Barney in disbelief. "Dig it, Barney, let's put it this way. If you don't get the fuck out of here now and stay the fuck away from here, I'm going to hurt you, man." He socks his palm with his fist for emphasis.

Barney looks at Cali and feels the pistol digging into his buttock. He suddenly remembers Mike's flame thrower. And he remembers Cali's words: "He was one of the guys that shot that guy Ryan."

"It's your house, Cali," Barney says. "I'll leave it up to you."

"Maybe you should go, Barney," she says. "I don't want any violence."

"Okay," he says, rising, "but I want you to know, Mike, I'm not afraid of you."

He smiles sarcastically. "You're making the right choice," he says. "Both of you."

He remembers the papers this time. He has Cali sign them at the door. She sneaks him a peck on the cheek. "See you *soon*, Booboo." She squeezes his hand.

2.

In spite of everything that's happened, Barney is confident that the state is going to fund the center, and he musters the energy to maximize this possibility. He visits all their families to reassure them about the Eddie affair, taking responsibility for it and promising that they will never again be so lax. He gets the enrollment back up to fifteen and increases Sue Ann's hours so she can help him teach.

He mobilizes Alice and Cali to help clean the place for the state inspectors who arrive one morning in mid-December to check the place out. The place looks good.

The inspectors, a group of three women, two white and one black, ask them difficult questions about discipline policy and program philosophy, but they answer well. By the time they're outside touring the yard, he's sure they're a shoo-in for the money.

The black woman, Ms. Judson, serious, with straightened hair, says to him, "You have a nice yard here."

Without thinking, he quips, "Well, of course we cleaned it up for you."

Her face drops. "You did?"

He realizes his mistake and back-peddles. "Just kidding."

He can tell by her penetrating look that she doesn't believe him. Her attitude subtly cools.

A week later they get a letter rejecting their request, ranking them nineteenth, with only the first sixteen programs receiving any funding. Barney is sure it's his quip that blew it for them.

3.

He tries to tell Linda Jean how restless he's feeling, and what he wants from her. He tells her, "You know Linda Jean, there's one word you could say that would make me want to stay with you. You know what it is?"

She shakes her head.

"It's the word 'go,'" he says. She looks at the floor.

Finally, he talks her into trying couples counseling. Through a friend, they're referred to a woman in Walnut Creek who does bioenergetic therapy, a system he can appreciate because it is based on the theories of Wilhelm Reich, whom Lenin had developing sexual policy for the infant Soviet Union until he got too far out, advocating free sex for adolescents. The therapist is a plump woman in her late forties with streaked hair and serious eyes, who lives in a vast, modern home with rosewood paneling, built, ironically enough, by Joseph Eichler, the same guy who built Geneva Towers.

In her office, she asks them to sit in a way that they think reflects the dynamic of the relationship between them. He doesn't really know what she means, so he just stays in the leather butterfly chair he's sitting in, but Linda Jean surprises him by sitting on the floor at his feet, which feels really weird.

They share what they like about each other. "I like how solid you are, Linda Jean. I like your willingness to participate in sexual adventures. I like how you are with my children, and what a good teacher you are. I like how well we've collaborated politically in the past."

Leaning on her elbow, she tells him nervously, "Barney, I like our sex, I like that you are a fighter for equality, I like how well you express your feelings."

You like how I express my feelings? He thinks. He wants to crawl through the floor hearing this. How embarrassing. That's the thing he's absolutely worst at. How little she knows him. But then, whose fault is that?

In summation, the doctor says in her measured professional tone, "You have some communication difficulties, but, as long as you are both committed, I don't see any reason why you can't work things out and stay together."

One phrase sinks like a rock in the pool of Barney's consciousness. "As long as you are both committed..." The words echo like the ripples from the rock. As long as you are both committed. He doesn't say anything, but he knows at that moment that he is not in fact committed anymore, and that he's going to have to leave.

How hard would it have been for you to just say, "Linda Jean, I'm scared. I don't even know what I'm scared of. I'm scared of growing old, I'm scared of dying, sure, like everyone. But most of all, I'm scared of my own fear, and this creates a feedback loop, as in fear of fear of fear of fear...ad nauseum. I'm scared, too, of telling you how scared I am, for fear that you will go away, not physically, perhaps, but that you just won't be there for me because of your own fear." You supposed it was fear alone which kept people apart, not just people in couples, but people in families, people in neighborhoods, people in cities, people in the whole world. Communism was foundering because of the fear people had of each other; indeed it stayed in power largely by perpetrating terror among the people, thus negating the one thing which might actually have made it work: overcoming the fear between people. But where would you start?

One of the things that must have happened in Jonestown was that the people dared to take on the fear of each other, dared to throw in their lot with the group as a whole, flew in the face of fear itself, only to confront the terror behind it, the fear of losing what unity they at least imagined they had, a fear apparently worse than the fear of death.

Dan White, too, he must have thought he was confronting his fear. Certainly he feared Moscone's power over him and Milk's homosexuality in equal doses, but what he failed to understand is that his real fear was of his own impotence and his own homosexuality. There seemed to be a grave danger that when you boldly took on your fear, you were really only confronting your anxiety, your fear of fear, your little fear that held the big fear in check, and, if you were not careful, you became what you feared the most.

One phrase of Cali's kept returning to your consciousness: "He was one of the guys that shot that guy, Ryan." That, combined with what Mike said to you just before he left for Jonestown: "I'm going to take your advice, man. I'm going to Guyana." The thought quietly percolated to the surface: If it hadn't been for you, Mike wouldn't have gone to Jonestown, Ryan wouldn't have been shot, and 900 people would still be alive...

SEVENTEEN

Kwanzaa

1.

For Jason's eighth birthday, early in December, Barney gives him a walkie-talkie, which costs more than he can afford. He carefully tells his son that it's partly a Christmas present. Linda Jean bakes him a wonderful chocolate sheet cake with a miniature circus train that circumnavigates the array of candles on a figure eight of track.

Meanwhile, Barney doesn't seem to be there at all. Cynthia used to accuse him of walking around with a paper bag over his head, but this barrier is thicker than that, it's like he's not in the universe, except that he's not anywhere else either, he's nowhere, frozen in a Plexiglas bubble that's floating outside the space-time continuum. It's not like death. In death, there are at least evanescent traces of past life, like the tingling sensations of an amputated limb. Where he is, Nowhere, it's like never having been alive, and at times, during the day, the temperature dips below absolute zero.

He is perfectly well aware that much of what he is not-feeling is directly related to the closing of the center, the collapse of his dream. Yes, he's depressed, what else is new? He considers himself a man with psychological awareness. No little depression is going to get him down. Not in his bubble, floating benignly outside the charted co-ordinates of the cosmos.

Responsibly, he sets the date for the actual closing of the center as December 20, the same day the public schools are out for Christmas, to give the parents a pool of baby sitters to draw on until they can find another center.

Linda Jean and Barney have a fight over how to celebrate the holidays. "I can't take Christmas this year," Barney says. "I can't stomach all that insincere joy in the face of everything that's happened. Let's celebrate Kwanzaa."

"Kwanzaa?" she says. "How are Jason and Ramona going to relate to that there? Besides, it's a phony holiday. There is no such African tradition, you know. Kwanzaa was invented by some nationalist from LA. The same guy whose organization used to fight the Panthers. Killed one of them I think."

He's surprised at how much she knows about this. "Can't remember his name though, can you? Neither can I. You know the sixties are over when you can't remember the names of the dead Panthers. So, this guy had some good ideas and some bad ideas. Kwanzaa was a good idea. It's about unity, collectivity, cooperation, creativity – not crass commercialism. A lot of people celebrate it now."

"It would make more sense for your kids to celebrate Hanukkah."

"Is that some kind of anti-Semitic remark? Hanukkah is a phony holiday too, at least the way it's been blown up to compete with Christmas. Their mother may be Jewish, but she doesn't bother with Hanukkah. She celebrates Christmas."

"Whatever you say, Barney," Linda Jean sneers. He's used to this, her agreeing without agreeing, and though he hates it, his revenge is to take what she says at face value.

He still hasn't told her of his decision to leave. He's waiting until after the holidays.

2.

One night, Linda Jean and Barney return home from food shopping, and, as they get off the elevator, they notice the door to their apartment is ajar. "Oh-oh," he says. The door jamb is splintered. They enter the apartment with a sinking feeling. His eyes dart to the stereo. An empty shelf. They've been robbed.

They check around hastily. The TV's gone. The camera from inside the closet. The typewriter. The toaster oven. The bedroom is in shambles, with the contents of drawers strewn all over the bed. The burglars were apparently looking for jewelry.

He calls the police and the Towers' security. Security sends a man right away to fix the door.

They stumble around in shock, waiting for the cops, checking here and there to see what else might be missing. All told, it's maybe $1,000 worth of stuff. Not a horribly big deal. Of course they have no insurance.

But that's beside the point. The point is, he tells Linda Jean, "How dare these motherfuckers come into our space! How dare them! God, it feels awful. It's like being violated. I'm sure rape is a lot worse, but this must be a similar kind of feeling."

Two hours later, two policemen come, a pudgy mustachioed Irishman and a slightly built Asian. Barney and Linda Jean tell them how they discovered the robbery. They tell the cops what they think is missing. Clearly bored, they write their report and tell them, "We'll check the pawn shops. Sometimes people's stuff does turn up, but don't count on it."

Barney doesn't mention to either the cops or Linda Jean his suspicions that somehow Mike is behind this thing.

3.

The center closes unceremoniously on the day of the longest night of the year. It has been a paradoxically warm and sunny day, but now it is dark. Cali, Alice, Sue Ann, and Barney huddle sadly in the office. "Hey, it was a good shot, Barney," Alice says in her gruff voice.

"I really admire what you were able to do," says Sue Ann in her Mississippi drawl.

He's thinking, do I look so down at the mouth these people think they have to reassure me?

"In some ways, it was the best thing I ever done," chimes Cali. "I learned a lot from you, Barney."

He looks at her longingly. He's been too out of it

to approach her lately, but he's thinking of giving it another go soon.

"What will you do now, Barney?" Sue Ann asks.

"Oh, I can go on unemployment again for a while. Or substitute teach. I can always do that. I'll get along."

They fall silent for a moment, and then all of the sudden a certain kind of light circulates between them, as if they have all come up with precisely the same idea at precisely the same instant. Cali verbalizes it first. "I get dibs on the tape recorder."

"I thought I might take some of these plastic dishes," says Sue Ann.

"Those big blocks will make some bad plant stands," says Alice.

"I'll take the desk chair," Barney says, "and all the envelopes."

They laugh as they claim their booty.

Linda Jean comes in from work and all of them stiffen, for different reasons. Cali has been uncomfortable with her ever since she and Barney broached the idea of an affair. Barney is having trouble being around her at all lately. The others are concerned that she will harshly judge their attempts to grab a piece of the crumbling pie.

"I want some of the doll corner furniture," Linda Jean pipes in. "That little table will be perfect for my sewing machine." They all laugh, relieved that the larcenous spirit has infected her, too. Although, one wonders, how can you steal from yourself?

4.

On the afternoon of Christmas day, Barney goes to Cynthia's to pick up Jason and Ramona, to the Victorian he painted red eons ago. He embraces Cynthia warmly, "Merry Christmas," he says. He kisses her eyebrows. She's wearing a new red velour robe.

He brings the children to the Towers. After their argument, Linda Jean has actually gotten into Kwanzaa and developed an inspired *Nguzo Saba*, like an altar, of the seven Kwanzaa symbols.

Ramona asks right away with her big-eyed innocence, "Daddy, you don't have a tree?" Her brown hair is cut off in a mop-top, as if her mother used a bowl over the top of her head.

"We're celebrating Kwanzaa this year," he tells her.

"Kwanzaa? What's that?" Monie asks.

Jason answers, "I know. I heard about it in school. It's some African holiday." There's a sneer in his voice. "We're not African." He has curly blond hair and oversized glasses which continually slip from his nose.

"Well, actually, we are, J. I hate to tell you, but all people originally came from Africa."

"They did?" Jason says.

"Yes, they did. And, the original people, our ancestors, were black, too."

"They were?"

Darryl, slouching in the corner chair with the stuffing coming out of the arm, quietly takes it all in, a bemused look on his face. He covers one side of his face with his hand as if he were embarrassed.

Linda Jean explains the symbols to them. "The straw mat stands for traditional African handicrafts," though Barney can see that this particular mat came from Japan. She points to the bananas and apples. "The fruit stands for *mazao*, or crops. The *kinara* is a candle holder like the menorah, only with seven candles, red, black, and green. Red for the blood we shed, black for the people, green for our mother earth." She looks through the book for the other Swahili words. "There's three *muhindi*, or ears of corn, one for each child in the family, you two and Darryl. Then, there's the *mishuma cha umoja*, or the unity cup, and the *zwadi*, or gifts, one for each of you."

"Can we open the presents now?" Ramona asks.

"First we have to light the first candle," Linda Jean answers. She does this. "Kwanzaa doesn't officially start until tomorrow, but we're starting it today so you guys can participate. Then we have to drink from the unity cup." She fills the wooden cup, which has rearing elephants for handles, with Gallo Hearty Burgundy. "In drinking from this cup, we are making a pact to maintain the unity of our family no matter what," she says. She reads a long-winded "Liberation Statement" from the Kwanzaa book, which pays homage to Nat Turner, Marcus Garvey, Martin Luther King, Jr., Malcolm X, and to the struggle for freedom. It ends with a shout of "*Harambee!*" a call to unity and collective work.

Jason and Ramona look at each other and echo the shout. Darryl sinks further in his chair.

"Now you can open your presents," Barney says.

They dive for the packages with their names on them, wrapped in last Sunday's comics. Ramona's eyes light up as she sees the View Master Barney has gotten her, with 3-D stories from Mickey Mouse, Winnie-the-Pooh, Hansel and Gretel, and The Legend of Sleepy Hollow.

Linda Jean hands Darryl his present, a shirt he doesn't like. "Paisley," he says. "No one wears paisley any more, Mom."

Jason's face falls as he discovers the felt dart board with the velcro ball Barney bought him. He is obviously disappointed. He bursts into tears.

Barney rushes to hug him.

"Remember? You got that expensive walkie-talkie for your birthday?" Barney tells him.

Linda Jean jumps on him. "Stop all that crying! You're too big for that. You're lucky you got anything."

Barney turns toward her. "Shut up!" he tells her, and he sweeps Jason into his arms and carries him back to the bedroom, where he holds him until he's all cried out.

When they emerge from the back, Monie confronts Barney sharply. "What about Santa Claus?"

Jason and Barney look at each other. "What about him?" Barney asks.

"Does he bring presents for Kwanzaa, too?"

Jason and Barney exchange glances. "Monie," Jason says, "I got news for you. There is no Santa Claus."

Monie, crestfallen, looks at Barney. "Sorry, he's right, Sweetie."

Monie seethes. She looks back at both of them square in the face. "Oh...yes...there...is!" she enunciates, with an incontrovertible certainty, as if she were affirming the existence of something as palpable as a chair.

Jason and Barney look at each other again, shrug their shoulders, as if to say maybe she knows something they don't. "Okay," Barney says. "Okay, Monie. You win."

5.

That night, in bed, after the children have gone to sleep, it just comes bubbling out of him like vomit: "I have to leave, Linda Jean." He's lying on his back, staring at the ceiling.

She doesn't say anything for a long time. She's curled up in a ball with her back toward him. He listens for tears or sniffles, but hears nothing but the howl of the wind outside the sliding glass door to the balcony. Just having let the words go, he feels lighter.

She unsprings like a cobra, turns toward him, screams, "Go, then!" and coils right back up again.

Whatever he expected, this isn't it. He freezes, continuing to stare at the miniature snow-capped mountain range of asbestos on the ceiling. Does she mean right now? After midnight on Christmas night?

He listens to the click of the numbers on the digital alarm clock, marking the minutes. The hum of the refrigerator. The elevator door opening. The wail of a cross-town siren. The heaving of Linda Jean's breath.

"I'll sleep on the couch tonight. I'll leave in the morning."

He takes the sleeping bag from the closet and goes to the front. He curls up on the couch. He's cold. He plans in his head what he will take when he leaves. Just a few clothes, some books, the camping stuff, the new boom box, the tapes. The burglars got most of their stuff anyway. He'll get the rest later. He thinks about their wedding tape, the one they forgot to play at their wedding, with Minnie Ripperton singing "Loving You," Linda Jean's choice, too sappy for him, ("Loving you is easy cuz you're beautiful..."), and his two choices, both by Gladys Knight, "It's Got to Be That Way," and "For Once In My Life," followed by a mutual choice, Al Green's "Let's Get Married." It bothered him at the time that he had two choices to her one, and he even asked her about it. Of course, she said "no problem," but the inequality was built into the foundation. He remembers the pang of irony he felt when he decided to use the other side of the tape to record the rest of the Gladys Knight album, beginning with "Neither One of Us," ("...wants to be the first to say good-bye"), a song that never fails to choke him up. He decides to take that tape, too, then he decides, what the hell, he's not sleeping anyway, he'll make another copy now, and he does so on the cheap replacement stereo they bought with the volume turned all the way down, so that all he can hear is some scratchy subliminal invocations of the tunes.

From the bedroom, he hears Linda Jean sobbing intensely now. He wants to go comfort her. He hates that he's hurting her, but he can't let her weaken his resolve. He thinks about asking her: Do you want me to stay with you because I feel sorry for you? His own eyes wet up just a little.

He doesn't sleep much. When he does, he dreams he is in Africa, deep in the jungle, and he's being hunted, but he doesn't know who it is that's stalking him. Is he black and being hunted by the white slavers? Is he white and being hunted by vengeful natives? Or is he being pursued by tigers, a species that he knows even in his dream doesn't exist in Africa?

As you wandered in and out of a hypnogogic state, you grilled yourself as to your reasons for leaving, for breaking Linda Jean's heart. Were you just wishing you were 25 again as Cynthia has implied? Did your apparent love for Cali make it clear that your love for Linda Jean was lacking?

Was it her fault because she loved you too much, more than you deserved? That her love was coming from some deep need in her, having little to do with you?

Or were you protecting her from whatever you started with Mike? Mike, who was blaming you for advising him to go Jonestown, where he was forced into killing Ryan, so that you could have Cali to yourself? Blaming you for causing the Jonestown Massacre?

And Dan White? Did you cause that too when you spoke to him so dismissively on the eve of his double murder?

Was it that knot of coldness, that snarl of ice, that lightless warmthless singularity in the small of your back that gave you the Midas Touch in reverse, where everything you touced turns to shit, or worse than shit, death?

Your heart pounded with palpitations of panic.

PART THREE

EIGHTEEN

Holy Innocents' Day

1.

The next morning, Barney says good-bye to Linda Jean's inert hulk in the bed. She plays possum. He piles Jason and Ramona into the red VW van, and they drive out of the Tower's garage with the wheels floating about three inches off the ground. A giddiness overcomes him as if he were a kid again, stealing his father's car. It's an unseasonably balmy day, an anomalous day, the sun is out, there are only a few puffy clouds, a gentle haze is in the air, a day out of sync with its time. "Let's go to the beach, kids," he says, "okay?"

"Sure," they say. He sees Mike standing on the corner and gives him a big smile and a wave. Mike glares back at him with a coldness that goes right through him like an icicle jabbed into his solar plexus. He wishes he'd ignored him like he usually does.

"Linda Jean and I are splitting up," he tells the kids point blank.

"Okay," says Monie, as if he has just told her they have to stop for gas. "That's fine," says Jason, with equal nonchalance.

He knows they've been through this before, twice in fact, once with Barney and once with their mother's second husband, but their apparent lack of affect disturbs even him. He knows they like Linda Jean a lot. "Is that all you have to say?"

"What do you want us to say?" Jason asks, reasonably.

"I don't know. I guess I thought you might have some feelings about it."

"It does seem kind of sudden," Jason says. "I didn't think you guys had been arguing that much."

"It might have been better if we argued more," Barney says. "It's a bad idea to keep feelings bottled up, you know."

"We know that, Dad," Ramona says, as if he's just told her the sky is blue. At Ocean Beach the gulls squawk with joy as they swoop from the sky, snatch choice remnants of yesterday's Christmas beach parties from the sand, and soar toward China.

They take off their shoes and run along the foam line, following the undulations of the waves just inside of getting their feet wet. Now and then they miss, the water plunges around their ankles, and they scream from the chill.

They clamber among the ruins of the Sutro Bath House, a maze of pools and tunnels left over from a grander time. At Land's End, they listen to the seals bark, put a quarter in the telescope, and watch them gambol on the rocks whitened with guano from the gulls, cormorants, and pelicans. He tells the children with a dramatic sweep of his arm, "This is it, kids, this is as far as you can go, the end of the United States."

"What about Hawaii?" asks Jason.

"Well, except for Hawaii, then."

They spend much of his change in the Musée Mechanique, a wondrous collection of slot machines ranging from Laughing Sal, a larger-than-life-sized mechanical clown-witch with a hideous cackle, the matriarch of the recently defunct Playland amusement park that had been across the street (now replaced by condos), to Super Pong and the very hot Ms. Pacman. They get their fortunes told by a mechanical gypsy. Barney's reads, "Beware of strangers, be open to new experiences."

They are entranced by the enormous farm scene which comes to life in its five foot square glass case at the insertion of a quarter. The hay bailers turn, the tractors plow, the dogs bay, the farmer swings his hoe, a circle of iron-bodied white women do needlepoint, a horse pulls a cart, a farmhand milks a cow, all to the rhythm of the banjo tune ("Camptown Races") which accompanies the dancing darkies in a corner by their tumbledown shack. "Look!" Jason says, pointing to the rollicking, black-painted, iron figures with a guilty smile, as if he is pointing out a naughty picture, which, Barney supposes, he is.

"That's racist," Barney observes.

"We know that, Dad," Jason responds.

Along the sea wall behind the Cliff House, a touristy restaurant, there's a small building in the shape

of a camera, with a sign that beckons "See the inven-
tion of Leonardo da Vinci! See the Camera Obscura."
They pay their money and enter a dark room with a
round screen in the middle of it, on which is project-
ed the surrounding concurrent scene, the ocean, the
Cliff House, the tourists walking by, the Great Highway.
You can always tell the tourists, because they're under-
dressed even on this temperate morning, expecting San
Francisco to be tropical. There's a periscope and a series
of lenses which focus the image more clearly than if it
were directly observed, a miniature world that looks
more real than reality. Monie sticks her hand in the
image of the water and giggles when it comes up dry.

"What's the big deal?" Jason asks.

"Well, the technique was invented by Leonardo. It
works like a huge eye, gathering in the light waves and
forming an image. It seems kind of magical to me."

"I'd rather play Ms. Pacman," Jason says.

"Okay," Barney says.

He gives Jason a few quarters for his game while
Monie and Barney play Super Pong, batting a light
beam back and forth across a net. Barney keeps trying to lose, but Monie misses every shot. He hits one
or two just to keep the game going, and she gets frus-
trated and quits when she sees the score.

Toward late afternoon, he takes the children to
Cynthia's. He's dying to talk to her. She emerges from
her bedroom to meet them in the hall. "Well, I did it,"
he says. "I left. And I'm feeling obscenely happy."

"You left, huh? Just like that? I'm sorry. Well, you

can't say you didn't try. Where will you be staying?"

"Actually, I was kind of hoping you'd let me stay here for a while."

"Really? I don't know, Barney, that doesn't feel right to me. I don't think so."

"Okay," he says, trying not to show how disappointed he is. "I'll probably sleep in my van, then."

"Good luck," she says, clearly impatient to return to her meditation, or whatever she was doing in her room.

"Thanks," he says.

When Ramona was just a baby, barely over a year old, and Jason just beyond toddling, you went with your comrades in the Party to a meeting of the San Francisco school board to support an integration plan. Protesting the plan were a dozen uniformed members of the American Nazi Party, decked out in brown shirts and black boots, swastikas taunting the crowd from their arm bands.

The auditorium was jammed with people. The Chinese board president gaveled the meeting to order, but order did not come.

"Throw the Nazis out!" the people were chanting at full voice. The hairs on your neck bristled with the excitement of confrontation. You could smell it on yourself. You had been to such confrontational meetings many times, but this was the headiest yet. Violence was in the air, thicker than San Francisco fog. The Nazis sat stone faced at attention.

A black woman teacher, Yvonne Golden, presumed by the Party to be a member of a rival sect, took the microphone and begian leading the chant. "Throw the Nazis out!"

Suddenly, you saw dozens of your own comrades pop up all around the phalanx of Nazis and jump them, clearly according to some plan to which you were not privy, acting out the chant quite literally. Fists flew, pandemonium raged. "An old fashioned Commie Nazi brawl," the papers would call it the next day. What were you supposed to do? Were you supposed to fight, too?

Uniformed police joined the fray. They must have been massed at the ready close by. You saw a man in a tan sport coat clubbing people right next to you. On impulse, you grabbed the swinging arm to stop it. You assumed that this was a Nazi in plain clothes. In fact, you will learn later, it was a plain clothes policeman.

The club didn't stop just because you intervened. It kept swinging, now crashing down on your own head. You tasted blood.

Moments later, you found yourself with six of your comrades crammed against the steel walls of a paddy wagon, bleeding from the forehead.

They took you to General Hospital and gave you 20 stitches above your eye. They charged you with felony assault on an officer (an officer?), disturbing the peace, and disrupting a public meeting. Your bail was set at $25,000. You were stuck in a felony holding cell with murderers and armed robbers. Would they lift your credential? They could. They might. You thought maybe your life was over.

Cynthia bailed you out by putting up the house. Especially after you explained how it was just an accident, that you were trying to prevent an assault rather than perpetrate one, she was sympathetic, but her eyes betrayed her fear.

You came to think of it as exciting. You were a celebrity for a brief while. You liked the attention.

You were removed from your temporary job. A brisk fight by the union got you reinstated.

The Nazis, reading your name in the newspaper, began to call your house. "We're watching you, Commie traitor!" they shouted into the phone.

Cynthia announced one day, "Barney, I can't stand it. I'm taking the kids to my mother's in Palo Alto."

"Come on, those chickenshit bastards aren't going to do anything," you said. Weren't you the victim here? Didn't you need her support? You couldn't understand how fearful she was. It didn't occur to you until years later that it might have had something to do with to you that the fact that she was Jewish.

She came back a few weeks later, but it was never the same again. You remembered clinging to Jason and little Ramona in those days, holding their little selves tight to your chest.

You left a couple of months later to pursue the struggle. You did your best over the years to stay close to Jason and Ramona, and you largely succeeded, but it wasn't the same as being there for them every day to kiss their childhood booboos or delight in their mastery of place value.

You ended up doing three weekends in jail with a gang of Iranian gas siphoners, Friday night to Monday morning, tortured with the boredom, but otherwise unharmed. The experience became a source of pride, a war wound from the movement. Four years hence, you still had that scar on your forehead.

2.

As Barney returns to Visitacion Valley, the sky grows dark, and he still has no place to sleep. He parks a block away from the Towers, down a hidden side street, just in case Linda Jean should be around. It seems silly for him to still be sneaking even though he's free, but he doesn't want to hurt her any more than he has to.

He sees that Mike is no longer on his corner. His stomach flutters as he rides the elevator up to the 19th floor.

Cali answers the door, hesitantly. "Barney," she says.

"Well, Cali, I did it, I'm free."

He hears a booming voice from inside the apartment. "Who the hell is it, Cali?" Mike.

"You left Linda Jean?" Cali says.

"Yep," he beams. "Can I stay here?"

"Here? Are you crazy?"

The voice from inside approaches. "I asked who it was." Mike's large frame darkens the hallway behind Cali. "You!" He seethes at Barney. "All right, man. You are really asking for it. Enough is enough. Step aside, Cali. It's time to teach this white boy a lesson."

"It's okay, Mike, he's just leaving," Cali says. "You know, school business."

"Cali!" Mike shouts. "That school closed, remember? Now get the hell out of the way and let me hurt him."

Mike lunges at Barney but Cali stands her ground between them. "No, Mike," she says. "Run, Barney!"

He runs. The door slams behind him, and he still hears scuffling behind it. He runs down the hall to the stairs, down the stairs, all the way this time, oblivious to whatever other dangers might lurk there. The exit door at the bottom flies open, no longer chained. He runs all the way to his van.

He spends the night sleeping in the back of the van at the beach, but he gets awakened by the cops who warn him that there's no camping allowed. "I'm not camping," he says, "I'm sleeping," but they make him move anyway. He doesn't get much sleep this way, but he likes being on his own, a piece of flotsam cast about by the tide.

He spends the next day enjoying his freedom, stocking up on survival supplies he thinks he may need, spending money he doesn't have, running up his Master Charge. He buys a Buck knife, a halogen flashlight, a precision compass. He's thinking he'll head for Deer Creek, but first he wants to go to the Holy Innocents' Day Celebration at Glide Church, a special memorial service for Mayor Moscone, Harvey Milk, and the 912 victims of Jonestown, so he spends this night parked along the panhandle leading to Golden Gate Park, a traditional area for hippies in vans, and the cops don't bother him.

As an atheist, he's not big on churches, but Glide is about as secular as you can get and still be a church. Cecil Williams, the pastor, is a portly black man whose dazzling dashikis, light shows, contemporary music ("Where have all the flowers gone..."), and political activism have earned him the wrath of the Methodist hierarchy. With his integrated congregation, charisma, and social mission, he is in many ways Jim Jones without the chicken guts and madness.

December 28th is the day marked to memorialize Herod's slaughter of all male babies under the age of two, which he ordered when he heard of the birth of a new King of the Jews – an appropriate day to celebrate the end of 1978 in San Francisco if there ever was one.

He decides to go for several reasons. He likes Cecil, whom he's met in various school struggles. He wants to grieve for Leonora and the others, and for the era that has ended with these events. He wants to meet women.

The church is in the heart of the Tenderloin, a district famous for its derelicts, prostitutes, and porno theaters, not accidentally in the shadow of the Hilton Hotel. The huge nave and the balcony are mobbed with people of all kinds for the afternoon service, a motley San Francisco collection, white haired do-gooders from Pacific Heights, white women with those telltale penciled eyebrows that let you know they're former addicts with black boyfriends. Street crazies. Gays in their jean jackets, cropped hair, and mustaches. Hippies in tie-dyed robes with hair past their shoulders and beards past their nipples, stinking of patchouli oil. Middle-class black families with finely scrubbed children in miniature suits, and blacks from below the underclass, winos who smell like they had their last bath in Herod's time. Day-Glo amebas from the light show writhe on the walls.

They sing a mournful version of "We Shall Overcome." Cecil exhorts them, "We are not here to blame but to forgive and to grieve the slaughter of the innocents."

Barney spots Jay first, about 10 rows in front of him, a tall man who towers above the others, sitting in a special section for people who lost relatives in Guyana. Then he sees Larry Cordell, his hair slicked back. Cordell sees Barney too, gives him a chilly look, and then points him out to his companion who turns to look. Mike. He stares at Barney long and hard, those piercing icicles darting from his eyes again. Then he sees Mike lean over and say something to a short, fat black man with long wavy hair like James Brown.

He decides he's not going to enjoy this experience sitting so close to their malevolent aura, so he squeezes and shoves his way upstairs to the back of the balcony. The choir does an amazingly soulful rendition of "Amazing Grace," which tears up his eyes so much that he closes them. When he opens them again, he sees that the short, fat, James Brown-haired fellow has elbowed his way to a seat just four rows away. He doesn't conceal his interest in Barney, but looks at him square in the face. Oh-oh, he thinks.

He's not particularly scared. But he's not real comfortable with this clown's eyes drilling into the back of his neck, so he decides to leave before the service is over. He eases his way out of the back door to the balcony without looking at him. He runs down the stairs. He hears footsteps coming after him, but they could be anyone's.

His van is parked in front of Turk St. Fantasies, where you can talk to a nude girl. There's a red-bearded, wild-eyed man leaning against the side of the van. "I'm a Vietnam vet," he says to Barney. "Let me wash your windshield." He is missing at least three teeth.

"I'm in a hurry."

"Let me wash your windshield," he repeats menacingly.

He looks behind him, sees no one following. "You know Mike?" Barney asks, almost as a joke.

"Mike! Sure I know Mike! Mike and me is buddies! Let me wash your windshield."

There's a lot of Mikes, Barney thinks, and he doesn't pursue it. He gives him fifty cents and pulls away, leaving him with his rag in his hand, washing the air. He notices another car, a big Pontiac, driven by an intense black man, pull out from the other side of the one-way street right after him. Of course, they've spotted his car and have it covered.

He makes a quick right, and the Pontiac doesn't follow, but a VW bug pulls out right behind him, a bearded white guy in glasses driving, a "Free Angela" bumper sticker on the front bumper. Barney drives real slow, trying to get him to pass, but he doesn't. Finally he stops, so the bug has to go around, but he keeps going slow, as if watching Barney in his rear-view mirror. A motorcycle, driven by a black man with aviator sunglasses takes his place behind Barney.

Barney speeds up, makes some more quick turns, finds himself back in front of Glide Church as the service is letting out, stuck in traffic.

He sees Jay, Larry Cordell, and Mike huddled together in the crowd. He sees them see him. He sees them run toward Jay's bronze Cadillac. But they're headed in the wrong direction up a one-way street. He manages to barge through traffic, run a red light, turn down O'Farrell, then Stockton by Macy's, scattering the crowds of after-Christmas sale shoppers like a flock of chickens. He crosses Market Street. He does a few more quick turns, James Bond style. There doesn't seem to be anyone behind him. He's shaken them. He relaxes.

He drives to his friend Bob's house in Bernal Heights, a bucolic neighborhood of little houses, a subset of the Mission District, with some of the streets still unpaved. He parks on Moultrie Street, a tiny street where his vehicle is unlikely to be spotted. Fortunately, Bob is home.

"I may be in danger, Bob," Barney tells him. "I'm being followed."

"Well, thanks for coming here, man," he laughs with his characteristic uproariousness. Barney bristles. "Just kidding, man. Who do you think is following you?" Bob has soft brown eyes nestled in granite features, thinning brown hair combed back. "A guy named Mike, you know, the boyfriend of the woman I was seeing, and his People's Temple buddies, that hit squad the papers call 'White Knight.'"

"Oh-oh. I thought you said nothing ever happened between you two."

"Nothing ever did."

"You're probably just being paranoid then. How's Linda Jean?"

"We've split up."

"No shit?"

"No shit."

"Well, that's it then, you're just all bent out of shape from the break-up, man."

"Maybe you're right, Bob. I agree with you that that's the most likely explanation. But you draw this conclusion too quickly, damn it. What if I *am* being followed? You know the old saw, 'just because you're paranoid, doesn't mean there *isn't* someone after you.'"

They bump up against the tension between them. "Here, have a cold one," Bob says, throwing Barney a Bud, his solution to everything.

Bob's flat is on the bottom floor, the basement really, and it's dark. It's furnished in Goodwill modern, with a green stuffed rocker and an orange-brown easy chair. A print of Van Gogh's sunflowers is tacked to the wall with push pins, next to a silk mandala of the Hindu pantheon, a memento of Bob's years in India. The front room, a combined living room and bedroom, is filled with tools, a huge concrete saw, plastic buckets filled with chisels, chalk lines, and hacksaws, several leather belts hung with hammers, tape measures, and Exacto knives. Barney sits on Bob's bed, made up of one flat sheet and an opened-out green sleeping bag with a plaid lining. Everything is covered with a nose-tingling patina of dust.

"Where are you staying?" Bob asks.

"In my van, basically. I think I'll go down to Deer Creek tonight, though."

"You're welcome to stay here if you want. I feel bad about you and Linda Jean because you are one of the few couples where I feel like I'm friends with both of you. But I was your friend first."

"I'd like it if you stayed friends with her too, you know. She doesn't deserve the way I'm treating her. But I can't help it."

"Sometimes you have to just go for yourself, man," he says.

They hang out some. They have a burrito at La Taqueria on Mission Street. Barney leaves for the Santa Cruz Mountains about 8 P.M.

As soon as he pulls away from the curb, it's clear they're all over him. It's difficult to say how he knows this. First, there's an old Dodge truck with a bearded white man right behind him, then he turns off, and a Buick with a mixed couple, the white woman driving, takes over. It seems they are coordinating this effort with considerable sophistication. The Buick follows him all the way to where Guerrero Street turns into San Jose Avenue. Then it keeps going, while its place behind him is taken by a big Harley with an equally big, leather-suited rider. The Harley follows Barney onto the freeway, 280 south, which proclaims itself "the most beautiful freeway in the world" – with some justification as it wends past the sylvan wilderness of Crystal Springs Reservoir and such communities as

Woodside where the Hearst's live (as everyone knows from the Patty Hearst case), its overpasses bridging the gaps between the rolling golden hills with uncommon grace – but he's not noticing this now, in the dark, he's noticing how his pursuers seem to swarm around the off-and-on ramps, one exiting the freeway while another enters to occupy the same position two car lengths behind him. It's the look of the drivers that give them away, their scruffiness, their intensity, their multiculturality, a rare thing in this San Mateo County of white bread suburbs. He figures their vehicles must be equipped with CB radios to coordinate all this, and he remembers reading that Jim Jones had a thing for radios. He hesitates to guess how many of them there are – too many, that much he knows.

He doesn't like the picture of him leading this chase into the dark and lonely desolation of the Santa Cruz Mountains, so he get off at Redwood City, hoping to fool them, crosses the freeway and starts back the other way. But they're not fooled. They seem to have covered every contingency, and he's beginning to get seriously scared. What do they want with him, these People's Temple survivors? Mike must have built up his role as an enemy. It's true that he delivered them their most recent local defeat with the childcare center deal. Now he wishes he'd just let them have it. It's likely that Mike blames him for persuading him to go to Jonestown. But he can't be as important to them as the likes of Congressman Leo Ryan, now dead, or his cohorts, who are probably being subjected to a similar ordeal. How many 'white knights' could there be? Of course, there could be thousands. Maybe the whole thing was planned. We know the suicide was rehearsed ("white nights" they called these rehearsals), maybe the aftermath too. Say they left behind just four fighters for everyone killed in Jonestown, that's 4000 people, all half-crazy from what happened to their comrades, pumped up with paranoia, searching for scapegoats to take the blame.

His mind races faster than the VW van, not a great getaway car with its 70 MPH top speed. Maybe they are just trying to scare him. They're succeeding. Maybe they want to kill him. People willing to squirt cyanide into the mouths of their own children are unlikely to be bothered by compunction. He gets off at Army Street, hangs a squealing U-turn onto Bayshore Boulevard, followed by their own squealing U-turns, heads up Cortland by the Goodman Lumber Co. and then winds his way around the tiny streets of Bernal Heights. He can't believe it, but he'll be damned if there aren't at least a dozen other cars apparently still swarming right along with him – though of course he recognizes that his rising fear is obscuring his judgment. He's trying to find Bob's street, Moultrie Street, but he's lost now. He has to just keep going but the streets are running out, all leading to the dark and uninhabited clearing at the top of the hill where there's some kind of spooky radar tower, and as he reaches the top, he's sure it's all over, they've got him surrounded, he ducks down his head waiting for the shots, he starts bawling like a baby, he's not ready to die yet, he sort of prays, please don't let this happen, I'll be a good boy from now on, he promises, and he suddenly turns off the street, onto the grass, down the hill, out of the swarm, into a dirt street, around a few more corners, and he stops right in front of Bob's house, jumps out of the car, pounds on his door to wake him up. When Bob finally lets him in, he throws his arms around him, shaking. He's safe.

"Barney, Jesus!" He pulls away from him. "You okay?"

"I know you don't believe me, but they're all over me, Bob."

"You're right. I don't believe you, Barney. I think you're losing it."

"Give me the benefit of the doubt."

He looks at him coldly. "There isn't any doubt."

"C'mon, Bob, how the hell do you know? There's always some doubt. Give me five percent."

"Barney, it's completely obvious. You're starkers. You're bonkers. You're nuts. You're totally out of your gourd. There's a hundred percent chance of that. But I'm an old gambler. If it will calm you down, I'll give it a two percent chance that there's some vestige of reality to what you say."

"I'll take it." Barney laughs. Bob gives him a Seconal, and as he falls asleep on Bob's floor, he realizes that he really is safe, that he did survive, that they had their chance to kill him, and they didn't, that they must merely want to scare him. But if they don't want to kill him, he has nothing to be afraid of. He dreams of getting together with Mike years later and laughing about all of this over a few beers. In the middle of the night, he wakes up to the noise of a gang of people in the street. He wonders what they might be doing to his van.

3.

He sleeps late, and by the time he's up the next morning, Bob has gone to work. He's feeling lightheaded, hungover from both the Seconal and last night's experience. His senses are off. The sun seems too bright, every little noise seems too loud. He's ready to go to Deer Creek though.

He checks the van. The door on the driver's side is unlocked, though he's sure he locked it last night. Inside, his stuff has been moved around. A box of books has spilled. Nothing is missing, though it feels like someone has been rummaging around. Maybe last night's chase threw everything out of whack. He's about to start the engine when he thinks "car bomb." He looks underneath the chassis, in the engine compartment, see nothing out of the ordinary. Closing his eyes, he turns the key. No explosion.

He's hopeful his pursuers have lost interest by now. No such luck. As soon as he pulls away from the curb, they're all over him again. Some of the vehicles and drivers look familiar from last night. Since they had their chance then and didn't kill him, he's much less afraid than he was. In fact, he thinks the situation is funny. All this fuss over someone as insignificant as him.

He hits 280 again, heading south. At every interchange, he sees the same kind of swarming, some of his pursuers get off, some others come on. He figures there's maybe twenty altogether, couldn't be more than that, who all fit the same profile. They drive old cars, they're black or bohemian looking, they look at him malevolently, as if they want him to know they're following him, as if the whole game is to make him feel it's him who's paranoid instead of them. He decides to ignore them.

When he gets to Cupertino where he has to turn onto Highway 17 toward Santa Cruz, he gets off the freeway and pulls into a parking lot behind a restaurant, hoping once again to lose them. He decides that someone ought to know where he is in case something does happen. He calls Linda Jean from the pay phone.

"I'm on the way to Deer Creek," he tells her. "I'm being followed by some People's Temple types, but I am in no danger."

"Are you sure?"

"I'm sure."

As he comes away from the phone, a man comes out of the men's room right behind the phone booth. He could have listened in on the call. Of course all these suspicious things could be coincidence, but there's just too many of them.

The place is called "Casa Hacienda," and the enchiladas he orders are as phony as the name. The man from the bathroom, a white man with African beads around his neck, sits down at a table nearby with his black girlfriend, an American Indian-looking man, and a white girl with long stringy blonde hair, a throwback to the sixties. Barney sighs. You just don't see that many mixed groups in this part of suburbia.

He decides to go on the offensive, no matter how ridiculous it feels. On his way out, he goes over to their table and says to them ever so politely, "Say, you folks know anything about White Knight?"

"White Knight?" the Indian says. "That a bar in San Jose, maybe?"

"No, it's not a bar."

"A chess piece" the guy with the beads says, smiling, baiting Barney.

"I know what it is," the blond woman says seriously.

"Good!" Barney says. "Then you tell Mike to call off his dogs, okay? Nothing ever happened between us. Got that?"

The girl tries to look puzzled now. "I'm not sure what you mean," she says, but something tells him she's not telling the truth.

"You know what I mean," he tells her and stomps out of the restaurant, newly empowered by his decision to fight back.

The others apparently weren't fooled by his attempt to hide behind the restaurant. At the first intersection after the freeway ends, as Highway 17 begins to wind into the mountains, he pulls off the road and gets out of the van. He's going to see what's what once and for all. Using a yellow legal tablet, he stands on the island in the middle of the highway and very conspicuously writes down the license number of every vehicle that could be part of the conspiracy.

He ignores the straight-looking people, the men in coats and ties, the old people, the new cars, the out-of-state license plates, the obvious tourists, the commercial vehicles, the vast majority of the cars. He only writes down the license numbers of older cars with occupants who fit the People's Temple profile, the non-whites, the scruffy types, the longhairs. Of course, he's exaggerating the numbers. But even if just a quarter of the numbers he's writing down have anything to do with the Temple, there are a huge number of people following him. In ten minutes, he's written down 80 license numbers. Oh-oh, he thinks. It's bigger than he thought.

A long-haired guy, stopped at the light, asks him what he's doing.

"I'm writing down the license numbers of the people following me," he explains. "That way, if something happens to me, there'll be some evidence."

"Well, I hope you don't have an accident," he threatens menacingly, obviously one of them.

Just to be sure he's on the right track, he waits until he catches one of them in a jeep actually talking on a CB radio. Just as he suspected.

Back on the road again, he's giddy with the numbers but elated with the power of fighting back. He feels much safer. He can still imagine this chase ending badly in the dark forests near Deer Creek, but he's increasingly confident of being able to outwit his pursuers.

Thinking he's safer going all the way to Santa Cruz, he passes the road to Deer Creek. Once in town, he stops at a 7-11 and calls Linda Jean again. He reads her his list of license numbers and makes her write them down.

He goes inside the store and buys a bottle of orange juice. He sees a young black woman buy a pack of Dentine. "That's all you're buying, huh," he says to her knowingly. She gives him a dirty look.

He follows her out of the store. She gets in a red Camaro. The driver is a white girl. Leaning on the window, he says to the black girl, "Do you want to buy a radio?"

"What?"

He shows her the list of license numbers. "I've got all these radios made by Puritan Template, and they're all in cars with these here license numbers. So you can tell Mike or whoever's ordering you around that if anything happens to me, there'll be hell to pay."

They look at each other with guilt all over their faces. "Okay, we'll tell him," the white girl says.

Now he's perfectly well aware that his rap sounds paranoid as hell, but he figures if he lets them know that he knows what's going on, they'll get the message, and if they don't know what he's talking about, they'll just assume he's crazy. He's pleased at the brilliance of this stratagem. His mind is racing; he's never felt so intelligent.

In the parking lot, he tries out his rap on several other suspects with similar results, although one guy just says "Fuck you," and walks away. Then the manager of the 7-11, a beefy, bald man, comes out and asks Barney what he's doing. He tells him he's writing down the license numbers of the people following him. The manager says he better stop or he'll call the cops.

So he moves on, decides to go to the Greyhound Bus Depot in downtown Santa Cruz, as public a place as there is. There's a minipark right next to the station with stone benches and patches of grass, which of course begins filling up with people as soon as he gets there. He sees the two Camaro girls, whose presence reassures him that he's not making this up. "Hey!" he greets them like old friends. "Did you tell Mike what I said?"

The girls look at each other and laugh. "Sure! Of course we did."

"What did he say?"

"He said... he said..." the white girl looks at her partner, "...he said you had nothing to worry about. You should go home, take it easy."

"He said that? For real?"

"For real," she answers, and then she and her friend double over with the giggles.

He accosts a few others with his rap. One young guy listens intently and asks, "Do you really have all those radios?"

Another, a black man, says, "I know just where you're coming from, man. Been there myself. Thing is, don't ever let them know how scared you are, got that? And be cool."

When he figures the park is filled with his pursuers, all trying to act like they don't know him, he decides to make a speech. He stands on one of the benches and addresses the people on the other benches and sprawled on the largest patch of grass. "Hey, listen up, people. Listen." He pauses for their attention. "I'm really sorry about Jonestown. It wasn't my fault. Whatever Mike and your other leaders are telling you, nothing ever happened between us. I'm innocent, I'm telling you. I'm being used as a scapegoat, just like you've been most of your lives. It's time to stop. If Jonestown had any meaning at all it's got to be this: DON'T FOLLOW LEADERS!"

A young girl with large blue eyes looks right at him sadly, and he can tell from the other sympathetic looks he's getting that his speech has had an effect. He goes into the echoing bus station and gives Linda Jean another call to update her list of license numbers. "Everything's under control," he tells her.

"Where are you?"

"At the Greyhound station in Santa Cruz. My strategy of dealing with them one by one seems to be working. I think their will is cracking."

"I'm coming to get you," she says.

"You really don't need to. Everything is fine. There's maybe a hundred operatives down here with me, but all they're trying to do is make me paranoid, and since I'm onto them, they can't possibly succeed."

"Wait right where you are, Barney. I'll be there in 90 minutes."

"No! I don't want you to come. I'm completely safe. I can handle this myself. Don't come! I mean it!"

"I'm coming anyway. Just stay where you are." She hangs up.

Damn. Now he supposes he has to wait for her in this grungy joint to allay her stupid fears. Her fear pisses him off. What does she have to be afraid of?

He might as well use the time to neutralize some more of them, numbers of whom have followed him into the station from the park. He tries a middle-aged woman who's been watching him, sitting by herself on one of the hard wooden benches. "Do you want to buy a radio?" he asks.

"*No hablo ingles,*" she pretends.

"Yeah, right," he says.

A bus pulls into the covered stall just outside the station. It's not a Greyhound. It has no markings on it at all, just like the buses that People's Temple would use to ferry their folks to and from demonstrations. Curious, he thinks. Disembarking from the bus is a mixed bag of people, blacks, hippies, Latinos, awfully similar to that same group of People's Temple demonstrators, and some of them look familiar to him, too.

Wait a minute, he thinks. A whole busload? For me? Could there possibly be that many of them left? Who knows, maybe the mass suicide inspired a peculiar type of person, "borderline personality," he's heard the type called, pushed over the edge by a dramatic event.

He can hear Mike explaining to them in his confused, jealous rage that Barney's the guy singularly responsible for bringing down their whole house of cards. But he's starting to tax his own credulity here.

"Where's this bus from?" he asks a clean-cut young man getting off.

"San Francisco. It's a special group."

"What kind of group?"

"A religious group."

"Oh really. It wouldn't have anything to do with... with Puritan Template, would it?"

"What?"

He takes a chance. "People's Temple."

"Not really. Well, sort of. We were on a revival mission, to heal the wounds of all that stuff in Frisco, you know."

"Heal the wounds."

"Yeah."

Barney can't believe how every piece of information he encounters confirms his worst suspicions. It doesn't occur to him that some other church might hold a revival to pick up the pieces of People's Temple.

The next person he tries his rap on says to him, "You seem to be under quite a bit of stress. I don't think you should keep doing this. Have you thought about getting some rest? There's a drop-in crisis center not too far from here."

Barney bristles. "I know what you're trying to say here. You're trying to get me to think I'm losing it. But I'm not falling for that trap. That's the whole point of this."

"You should think about getting some rest."

He is weary. He sits down on the bench and lets them swarm around him for a while. They don't seem prepared to make a move on him yet. They're probably waiting for dark.

4.

Linda Jean comes with Bob in Bob's truck, then drives the van to Deer Creek while Barney crouches in the back. He's hoping that having her drive will fool his pursuers, and he's relieved to notice that no one seems to be following them back through the mountains in the fading light of a long day. Fortunately, the road had been fixed since the last time Barney and Bob were there.

The quiet of their redwood grove is sublime, but Barney is furious at Linda Jean for having "rescued" him. "If you loved me," he tells her, "you would have listened to me. I told you I was in no danger. Say it. I want you to say it. 'I don't love you any more....'"

She says it, looking at the ground, whispering, "I don't love you any more..."

"'...because if I did, I wouldn't have come.'"

"...because if I did, I wouldn't have come."

Bob builds a fire and Linda Jean cooks up some hamburgers. Barney tells Bob, "I know the numbers have spiraled beyond belief. I know it's hard for you to believe that there were a hundred cars after me this afternoon. I know the most plausible explanation is that I'm crazy, but I still need your concession of a two percent chance that this is happening to me.

Because it is happening to me."

"No way, Barney. I'd be doing you a disservice if I lied to you. There's not one chance in hell that you are not imagining this whole thing."

"The trouble is," Barney says, "people have so much more at stake in maintaining their own fragile sense of reality that they can't be trusted to judge anyone else's. We've been friends a long time. If our friendship were on the line, would you reconsider?"

Bob hesitates, looks at Barney with sadness in his eyes. "No," he says softly, and the little word goes straight to his heart, like an air bubble in the bloodstream. This betrayal, that Bob would sacrifice their friendship to preserve his own understanding of reality, hurts more than he can say.

Barney wanders off by himself down to the rocks they've named Barney's Rocks because he likes to sit on them so much. He sits on the biggest one, on a moist patch of moss, the last vestiges of daylight abandoning the sky. A cold breeze wafts up the creek, and for one terrible moment, he grasps how alone he is. It's not about being outside the known universe anymore. It's like being in a whole other universe every bit as vast as the one we learn about in school, with ten billion galaxies of ten billion stars, a few of which he can see are now blinking on in the sky, but being here in this whole other universe all by himself, the very first cell to be conscious of itself, or, far more likely, the last.

What if he is making this up? What if he is just being paranoid and there really hasn't been anyone following him all day? This thought has never occurred to him before, and it fills him with the worst kind of dread. Because the awful implication is that there is absolutely no way to know. At this moment, under a darkening sky, he can trust no one's judgment of what's real – not his wife's, not his best friend's, and worst of all, not his own. Which feels not only like wandering alone in an alien universe, but not as his old familiar self, the bungling but lovable fool who juggles the pieces of his life, rather as an alien creature lost in an alien universe. The air is thin and smells of unearthly gases. As he looks around, the most elementary distinctions between things disappear. He can no longer recognize where the leaves end and the trees begin, nor remember what either the leaves or the trees are called, he can no longer understand the distinction between the rocks and the water rushing over them, and suddenly he feels that he isn't alone, that he's surrounded by blank white faces with round empty eyes hovering menacingly in the air, laughing at his predicament, perhaps pieces of his self that the juggler has dropped, or perhaps the true inhabitants of this alien planet, and this vision fills him with so much terror that he flails his arms at these creatures and runs back to the campsite where he sits on a log, watching the fire, imagining that a flame-thrower has come along to obliterate his hollow-eyed resident demons, in the silent company of the strangers who had once been his wife and best friend, only slightly reassured by their faint familiarity.

NINETEEN

New Year's

1.

Barney makes Linda Jean drive back to the city the following day, while he crouches in the back of the van, certain that his pursuers will have given up by now or at least that they will have lost track of him after their night deep in the woods. As soon as they hit the highway though, there they all are again, apparently having patiently spent the night driving back and forth on the county road that runs between their dirt road and Highway 17. "Jesus! I don't believe this," Barney says as he begins a new page of license numbers on the yellow legal tablet. Many of the cars and the numbers have a familiar feel to them, and he realizes that he has them now, he has the proof he needs, all he has to do is compare the list of numbers from yesterday with the list from today and find out from the Department of Motor Vehicles who owns the cars that appear on both lists. Then find those names on the list of People's Temple members which surely the FBI will have by now.

Linda Jean behaves as if she totally believes his version of what's happening, but, of course, he can't trust her, she believes too easily, while the others doubt

too easily. He never imagined reality to be so difficult to check. It is clear to him that at least some of
the reactions he got from strangers yesterday, which
seemed at the time to confirm his interpretation of
events, really came from people who, for reasons of
their own, thought it best to humor him.

The first thing he does when they get back to his
former home in Geneva Towers is to fish out the .25
automatic pistol from under the mattress and slip it
into the back pocket of his jeans.

He is not surprised to note out the window that
Mike is not at his usual post on the corner.

The next thing he does is call the FBI. How ironic
to be allied with them. The investigator he talks to
sounds sympathetic at first. He says there is no list of
People's Temple members. "Ever since Watergate," he
complains, "our hands have been tied." When Barney
mentions that he thinks there are about 100 People's
Temple survivors following him, the G-man transfers
his call to some bureaucratic flak whose job it is to get
rid of kooks. "The FBI doesn't conduct investigations
based on unsubstantiated claims of individuals. I
suggest you contact your local mental health agency,
which is better equipped to handle your problem."

The San Francisco Police are more encouraging.
"We've received numbers of calls like yours, and frank-
ly we don't have the resources to check on all of them.
I know it sounds strange, but if something were actually to happen to you, you know, if a crime is actually
committed, then we could investigate."

He tries a private investigator from the yellow pages. "Do you have any idea how much it would cost to check out all those license numbers?" he says. "The Dept. of Motor Vehicles charges five dollars for each one, and you say you've got 200 numbers? That's a thousand dollars right there, and that doesn't begin to cover our fees."

He tells Linda Jean to recopy his lists of license numbers, scrawled helter-skelter all over the legal tablet, and to note any concordances between the two main lists. After an hour of copying, she's about half done and has found no matches.

In the mid-afternoon, he ventures out in the van to find out if he's still being followed. After 15 minutes, it's clear that he is, and he ducks back into the apartment.

He calls Cali. "Things have gotten a little strange, Cali," he says.

"Strange? How do you mean?"

"It's hard to explain."

"Where are you now?" she asks.

"Er, well, I'm still in Linda Jean's apartment, it's a long story."

"I thought you left her, you liar. You want to come over?"

"I don't think that would be such a good idea, Cali. I think your hubby Mike is seriously messing with me."

"Oh, don't worry about *him*, he ain't shit," she says, and for the first time he notices the drug-induced slur in her words. "He hasn't been around for days."

"Yeah, I know. He's been around me. Or his hench-people have."

"Really? You've seen him?"

"Not exactly. Or I did a few days ago when this thing started happening, him and Larry Cordell and Jay."

"The three stooges. What 'thing'?"

"They're after me, Cali."

"Oh," she says, noncommittally. "Who's after you?"

"I told you. Mike. And about a hundred of his friends. You know, 'White Knight.'"

"Oh," she says.

"You believe me, don't you? You know what he's capable of."

"Barney, I don't know what to believe. Everything's been so crazy."

He can tell by her voice that she's among those who too easily dismiss his story, so he tells her "I have to go now. See you later," and hangs up, at a total loss as to what to do next.

2.

He lies on the bed that night as far as he can get from Linda Jean. He wonders why he's even in the same bed with her. He can hear people interpreting this "craziness" as a way for his unconscious to steer him back to her, but he doesn't buy it. He fades in and out of sleep all night, now and then peering out the window at the complex ballet the People's Temple cars are performing to make sure he's covered.

At four in the morning, he gets an idea. If he could get Linda Jean to see how these people react when he confronts them with his knowledge of what they're up to, when he gives them his paranoid rap, if he could prove to her that he is in fact being followed even at this hour, if he could dispel the last vestiges of her doubt, then he could have her back as an ally and together they could figure out what to do. And maybe there would even be a small chance for them, for their marriage.

He gets dressed, checks to see if the gun is still in his pocket, and wakes her up. "Linda Jean, I'm going out now, down to the 7-11 on Bayshore to confront these people, and I want you to come with me, to see for yourself how they react." He goes around the apartment, flashing the lights on and off to let them know he's coming out.

He hears Linda Jean talking on the phone.

"Who are you calling?" he demands to know.

"Just my sister, to let her know we're going out."

Minutes later, the doorbell rings. Barney answers it. There's two policemen at the door. He's elated to see them. At last, someone will believe him. He wonders who called them.

One of the policemen, the same big Irishman who investigated their burglary, pat searches him, finds the gun and a lid of marijuana in his jacket pocket. He shows the gun to his Asian partner. "It's okay," the Irishman says, "he hasn't left the apartment with it yet." He dumps the marijuana down the disposal. Barney tells them his story.

"I was at the Holy Innocent's memorial at Glide Church a few days ago. I noticed some people there from People's Temple, one guy especially, named Mike Davis, who has a serious grudge against me. I think he got the rest of the White Knight squad of People's Temple survivors to believe that I was their number one enemy, and they've been following me for the past three days. They're out there now."

"Okay, Barney," the Irish cop says evenly, "we're going to take you in on a 5150, a seventy-two hour hold for a psychiatric examination. Put your hands behind you, please."

"Oh, wow," is all he can say as they snap the handcuffs on his wrists.

Linda Jean comes down the elevator with them and gives him a forlorn look as they load him in the squad car. They take him to General Hospital, where, though he is as calm as can be, they strap him to a wooden bench, two-point restraint it's called, a leather belt around one wrist and one ankle.

An hour later, they take him to a small, plain, white room. He tells his story to a bored social worker, a young woman who's heard it all before. Then they take him, strapped to an ambulance bed, to Langley-Porter Neuropsychiatric Clinic, near Golden Gate Park, where he's assigned a room on the locked ward.

3.

There is no padding on the walls at Langley Porter, there are no medieval torture devices, no madmen bouncing around in straitjackets or chained to the walls. In fact, the place is more like a college dormitory than a hospital – except that the door is locked. The rooms are painted in calming but cheery pastels and paneled with blond wood.

Most of the inmates are medicated, which means they shuffle around the hallway in a dense fog. The intake worker is a young blond man with wire rimmed glasses who resembles Barney ten years ago. Barney talks him into allowing him to skip the tranquilizers. He's actually feeling amazingly good, as if this were the most interesting thing that has ever happened to him, to hover along the fuzzy line between consensual reality and individual experience, between what other people believe is real and what he's experiencing. He interviews everyone, the psychiatrist, the social worker, the ward staff, the patients, in a deliberate attempt to find someone who will neither disbelieve nor believe his story too readily. He's astounded at how difficult this is. The professionals, to a person, dismiss his story as the ranting of a paranoid. They do this in different ways. The portly psychiatrist does it by simply smiling benignly through his whole spiel, as if he were listening politely to someone speaking in a foreign language of which he, the doctor, knew not a word. The social worker, a mousy woman in her forties, fighting burnout, asks him during his first group session why he is here.

"I was being followed by up to a hundred People's Temple members intent on avenging Jonestown, and I couldn't get anyone to believe me."

"I see," she says, casting her eyes downward with disdain.

The other patients gravitate to HIS side. A pudgy boy of about nineteen, sent here for stabbing his brother with a kitchen knife, comes up to him after group and says, "I believe you, man," but his desperation for Barney's friendship oozes from the baby fat of his face.

Another patient he tries to reach, a fierce and muscular black man of about 30 who calls himself Chairman Mao, puts him off when Barney asks him why he's in here by telling him he killed 25 whites.

"Really?" Barney says, playing along. "How can you keep count?"

"Oh, I can count, man, I can count," he says, squinting at Barney hungrily as if sizing him up as his next victim.

Barney decides to do for Chairman Mao what he really needs someone to do for him. He tells him, "I think you're trying to scare me, but after what I've been through with the People's Temple, I'm not scared. Do you want me to leave you alone?"

He glares at Barney for daring to challenge him, but shrugs his shoulders.

"If you want to talk about it for real, I'll listen," Barney tells him.

He gives Barney a thin smile. "Thanks," he says, and shuffles away. He doesn't exactly smother him with warmth, but Barney is encouraged by his response.

The psych tech staff treats them all as if they were children. They see everything the inmates do as a symptom – if they frown, they're depressed; if they smile, they're in a manic phase; if they don't eat, they're acting out; if they devour their food enthusiastically, they're demonstrating hyperactive behavior.

That night is New Year's Eve, of all things, and Barney wonders why he hasn't heard from Linda Jean. After their cardboard turkey dinner, the staff throws a lame party in the lounge, complete with paper hats and those noisemaker things that honk, unfurl, and stand out like an erection when you blow into them. The patients quickly tire of blasting them in each other's faces. They toast the new year with sparkling apple juice at 9 o'clock – New Year's in New York – since the drugs preclude most of the inmates from making it halfway conscious to anywhere near midnight.

After a game of chess with the guy who looks like Barney, one of the friendlier staff members, the other patients have mostly crashed, and Barney finds himself alone in the lounge with a nervous and homely young girl he's written off as the least likely person to connect with. She tiptoes about invisibly, clutching a worn teddy bear and a Bible wrapped in a towel, and never says a word to anyone. Her black hair is chopped off unevenly short as though she cut it herself. She has a birthmark the size and color of a Reese's Peanut Butter Cup on her cheek, wears big, black-rimmed glasses, and has no chin. Most of the time she stares at the ground.

"What's your name again?" Barney asks, having forgotten it from group.

She mumbles something he can't hear.

"What?"

"Ursula."

"My name's Barney. Why are you in here?"

She looks around as if hopeful that he might be addressing someone else. "It's just too scary out there," she whispers.

"What are you afraid of?" he asks gently.

"Everything."

"Everything?"

She looks around again, this time to make sure no one else is listening. "My father."

"Why him?"

She clams up.

"You don't have to tell me. Only if you think it might be helpful. I don't have any ax to grind with you. I'm really just passing the time until I can get out of here."

"Do you really want to get out?" she asks, her voice gradually increasing in volume.

"Yeah, don't you?"

"No way," she says. "I feel safe here. But, if you want to get out, you have to tell them what they want to hear."

"What do you mean?"

"What you told them in group sounded paranoid. Even if all those people *were* after you, you've got to pretend it was a delusion, otherwise you'll never get out. I know, because I've got the opposite problem. All I have to do is keep telling them my father's been raping me, and they'll keep me here forever."

"Has your father been raping you?"

She looks around again. "Yes. But he's an important doctor himself, and he knows how to get around all the investigations. So there's no physical...evidence, you know?" She turns bright red at the word 'evidence.'

"So no one believes you."

"No one. They say I'm angry at him for leaving my mother, which I am."

"Doesn't she believe you?"

"Nope. She says that for all his rotten qualities, he'd never do anything like that."

"I can see why you want to stay here."

She smiles at him wanly. "What about you? Do you really think all those people are after you?"

"I don't know. The hard part is I don't know how to find out. It really, really felt like there were a lot of people following me. But I can't figure out how to fucking tell, you know? It's maddening. Either people just discount my story so completely that I know they're just trying to preserve their own fragile sense of reality, or they believe me absolutely from some place in themselves that's needy for my approval."

"Ah," she says, beaming understanding.

"I mean I know the most plausible explanation for what's happening to me is that it's my guilt from leaving my wife that's following me down the freeway, or maybe it's her pain that I don't want to feel."

"Tell that to the group tomorrow. That'll get you out."

"You think so? Really?"

She shrugs her shoulders. There's a short silence between them. Then she asks, "What would it feel like if you just felt it, the pain I mean?"

Barney starts to shake. "Oh God, I don't know, it's overwhelming. It's like what a horrible heel I am for abandoning this poor black woman, that's part of it, the guilt. But mostly it's this indescribable fear." He covers his face and trembles some more. Tears well up in his eyes and he can't stop them. Ursula moves in next to him and puts her arms around him, which makes for more tears.

One of the psych techs, a man with dark unruly hair, barges in the lounge and glares at them. "What's going on? You all right, Barney?"

He straightens up, pull away from Ursula. "Yeah, I'm okay. We were just talking."

"Doesn't look like talking to me. I'm going to call your doctor. I think you need to be medicated."

"No, I don't," Barney says firmly.

"I think you do. It's time for both of you to go to your rooms."

Barney looks at Ursula, prepared to be defiant. She shakes her head at him. "All right," she says.

When he's in his room getting ready for bed, the psych tech comes in with a big red pill and cup of water. "Here. Your doctor says you should take this."

The picture of compliance now, Barney says, "Thanks," throws the pill in the back of his throat, and takes a slug of water. He artfully detours the pill to a hiding place under his tongue until the psych tech leaves the room, then he spits it out. He lies on his bed and trembles some more, amazed at the healing effect of the shakes and sobs he allows to spasm through his body. It's as if his nervous system were violently unscrambling the snarls of neurons that have disconnected him from the world in recent days, weeks, months, who knows when it started?

You were nine years old. You were a solitary boy who spent much of his time puttering in his laboratory, located in an old shack in the woods, at the top of the hill behind the big house. You were not happy with your family life, where your frequently drunken father sucked up all the attention leaving nothing for you and your sister Pookie. You were not happy with your place in the pecking order at school, where the other children picked on you for being spastic at baseball, where the best image that you could project is that of the "mad scientist," at a time when nerds were still unfashionable. You wanted out of this world. You painted a skull and cross bones on the door to your lab with radium paint so it glowed in the dark, and you holed up in there designing a rocket to the moon. One day, you were ready to test your first prototype, a jet engine, constructed of two orange juice cans soldered together with a strip of copper tubing between them. You took the device just outside the door to the shack. You poured the white gas in the upper can. It was supposed to drip into the lower can, the combustion chamber, and mix with the air there, where, once ignited, it would create thrust. You tried to ignite it using your grandfather's old brass blow torch. You pumped the torch up as far as you could. You turned the valve. You kept trying to light the torch with a match, but the matches went out. Finally, it caught. A tongue of flame six feet long lept from the torch into the shack as if from a flame thrower. The white gas in the orange juice can ignited all right, and so did a pile of oily rags in the corner of the shack, which in turn ignited the dry wooden structure of the old shack itself. You ran out of the shack and down to the big house where you shame-facedly yelled "Fire!" at your mother as if it were an act of God, and she called the fire department which arrived on the scene moments later in a big pumper truck and put the fire out, but not before it has destroyed the shack. You didn't get in trouble because you never let on that it was you that started it. You were racked with guilt, but you also knew that it wasn't you that left that pile of oily rags there. You would never know if the fire would have gotten out of control without those rags. Or if, finally, the fire had been your fault or not. A few weeks later, you were rummaging around the ruins and you found nestled in the foundation a charred, corrugated box, one of the few things not totally consumed by the fire. You looked inside the box. There were dozens of masks inside, you knew what they were, you'd seen them before and asked about them, they were death masks, plaster of Paris impressions that your grandfather, an amateur sculptor, made of his colleagues in the medical profession, models he would never have a chance to use to make busts of them, but now their whiteness was streaked with black soot from the fire, swirling from the hollow circles of their eyes, just as their spirits must have left their bodies in the moment of death, and the sight so frightened you that you lept out of the foundation and ran back to the house even faster than you did when the shack was burning, never to return to this spot, or even, until now, to this memory.

4.

On the evening of New Year's Day, Linda Jean brings Jason and Ramona to visit him. All three of them hug him extra hard. Seeing himself through the children's eyes, he's gripped with the awful sense of being "crazy." What must it be like for them to know their father is crazy? His eyes wet up with tears again, as they've been doing all day.

Ramona has brought the Viewmaster Barney gave her for Kwanzaa, a touching gesture on her part, probably to show him how much she likes it. She and Jason sit on the vinyl couch in the visitor's lounge and trade the viewer back and forth while Linda Jean and Barney trade banalities.

"What story are you looking at, Monie?" he asks her.

"Hansel and Gretel," she says.

"You know, the one where the children get away with murder," Jason interjects. "You used to say that."

"That witch was going to *eat* them," Monie says, her voice rising stridently.

"What about that father, I want to know," Barney says. "What kind of father would let the stepmother talk him into abandoning his own children?"

"Really." Linda Jean, the stepmother, laughs.

"He didn't *want* to," Monie says shrilly in his defense. "She *made* him."

Jason says, "Monie, you just love to argue."

"I do *not!*" she screams, her vehemence out of proportion, and they all look at each other and crack up. Even Monie has to laugh.

Barney's throat lumps up again over just how 'normal' they're all acting, despite where they are.

"I got you a little something," Linda Jean says to him. She gives him a skinny package wrapped loosely in red tissue paper. Inside is a rough, wooden carving of a deranged-looking knight holding a jousting lance. Barney smiles.

"You know who this is, don't you?" he says.

"No, I just saw it in a junk store window, and it reminded me of you."

"Don Quixote. He was famous for tilting at windmills." He's all the more charmed by the fact that she doesn't even know this, and yet intuitively understands this knight-errant as his mentor.

5.

He follows Ursula's advice and tells the group the next day that he's figured out that it was Linda Jean's pain following him down the freeway, and that he's ready to get out of here and go back to her. The last part surprises him until he says it, and then it just seems obvious. The social worker lights up. He goes on. "I'm a little mad at her for calling the police" – as he's figured out she must have done – "but I know how much she hates the police, and how hard that must have been for her."

After group, he's feeling elated, and he calls Linda Jean. "I'm sorry for everything, Jeannie," he says, "and I'm ready to get back together with you and give it another shot."

There's silence at the other end of the line.

"Jeannie? Isn't that what you want?"

"I don't know what I want any more, Barney. You've hurt me. I don't think you have any idea how much you've hurt me. I'm afraid something snapped between us this past week. It can't be undone so easily. Maybe not at all."

He can't believe he's hearing this. It never occurred to him that his decision to leave might not be revocable. "Jeannie! Please! I want to come home! What happened to 'I'll always love you no matter what'?"

"It's not that I don't love you, Barney, you know that. It's just that I need to be on my own for a while. You showed me that it was no good for me to depend on you the way I did. And you hurt me so much, Barney. I can see now that you didn't mean to, that you were out of control and that there, but the pain is too much. I can't risk going through this again."

He feels like it's her kicking him in the kidneys this time, and then pushing him off the Golden Gate Bridge. Standing on wobbly knees at the public pay phone in the hall, he lets the tears flow down his face while psych techs and patients steal wary glances at him. He can't tell whether Linda Jean is crying or not.

Finally, he's able to speak again. "It was you who called the police, wasn't it?"

She's silent again. "Yes," she says finally.

"It worked. It was a hard thing to do, but it stopped the craziness, who's ever it was. White Knight hasn't followed me here, and I don't think they'll still be after me when I get out. I think they got what they wanted, to drive me crazy."

There's another pause. "I'm sorry, Barney." There are tears in her voice now. "Bob says you can stay with him for a while, until you can get your own place."

It's his turn to be silent. "Okay," he says. He knows there really isn't anything more to say.

You remembered the earlier fire, when you were four. You were playing with your sister Pookie upstairs in what your family still called the maid's room, though the maid was long gone. There was a closet with old clothes in it. You found a new metal tea set, a hidden Christmas gift for Pookie.

"Let's have a tea-party," Pookie said, and she dressed you in a top hat and an old dress of Mommy's, while she put on a pill-box hat with a veil and Daddy's tuxedo jacket.

She ran to Mommydaddy's room and fetched two Lucky Strike cigarettes. You ran downstairs and brought back the big silver table lighter.

"No, Barney, no," Pookie said, waxing parental.

You kept flicking the lighter, watching the flame.

Pookie said, "I smell something funny." She looked out the window in the hall. Smoke was pouring out from between the shingles of the roof.

You dropped the lighter. Pookie ran to get the caretaker, who called the fire department, which put out the fire, but not before the second floor of the house was burned up.

When you asked, your father told you that the fire was started by a squirrel shorting out the faulty electrical wiring, but you would never be sure that it wasn't you with the lighter that caused it.

6.

That night on the way to bed, Barney runs into Chairman Mao, who beckons him to follow. Now, what, he thinks, he's going to kill me? Instead he pulls out a joint and offers to share it. They smoke back in forth in friendly silence, the sweet ritual of weed which is almost as delightful as the drug itself. Since paranoia is behind him, he gets the euphoric treatment. He thanks the Chairman profusely and, with a beatific smile, climbs into bed. He stares at the ceiling.

You stared at the ceiling and saw, not the white, perforated sound-proofing tiles of' the hospital ceiling, but the knotty-pine ceiling of your boyhood room, the knots assuming the most frightful incarnations: rabid squirrels, slithering snakes, clubs with double bulbous handles, suggesting something unspeakable. In the hiss of the hospital radiator you heard the sound of a shower. You were two years old.

Your father was away in the war for the first year and a half of your life removing cataracts from the eyes of Chinese warlords and as a result you hardly knew him. What you did know of him scared you. He was gruff. He was often mad. This one night he seemed in a happy way after a few drinks. It was time for your bath. He had another idea. He wanted to take you in the shower! You've never been in the shower before. He got naked. You got naked. He held you in his arms. The water was loud and steamy, scary like him. But once inside it was warm. You were close to him, skin to skin. You'd never been this close to him or perhaps to anyone. His chest hairs tickled your nose. He soaped you up and you slipped and slid against him. It felt good. You noticed your little pecker stiffen. He noticed too and got a strange look on his face. You felt yourself slipping, sliding down his body, all the way down. Your face was next to his big pecker and you saw it too was standing up.

Suddenly, he shoved it in your mouth.

You gagged.

This was happening. This couldn't be happening

The shower was over.

You were in shock.

Your father handed you off to your mother like a football. She dried you off and dressed you in your Bugs Bunny foot pajamas. She put you in your crib.

She propped a bottle, stuck the nipple in your mouth. Fresh from violation, your mouth spit it out.

A wave of fury came over you.

You screamed. You wailed. You let out your rage at the top of your lungs.

Your mother kept trying to stick the nipple in your mouth, but you would have none of it.

Finally, at her wits end, she came at you with a look on her face like the big bad wolf and shoved a pillow in your face to shut you up.

You shut up. As your body incorporated an ache of epic proportions, you drew one conclusion: you are on your own here.

As you lay on your hospital bed, you could never be sure if this happened or not. This happened. This couldn't have happened. There was of course no way to tell. Thus were you stuck with this ontological doubt at the dawn of consciousness.

They call him to the office the next afternoon and tell him he can leave as soon as he settles the bill. The man with the unruly hair hands him his statement.

The bottom line reads $3,462.71.

"*What?*" he screams. "What the hell is this? I was *forced* to come here. You mean I have to pay for it?"

"I'm afraid so," he says. "How much could you afford to pay on it each month?"

"None of it! I'm fucking unemployed!"

"Unless you sign an agreement to pay your bill, I'm afraid I can't authorize your release."

"And you're the ones calling *me* crazy?"

He shrugs, not without sympathy.

"Okay, I'll sign anything to get out of here. I'll pay you five dollars a month."

"Okay," he says. "Sign here and you're free to go."

He signs "Barnard Blatz" and then prints "under protest."

Outside, it's a brand-new year, 1979. As he waits for the bus on Parnassus Street, on a hill overlooking Golden Gate Park, cars pass him by with exhilarating disinterest. The sun warms his face. The singing of the birds has never sounded so sweet. There's a hush in the air that smells of lilacs.

TWENTY

White Night

1.

Barney lives on Bob's floor for several weeks. He decides right away to forgive him for letting him down and be grateful that at least he was totally honest with him when he refused to yield to his demand that he give his "paranoid" story a two percent chance of having some basis in reality. By mutual consent, they don't speak of those strange events at year's end.

In the ensuing months, he settles into a one-bedroom flat with high ceilings in an old Victorian house in the Western Addition. Mildew flourishes in the bathroom, cobwebs festoon the corners, the doors and trim are painted with flat white instead of enamel so they pick up every smudge, holes in the yellow-green-plaid linoleum in the kitchen reveal a subfloor of newspapers going back to 1935 ("Visit Germany, Land of Gemutlichkeit") – but it's home.

After humiliating himself before certain administrators, he has managed to get himself rehired by the school district – only part-time, but it keeps him going. He has a class of four-year-olds at a small two-room center near where he lives. Once again, he's trying to figure out how to give them their freedom, how to let them have their feelings, how to avoid massacring their dreams with the demands of consensual reality – but without ignoring those demands either. He's putting his life back together.

He's seen Mike once, when he was moving his stuff out of the Towers. He was standing on the corner, by himself. Barney waved to him, gingerly. Mike waved back and gave him a big smile. He decided right then that he would never know whether he and his people had been following him or not. Never. It was one of those things, one of those irritating things that you just have to accept as unknowable if you want to stay in touch with the consensus.

And he does want to stay in touch. Madness is an experience that everyone should have once in their life, but once is plenty. The experience has left him, on the whole, less anxious – anxiety being the fear of fear, and now that he's stared wide-eyed at the raw stuff of terror, it isn't so scary any more, psychosis as the ultimate cure for neurosis.

In the current parlance that he once would have scoffed at, he's learning to "feel his feelings," no small thing. He's learning that if he allows himself to tremble, if he allows himself to cry, if he allows himself to laugh uproariously at the embarrassment of trembling and crying, he can not only tolerate feeling his feelings, but he can also heal himself. It would be nice to have help with this, but for now, he's on his own. Trust will be a long time in returning, and he has to start with himself. Much of the time what he is feeling is a dull ache in his chest for what he has lost with Linda Jean.

Alice invites him to a costume party for Mardi Gras to celebrate her new job as an assistant manager at Mervyns. He decides to go dressed as himself. It's supposed to start at nine, but he's hung around the black community long enough to know better than to get there much before midnight if he doesn't want to be first to arrive. It's an odd feeling riding the elevator in the building where he no longer lives, with people he doesn't recognize who glance at him with an indifference he once mistook for hostility.

Turns out Alice herself is the only one in costume, dressed as the creepy skeletal death figure from the movie "Black Orpheus," in a black bodysuit painted with Day-Glo bones, but when no one else shows up in costume, she takes hers off and puts on a snazzy silver jogging suit.

The living room is dark and smoky, hung with balloons, clogged with people dancing. Barney is the only white person, but he hardly notices.

Linda Jean, in a red denim jumpsuit he gave her for Christmas a few years back, is cordial, but she keeps her distance. She's straightened her hair. It seems as if women always change their hair dramatically when their relationships end. He dances with her to Martha and the Vandellas, "Dancing in the Street."

"Remember this?" he says. "We used to imagine this song coming to life on the night of the revolution."

"We had such high hopes," she says. There's sadness in her voice.

"You getting along okay?" he asks.

"You know me, the tough skin of an elephant," she says, bitterly. "I'm okay, though. I guess I did depend on you a lot. Too much. I'm stronger now."

"I am too," he says.

He looks into her eyes all the way back through the years they had together and gathers in the moments of closeness like a net full of silvery minnows glinting in the sunlight. They dance the next one, too, Otis Redding, "Try a Little Tenderness," slow and close. There's an easy familiarity to their embrace. As the song ends, their lips touch. They kiss long and hard. He thinks of their first kiss eons ago in the van. A bubble of warmth envelops them.

Terrified that they might burst the bubble, they don't say anything, they just keep hanging out together, drinking brandy after brandy, enjoying themselves, attracting a wink from Alice who, like them, is looking for a storybook ending. Barney is smart enough to know better than to develop expectations, but he's thinking that at least they will go home together tonight, home to her apartment, home to their old home together.

They're necking contentedly on Alice's brown-gold couch, when the entire apartment vibrates with the fierce wind from the hallway as Cali Robinson makes her entrance.

A chill comes between Linda Jean and Barney as Cali squeals greetings to Alice, "Hey, Girlfriend!" and

grabs the attention of the party as if there were a spotlight on her, dressed in her red leather micro mini,
white tights, a white silk blouse.

He suddenly has a violent urge to pee, and he gets
up from beside Linda Jean. "I'll be right back," he tells
her. "Don't go away."

When he comes out of the bathroom, Cali is standing in the hall as if waiting for him. She pushes him
back inside, saying, "I have to use it, too." She kisses
him and rubs her body all over his. She pulls out the
inevitable fold of paper with the white powder on it
and invites him to snort some off her long, pink fin-
gernail. He accepts.

"Where's Mike?" he asks.

"You still scared of him, Booboo? He's out there
somewhere. You didn't see him?"

"Jesus, Cali, no! I can't afford this. Let's leave it
alone, okay?"

"Sure, Boo, whatever you say."

They emerge from the bathroom separately,
Cali first, Barney some minutes later, but not late
enough to avoid Linda Jean, who's been waiting for
him in the adjacent bedroom. She's drunk now, and
furious.

"God damn you!" she screams. She pounds her fists
on his chest. She kicks him in the shin. He crumples
and tries to protect his face, but she gets her fists past
his arms without difficulty. She hits his nose; he tastes
the blood flowing. She pulls his hair. "How could you!
With that junky! To think I almost...."

"Linda Jean," he whines. "Listen. It's not what you think."

But she is in no mood to listen. She keeps pummeling him until all he can do is curl up on the floor like a fetus.

Alice finally grabs Linda Jean from behind, pulls her off him, and pushes her into the bedroom. He can hear her sobbing.

He stumbles back into the bathroom and cleans the blood off his face. His shirt, too, is covered with it. One of his eyes is half shut.

He works his way back through the crowd toward the door. As he's about to leave, Mike spots him. He smiles and shakes his head at Barney's disheveled self as if he has no idea what the fight was about. Just as well, he thinks.

Overcome with profound fatigue, he heads for home, his cozy new home, where there's no one to answer to or, for that matter, to stroke his forehead.

2.

On Monday, May 21, 1979, just before 5:30 P.M., he's sitting at home, relaxing from work, watching "Wheel of Fortune," something he never does, waiting, like most of San Francisco, for the verdict in the Dan White murder trial. The phrase on the board reads: "Th- d__rm__s_ s__d, k__p y__r h__d." One of the contestants has just asked to solve it, even though, feeling stupid, Barney can't. A bulletin interrupts the show.

"This just in," the shrill announcer says, a boyish-looking man Barney remembers from their press conference at the Towers. "The jury has reached a verdict in the Dan White murder trial. After three days of deliberation, the foreman announced to a silent courtroom that 'we the jury find the defendant Dan White guilty of the crime of voluntary manslaughter in the death of George Moscone.' There were tears in the eyes of the district attorney, and Mary Ann White broke into sobs as the foreman continued to report the verdict for the death of Harvey Milk as well...."

"Voluntary manslaughter!" Barney says aloud. He thinks, isn't that like hit-and-run? He's not the only one who is shocked that the jury bought the defense argument that White was under the influence of an "irresistible impulse," brought about in part by his addiction to junk food, Twinkies in particular.

The new mayor, Dianne Feinstein, the chief benefactress of the murders and a former ally of White's on the board, as the conspiracy theorists have noted, comes on screen to calm the town which must by now be seething with rage. "I think it's important for this town to pull itself together again," she says. Barney doubts that people will be so easily consoled.

A gay leader on the tube says, "What this verdict means is that it's now open season on fairies."

Barney lives only a few blocks from City Hall – he can see the green dome from his window – and as the sky grows dark, he senses a great deal of commotion there. He decides to check it out, to express his note of protest too. Even though he feels for White, there's no way he thinks White should get away with what he did.

By the time he gets to Polk and McAllister, rocks are flying toward the graceful edifice, cathartically smashing its windows, one by one. The crowd of thousands appears to be mostly gay, the result of a spontaneous march from the Castro district. They cheer each hit.

Barney maintains his stance as an observer as long as he can. He watches while the police Tactical Squad makes periodic, club-swinging assaults on sections of the crowd; he watches while the crowd isolates and beats up a number of individual police officers.

When a group near where he's standing solicits his help in overturning a police car, he can no longer resist turning his fear into excitement. He joins in the satisfying effort and applauds when someone dips a newspaper in the gas tank, lights it, and throws it in the squad car's smashed window. He cheers, too, when the overturned blue-and-white car bursts into flame.

But the fire quickly brings forth images of melting faces, which extinguish his delight and fill him with another rush of fear. When the teargas canisters start to fly from the police lines, he decides it's time to leave. He works his way to the edge of the crowd and spots a familiar face as he approaches Van Ness Avenue.

"Cali!"

"Barney Blatz!"

They embrace. "Where's Mike this time?" he asks, looking around warily.

"Don't worry, Booboo. Mike's in jail. Got caught fencing stolen cassette decks again. You're safe this time."

"It doesn't feel too safe right here, with the cops running amok. Let's split, okay? God, it's good to see you," he says. "I live right around the corner."

They walk to his new place, holding hands. "Cute," she says, surveying his messy bachelor pad with its Escher and Hieronymus Bosch prints all over the walls.

In minutes, they are all over each other. He has his hand inside her pink angora sweater and he's working on unbuttoning her Levi's. They waste little time on foreplay, fearful that they'll be interrupted by a nuclear war or at least an earthquake before the climax. It's as if they'd been waiting years for this. They make furious love on his bare mattress and come together minutes after he's inside her wetness.

"I knew it," she says. "You make all the right moves. You're stuck with me now, Barney-barn-barn."

He can't believe this is finally happening, this dream is finally coming true, and yet somehow it feels like no big deal. With a wry smile, he tells her, "I think it was Mark Twain that said be careful what you wish for because you just might get it."

But when he goes to use the bathroom, he does feel his body smiling all over. He lets his imagination glimpse what their life together might be like, how she'll wait for him to come home from work naked on the bed, and he'll wean her from drugs by the boundless energy of his love, how together they'll reinvigorate the revolutionary movement, to the tune of "Dancing in the Streets."

When he gets back to the bedroom which is not much larger than the mattress on the floor, cubed, she's dressed again. "I got to go, Barn-barn. I'll call you tomorrow."

"Already? How will you get home?"

"Don't worry about me none, Boo. I've got some friends in the neighborhood I need to see."

He realizes she's going to score more drugs. "I don't like all the drugs you take," he says.

"Hey, Barn, that's me, I yam what I yam. You don't have to do them with me, you know. I'll be back tomorrow, don't fret yourself. You're my man, now." She gives him a passionate kiss, fills his mouth with her tongue.

As soon as she leaves, he has a funny feeling. Still naked, he picks up his black Levi's lying in a heap on the floor and looks in his wallet.

"Oh, shit," he says out loud to the cockroaches. His Visa, his Master Charge, and his driver's license are sure enough missing. He has to laugh.

He rummages through his disorderly files of old bills and calls the 800 numbers to stop his cards, only slightly embarrassed to explain that they were stolen from his wallet in his own apartment.

Then he writes her one last poem on his yellow legal tablet.

Wisp of a witch
who lives in the sky,

I blow my nose
in your tissue of lies.

Blackbird,
Bye-bye.

He knows it's not quite that simple. He lies back on his bed, alternately laughing, crying, sobbing, raging, shaking, running the gauntlet of feelings he can finally feel. So wonderful to feel your feelings, he thinks sarcastically. Be careful what you ask for. Quick! What can I numb them with? Weed, coke, more sex, brandy... But he's stuck with them. Those substances are not going to work anymore. He's lost everything, yet a peculiar calm comes over him. His lifelong anxiety is gone, at least for now. Maybe the next chapter of his life will be a little less intense. Maybe.

He sticks the poem in a brown envelope stolen from the school district, stamps and addresses it, throws on his jeans, and, shirtless and shoeless, runs to the corner mailbox in the early evening fog.

Acknowledgements

Many people helped me on the journey toward publication: Jo-Anne Rosen and Mark Lapin for helping to put the book together, as well as their support in our writer's group, along with Ruhama Veltfort, David Belden, Sally Abbott, Naomi Cooper, and Kyla Houbalt.

Thanks as well to Jack Slater, to my children Ben, Zena, and Slater. To Richard. And to my wife Gloria who never lost faith in me.

Henry Hitz taught pre-school for 30 years in the San Francisco public schools and has been organizing parents in Oakland for the past 15 years. He has published stories in *Cube Literary Magazine, Instructor Magazine* and *Moonfish*. His first novel, *Tales of Monkeyman*, won the Walter Van Tilburg Clark Prize. He blogs at http://whiteknightsf.blogspot.com. Asked if *White Knight* was autobiographical, he replied, "Yes and no."

CPSIA information can be obtained
at www.ICGtesting.com
Printed in the USA
LVOW13s0631240517
535631LV00007B/102/P

WHITE KNIGHT

or how one man came to believe that he was
the one who caused the San Francisco City Hall
killings and the Jonestown Massacre

a novel by
Henry Hitz

White Knight:
or how one man came to believe that he was
the one who caused the San Francisco City Hall
killings and the Jonestown Massacre

© 2015 by Henry Hitz

ISBN: 978-1-941066-10-2

Library of Congress Control Number: 2016930090

Front cover design by Mark Lapin
Book design by Jo-Anne Rosen

Cover photos by Henry Hitz
The implosion of Geneva Towers Apartments,
May 16, 1998

Wordrunner Press
Petaluma, California

To Earldean

who has suffered the most for this story